Before she start[...]
in I.T. until she [...]
journalism and [...]
Health & Fitness magazines as well as newsletter
content and media releases for a not-for-profit
organisation. In 2011 the fiction bug bit and Helen has
been writing fiction ever since.

Helen J. Rolfe writes uplifting, contemporary fiction
with characters to relate to and fall in love with.
Snowflakes and Mistletoe at the Inglenook Inn is her
tenth novel.

Find out more at www.helenjrolfe.com, and follow her
on Twitter @HJRolfe.

## ALSO BY HELEN J ROLFE

The Friendship Tree

Handle Me with Care

What Rosie Found Next

The Chocolatier's Secret

In a Manhattan Minute

Christmas at the Little Knitting Box

The Summer of New Beginnings

You, Me, and Everything In Between

The Magnolia Girls

# Snowflakes and Mistletoe at the Inglenook Inn

Helen J. Rolfe

This book has been edited in British English (BrE) and therefore uses British spellings.

*For my wonderful friend, Pam, who accompanied me while I carried out my research on a recent trip to New York, and who successfully negotiated access to the Grand Ballroom at The Plaza!*

# Chapter One

*Darcy*

*Three weeks until Christmas*

Darcy Spencer was still getting used to calling the Inglenook Inn her home, as well as her place of work. For the next eight weeks she had the prodigious responsibility of running the boutique hotel in the heart of Manhattan's Greenwich Village. The owner, Sofia, was relying on her to do a good job, and, more than that, Darcy wanted her time in charge to be a raging success. She'd worked hard to build a career in the hotel industry and this could propel her to another stage. Quite what that stage was yet, she wasn't too sure.

When Darcy heard the impatient ping of the Skype call coming through she had no choice but to race, half-dressed, to the desk in the communal lounge situated on the entrance floor just after you came through the front door of the brownstone. She knew the call would be from Sofia, and Darcy didn't want her to feel she had anything to worry about if she didn't answer straight away.

She sat at the desk, took a deep breath, and pressed the button to accept the call, attempting to look as unflustered as was humanly possible. Sofia's friendly face smiled back at her all the way from Switzerland, where she'd flown to be with her daughter, Gabriella, who was going through a second pregnancy and suffering morning sickness that sounded bad enough to put even the cluckiest woman off having babies.

'Darcy, hello!' Sofia's hand blocked most of Darcy's view as she waved enthusiastically at the girl she'd entrusted with her business.

'Hi, Sofia, how are you? How's Gabriella?' Gabriella had been Darcy's best friend since they were in second grade and Sofia had often treated Darcy like a second daughter. When she'd been asked to manage the Inn in Sofia's absence, Darcy had felt honoured as well as terrified about the level of responsibility that came with this position.

'She's not too bad, considering. She's sleeping at the moment or I'd have her chat to you.' Her voice came over nice and clear, for which Darcy was grateful. Skype had been temperamental the last few days and when it played up it drove her crazy. 'Kyle is sleeping too, which is a blessing.'

'Tiring you out is he?' At fifty-five Sofia was young enough to have fun with her grandson, and he probably gave her a welcome rest from running the Inglenook Inn, but Darcy suspected she needed her down time too.

'He's quite exhausting, but utterly gorgeous.'

'I bet he loves having you there.'

'He does. And thanks again, Darcy, for stepping in at the last minute. Please tell me you sorted out the Christmas tree.' She clasped her hands together in a prayer position.

'It's all arranged, don't worry. It won't be arriving for almost another week, but we've got one, and I'm assured its stunning and worthy of being put up in the lounge.'

'I'm so sorry I didn't place the order.'

'It's fine. Better late than never, I say.' Sofia thought she'd emailed the tree company with the order but it had still been sitting in her drafts folder when Darcy checked why the tree hadn't arrived the day before Thanksgiving.

Sofia had been in a total panic but Darcy had turned her attention back to her daughter and Switzerland, and taken the reins from there.

'Well, thank you for sorting it out.'

'It's my pleasure.' She hoped she'd go on describing the job that way. She hoped it wouldn't get so hard that she'd want to jump on a plane and go as far as Europe herself.

'You certainly look the part,' Sofia nodded, taking in the suit jacket and smart shirt Darcy was wearing. 'And you still have a hint of the English accent you picked up in London.'

Darcy grinned. She hadn't been back from her travels all that long. 'Thanks, I think.' She put a hand to her dark hair, pinned up in a chignon as it usually was when she was at work. Ever since she'd got out of the kitchens and away from being a chambermaid in her quest to take the hotel industry by storm, she'd prided herself on dressing well. In this current role she would be the first face guests set eyes on, the first point of contact, and at all times she was representing the establishment she worked for, which meant standards couldn't slip.

She was thankful Sofia couldn't see beneath the desk right now or she may not be so impressed. Earlier this morning Darcy had checked the retreating form of the Inn's only guest as he left for work in his usual business attire – dark suit, well-fitted – and fled down the front steps of the brownstone, hailing a taxi with a yell and a raise of his hand that revealed just a small section of his shirt sleeve. After he'd left, she'd ducked across the street to the corner of the next block and grabbed a takeout caramel macchiato. She intended to drink it as she updated paperwork, called the delivery people to check the Christmas tree was definitely arriving at the appointed time, and generally had a breather before she got everything ready to welcome new guests this afternoon and ensure the top-floor apartment was kept as their businessman guest expected.

Her plans had gone awry however when she took the top from her macchiato the second she came in from the cold and somehow managed to stumble in her heels and slop at least a third of the contents over her navy skirt. Muttering to herself, she'd taken the skirt off. The liquid hadn't hit her stockings so without another guest in sight, she'd traipsed downstairs to the laundry and popped it straight into the machine. It was as she was taking the stairs up again that she heard the laptop on the front desk and the incessant Skype ringtone that would go on and on until it was answered.

Over Skype now, Sofia asked more about their guest list for the coming weeks and Darcy filled her in. 'The guest you checked in last week before you left is quiet as anything. I think he must work a lot.' At least that's what the well-used office desk and the lines of suits upstairs had told her when she'd made up the bed yesterday morning, replenished refrigerator supplies and the light refreshments. She was too professional to pry, but unless you were blinkered you couldn't help picking up on guests' behaviours and lifestyle. Besides, understanding people was all part of the hotel business and something Darcy took great pride in.

Darcy re-checked the book on the desk where guest details were recorded. It was on the computer too, but Sofia, and Darcy, liked to be able to have the list on hand. 'I have a family checking in this afternoon plus another couple,' she told Sofia, 'but nobody will arrive before four o'clock so it gives me a chance to get organised.'

'That's good. Did you send the accountant the latest spreadsheets?'

'Sofia, you've no need to worry, I promise. I sent everything to him. The rooms upstairs are almost ready for the next guests, and the new boiler in the basement is still going strong.'

'Darcy, I don't know how to thank you, I really don't.'

'Letting me stay here is reward enough, not to mention when I get to put this stint on my résumé as I look for a job.'

'Well I'm glad it's working out. It's a weight off my mind. And who knows? Maybe one day you can take over from me when I'm too old to climb all those stairs.'

'They're hard work even for me, especially going down to the basement.'

'No moaning from you. You're in your late twenties…maybe in another thirty years you can talk like that.'

Running the Inglenook Inn was something that had happened by chance. Darcy had been travelling for five years, coming home to New York on only a few occasions. She'd worked in hotels in Sydney, Australia, a small town in Ireland, then she'd moved over to Scotland, where she'd found work with a large hotel chain. She'd finished up in London, where she'd worked first as a waitress and then as a kitchen hand, washing up for hours on end. Finally she'd managed to secure the role of front-of-house supervisor, which she'd loved until the position was snatched out from under her when a misunderstanding led to her resignation and subsequent return to New York. She'd wanted to gain far more experience before coming home, but the best laid plans hadn't quite worked out that way, which was what made this role at the Inglenook Inn perfect in its timing. It was the chance to prove herself all over again and move forwards.

'I sneaked another look at the new website this morning,' Sofia told her now.

'It's really easy to use, isn't it?'

'Dylan did a brilliant job. The photographs sell the place. Fingers crossed for lots more bookings.'

On one of Darcy's visits home to New York, Sofia mentioned she'd never been able to knit and she longed to be the type of grandparent who could make cosy woolly sweaters and accessories for her grandchildren. Darcy had taken Sofia along to the Little Knitting Box, a store in Inglenook Falls that had originally started out not far from where the Inn was situated now. There, Sofia secured some strong friendships as chatting took her mind off her divorce and endless talk of lawyers, financial arrangements and property settlements. The owner of the store, Cleo, introduced Sofia to her other half, Dylan, a freelance website designer, and it wasn't long before they were talking business and the development of a whizz-bang website for the Inn.

'All you youngsters have helped me enormously,' said Sofia. 'Are you still knitting?'

'When would I have the time?' Darcy rolled her eyes. 'But yes, I'm fitting a little bit in when I can. I'm attempting to knit a sweater for Kyle. The last time I attempted a similar project, it ended with me unravelling the entire thing.'

'Practise makes perfect,' Sofia encouraged.

'Yes, but I'm so slow it won't be ready for Christmas. It should be ready for his birthday in February though.'

'It'll still be cold then, don't you worry.' Sofia's smile radiated warmth. 'And how's Rupert, our resident chef?'

'He's fine, even without you here mothering him.' She grinned. 'He's very reliable. He's here well before his start time every day to do the evening meals as requested, and we've been talking at length about the menu for the Christmas lunch.'

Darcy was more than capable of making light breakfasts, lunches or snacks at a guest's request, but she was grateful Sofia had employed a part-time chef who came in to do the fancier dinners, because Darcy knew she'd have no hope of doing it herself. The closest she'd come to gourmet was shopping at Zabar's and arranging foods on a plate to look appealing.

'Is it snowing there?' Darcy peered more closely at the screen. She still hadn't had a chance to duck out and get another coffee and already she was planning in her mind to finish the Skype call with Sofia, run upstairs to the two-bedroom apartment that was hers for the duration of her stay at the Inn, pull on another skirt and then treat herself a second time, hopefully with much more luck.

'It certainly is, and it's beautiful. We had a light flurry this morning and already Gabriella is talking about getting Kyle to take up skiing. He loves sledding. Start them young, that's what she thinks.'

'She's a great mum. I'm sorry she's having such a hard time.'

'Me too, but she's got me to help while Trent is at work.'

They talked some more about how Trent's job over there was going and although Darcy knew Sofia missed her daughter incredibly, it was good to see how happy her friend was in her marriage and how settled they were in coupledom and family life. Trent had a good job, earned excellent money, and Gabriella was taking motherhood in her stride. Darcy had to admire her for it. It wasn't the lifestyle she'd choose – being financially dependent on a man.

'I'm going to have to get on now, Sofia.' She knew if she chatted much longer, not only would she be pushed to finish all the paperwork and prepare the guests' bedrooms before the next set of arrivals, but she'd also be cold if she didn't get some clothes on her bottom half. She hadn't lit the fire in here yet, but she'd do it in time for the next guests. It gave the Inn a cosy feel, stepping off the Manhattan sidewalk into a little slice of heaven.

'I'll ask Gabriella to call you later or text at least,' said Sofia. 'Do you have any questions for me?'

'Everything is in hand. And we have another booking for January, and two more for the start of February.'

'That's great.'

It was, but she wished Sofia would make some changes to boost bookings even further. Darcy's head had been buzzing the last few days with ideas, but how could she make any suggestions without offending Sofia or sounding like a know-it-all?

'I'm nervous that I won't be there for Christmas,' said Sofia.

'I know you are, but you've got me. I will not let you down.' Especially not after what she'd done without Sofia's say-so. She'd almost admitted it but she didn't want to add to Sofia's worries in case it didn't work out for the best. 'If this Christmas does well and you want to do it again, there's so much you could provide for guests. You could offer gift-wrapping to fraught parents with kids in tow who need Santa gifts hidden and then miraculously appearing under a tree; you could offer babysitting services for couples to have a romantic night out; you could book activities around the city for those who have no idea how to spend the time or what will be open and what won't be.'

'I wish I could afford to employ you permanently,' Sofia smiled. 'You're full of ideas and I need them.' Darcy was on the verge of saying everything she'd thought about, but it would be too much, too soon, especially with Sofia away. 'Are you sure you want to go and work for a big hotel chain where it's impossible to know all the guests' names?'

'That's always been my aim, but who knows – this place is wonderful, in a different way. Maybe I could set my sights on something smaller.'

'I'll let you go then, Darcy. And thanks again. Do call me anytime, day or night, if you need anything.'

'I promise I will.' With impeccable timing she heard a small voice in the background and Sofia had to turn her attention to Kyle, who'd woken from his nap.

Darcy closed down the Skype session and shivered. The heating was on but with only stockings on her bottom half, she felt the cold that tried to sneak around the window panes and in through any crack it could find. She was about to scoot upstairs and grab another skirt when she heard the front door open. It creaked, brought a rush of cold air in, and then it clunked shut. Darcy froze behind the desk. It couldn't be Rupert – he'd said he wouldn't be back for at least an hour – and it couldn't be Mr-I'm-addicted-to-my-job from upstairs, because, well, he was addicted to his job. But when footsteps in the hallway halted before they took the stairs, it was the man in the dark suit that appeared.

Darcy adopted her best professional face. Usually she'd be out from behind the desk to greet a guest, deeming it the most polite thing to do. But how could she do that when she was partially dressed? Instead she looked up and gave him her friendliest smile.

'Sorry to disturb you, but I was wondering if you had a menu for lunch.' The man approached the desk when Darcy didn't make a move.

As much as Darcy felt rude by not getting up, she couldn't do anything but stay put. She tugged at the bottom of her shirt as though it could cover a little bit more in case he were to peer over the top. She extended a hand. 'I'm Darcy, I don't believe we've met.' Although, when he took her hand and his chocolatey brown eyes looked deep into hers she could've sworn she'd seen him somewhere before.

'It's good to meet you, Darcy. I'm Myles Cunningham, I'm staying on the top floor.'

'It's lovely to meet you. And I hope everything is to your liking, sir?' He was an Englishman in New York and it made her smile to hear his accent, the familiar intonations she'd heard during her time in his country. With her quizzical nature she wondered what brought him to New York in the first place, but she was more concerned at her lack of skirt right now than his personal life.

'Please, call me Myles,' he answered. 'And everything is fine. I'll be working from the office upstairs for the rest of the day. I'd like to arrange to have some lunch up there, if I may.'

Darcy turned the best she could without baring all and plucked a lunch menu from the pile on the shelf behind her. 'This is the menu, or if you'd like something a little more, I'd be happy to go out to the deli and pick something up for you.'

He perused the small piece of card and seemed impressed enough. The apartment he was staying in was his for at least a couple of months, so this was a lucrative client and Darcy needed to impress him. She wondered, was he lonely up there for hours on end, when he wasn't in the office? The top floor was their most palatial apartment here at the Inglenook Inn, with its classic vintage brown Chesterfield sofas in the lounge area and pocket doors that could be pulled out to create an extra bedroom if guests required. In the master bedroom was a deluxe bed with the finest white linen and a chaise longue at one edge with a view across the rooftops of Manhattan, and she wondered whether he ever stopped working long enough to take in his surroundings. There was a mirrored mantel in the lounge, sitting over an ornate but unused fireplace, with tall candlesticks on either side, and above the office area and the desk easily capable of sitting three or four people, was a skylight that gave away the time of day depending on whether the moon and stars or the sun came out to play.

'I'll take the club sandwich, please.' His request jolted her out of her thoughts.

Darcy had a habit of observing people and trying to work them out, and it was often far too distracting. 'What time would you like it?' She made a note on the scribble pad beside her.

'In about an hour if that suits.'

'Of course it does, sir.' She wrote the time down.

'Myles.'

'Excuse me?' When he smiled she said, 'Oh yes, Myles.' Usually confident with guests, she was turning into a teen impressed with a man older than her and dressed in clothes worthy of a feature in *GQ* magazine. To make matters worse, he seemed amused by her uneasiness and she tried desperately to think where she might have seen him before. He definitely looked familiar.

'Thank you, Darcy. I'll see you soon.' He turned to leave the lounge, briefcase in hand, coat over one arm, suit jacket in place with the same cuffs she'd seen earlier that morning still pristine white and measuring precisely how they should in relation to his jacket sleeves.

She waited for him to go and when she heard his footsteps on the stairs and their gradual fading away as he went all the way to the top floor, she braved getting up from the desk. She tiptoed in her heels across the wooden floors and peered around the doorway into the hall. Apart from the usual comings and goings on the street outside, the brownstone was silent with their single guest now ensconced in his apartment, so she took the stairs one at a time, her hand careful not to knock the Christmas garlands she'd twisted round the bannisters with their tiny twinkle lights shining their enthusiasm.

She cursed under her breath when she dropped her key on the floor right outside her apartment, but nothing could match the feeling that whipped through her body when she turned the key in the lock and realised she had an audience, because there was Myles at the foot of the stairs on her floor obviously debating whether to pass the scantily clad woman in the hallway or whether perhaps it was best to hover until she disappeared inside. He must've come back down the stairs so quietly she hadn't heard him.

She flew into her apartment and shut the door without a word. She leaned against it and had no idea whether he'd gone past yet or not.

All she knew was that this wasn't the impression she wanted to leave on a guest, least of all when she was doing her best to make this season successful for the Inn and for her. After her spectacularly bad departure from her job in London, she needed to make this something good, for her self-esteem and confidence as much as anything else.

She hastily found another skirt, pulled it on and hoped she wouldn't have to face Myles when she came out of her apartment and shut the door behind her, but it was as though the man had a radar.

'Hello, sir.'

'M—'

She shook her head as though it would help her mind get straight. 'I know, Myles. I do apologise.'

'No need.' He looked amused and she hoped he wasn't thinking about what he'd seen earlier.

'Can I get you anything?'

He was staring, that was for sure. 'I'm sorry, I just feel as though we've met before.'

'I don't think so.' She smiled. She didn't admit the same thought had crossed her mind earlier.

He seemed to accept her claim. 'Could I please ask for a bottle of beer to be brought up with my lunch?'

'Of course, I'll bring it to you with your sandwich. Any preference for which type?'

'I'll leave it up to you.' His eyes didn't leave hers.

More confident fully dressed, she turned to go down the stairs and left him hovering in the corridor, fully aware he was still watching her. It was only as she reached halfway down that it dawned on her. She had seen him before, and she remembered exactly where.

13

He must've realised the same thing at the same time because when she turned to look back, he'd taken a few steps along the corridor to close the gap between them.

He shook his head. 'I don't believe it. Darcy Spencer. We meet again.'

# Chapter Two

## *Myles*

Myles opted for a run around the Jacqueline Kennedy Onassis Reservoir later that afternoon. He was still in the early days of living in Manhattan and he wanted to get a feel for the place, which meant venturing away from Greenwich Village, where he was living, and the Financial District, where he spent the rest of his time at the office.

Myles took the subway and followed it all the way to the Upper West Side 86th Street station. He wondered how long it would be before this all felt as familiar as taking the tube back in London.

He made his way to the start of the loop, using the walk from the subway as a warm up. He ran a lot in London – it kept him sane – and since arriving in New York he was determined to at least make time for that amidst his enormous workload, even if he didn't make time for much else. He'd always been the same way. Work came first, no question about it. But today he'd found it impossible to concentrate when he'd sat down after his lunch, and now physical exertion was the only solution if he wanted to be at all productive. He still needed to put together a funds flow model for the deal he was about to close, but the only thing that was flowing at the moment were his thoughts.

Darcy Spencer. The name was set firmly in his mind as well as the image of her long legs in stockings, the hint of suspenders creeping up the tops of her thighs, and the heels that did nothing to deflect his attention. He hadn't recognised her at first. He'd hovered at the bottom of the stairs, hoping to save her embarrassment by letting her go inside her apartment before he moved again. He'd come down to ask for a beer with lunch, a beer he'd subsequently left and put in the fridge for later on. Unfortunately, Darcy had seen him before she'd opened the door and he'd been embarrassed for her. He'd felt like some kind of stalker, lurking in the shadows. But that was nothing compared to how he'd felt when he realised he knew her from London.

It had been a work Christmas party at a swanky hotel in England's capital and he'd attended along with his colleagues but had been the most sober of all of them. With an important client meeting the next morning, letting go hadn't been an option for Myles that evening. He'd joined in, pretending he was as inebriated as the others, who were all getting into it with rooms upstairs waiting for each of them. It had been no expense spared by the firm he was working for, but when some of the partygoers cranked up the Christmas cheer, more than one of them getting it on with the women in the office or, in one case, with a waitress who was topping up their glasses all night long, he knew it wasn't going to end well.

One of the other waitresses was friendly and a bit flirty with Myles's colleague, newcomer to the firm, Brian, but when it came down to it she wasn't interested in anything more. All she wanted was simply to do her job and make them feel welcome. But Brian had a hard time understanding the word 'no' and Myles had had to step in and help her out. Brian hadn't been too pleased, his pride was dented, and when Myles wasn't looking Brian had tried it on with the girl again. He'd earnt himself a big slap across his cheek but, surprising everyone, had groped her one more time. Myles, with the help of another colleague, had escorted Brian to his room, where they pushed him in and he collapsed on the bed. Myles had wanted to go and see if the girl was OK but by then he needed some headspace and so grabbed his laptop from his room. It wasn't yet nine o'clock so he found the restaurant area and ordered a strong black coffee, the perfect hit for him to get some preliminary work done. People commented on his work ethic, saying it was more like a religion to him – and it was. His parents had paid for top schools for his education, and after his father and grandfather had made themselves a success in the business world, Myles had always wanted to do the same.

Myles had two cups of coffee and enjoyed the quiet, low-lit corner of the restaurant, where he worked through everything he would need for tomorrow. He'd prepared a PowerPoint pitch for a new client and, now, he felt he knew it backwards. It was exactly how he liked to go to a meeting, prepared and ready for any questions, any change of direction that he could use in his favour.

Just after midnight, Myles packed away the laptop and up he went to his room. The hotel was plush and the bed as comfortable as any he'd ever slept in, and despite the caffeine hit, as soon as his body went from vertical to horizontal and his head sank into the luxurious feather-and-down pillow, he was out like a light.

At 3 a.m. the fun started. He woke up to the sound of the phone and when he answered was told it was the wake-up call he'd requested. He explained they must have the wrong room and put the phone down, but he couldn't get back to sleep because he was itching all over. He tossed and turned, he scratched incessantly, and after a pitiful attempt at more sleep, he got up. The skin on his arms, across his chest and up his neck was bright red and the only relief he found was by taking a shower. He'd wondered whether he was allergic to the washing powder the hotel used on the sheets, but when he cleaned his teeth and looked in the mirror to see his white smile was more red than anything else, he realised someone was playing games. And putting some kind of dye on his toothbrush had pushed him too far.

Fuming, aware he must've been the brunt of a practical joke, Myles realised he had no spare toothbrush to use. He wondered which one of his colleagues would've had time and been sober enough to do all those things that had made his night so terrible. He packed up his suitcase and considered how he was going to investigate this. He felt he couldn't let it go. He hated practical jokes, had never found them funny. As a boy he'd boarded at a school where practical jokes had happened all the time – it was almost a rite of passage – but he couldn't stand them then, and he certainly didn't appreciate them now.

He got in the elevator and said hello to the two chambermaids, who were gossiping about something or other, and he was so engrossed with thoughts of the presentation this morning and how he was going to cover up the unsightly redness on his neck that he almost missed the snippets of their conversation that told him those practical jokes had been nothing to do with anyone at work.

'Serves him right, the bloody pervert,' one said to the other, who burst out laughing.

Whispering, the other girl said, 'My brother said that powder she used works wonders. He put it on a teacher's seat once and the teacher was scratching his arse the rest of the day.'

Myles didn't turn round and willed the elevator to move even slower so he could hear more. All he needed was for these girls to say the name of the person responsible, the person they thought was so funny.

'Hope his head was pounding when he answered the wake-up call,' one of them sniggered.

Myles was so angry he stared straight ahead all the way to the bottom floor as the pair smugly revelled in someone else's ingenuity.

He wondered how funny it would be when he finished with them.

He marched up to the front desk. He saw the girl from last night, the one his colleague had hassled way too much, and he wanted to ask if she was OK but he had other things on his mind now as she hovered with another girl, who had on a shiny brass name badge. He looked closer. Darcy Spencer, Deputy Front of House Manager.

'Are you in charge?' he demanded. The girl from last night went on her way with a set of keys.

'I am, sir. May I help you?' Her smile almost dazzled him, her dark curls fell delicately to frame her face and a hint of an American accent made her interesting, but he wouldn't be distracted from what he needed to do.

'I have a complaint, a very big one.' He scratched at his neck again. He just hoped his teeth were at least a little less coloured than before, but he needed to buy a toothbrush before he went anywhere near a workplace.

She didn't look overly worried. 'And what seems to be the problem, sir?'

He explained the shenanigans of last night: the wake-up call, the itching powder, the food colouring. She kept a straight face the entire time.

'I want someone to be held accountable,' he demanded.

'I understand that, sir. May I ask, were you a part of the Christmas party last night?'

'I was, but what does that have to do with anything?'

'I'm just trying to ascertain what may have gone on, that's all.'

'I thought it was a colleague.'

'It sounds the most likely.'

He made a face. 'That was until I overheard two of *your* people congratulating whoever pulled the stunts at how well they had gone and how funny they were.'

Her face drained of colour and her ice-blue eyes looked worried now.

'Did you hear what I said?' He scratched at his neck again. He was in no mood for this and he didn't have time to waste. He'd be presenting to potential clients in less than an hour and prayed the persistent itching would subside by then.

'I did, sir.'

'So what are you going to do about it?'

'Is there a problem?' An older gentleman in a dark suit with a similar brass badge brandishing his name and that of the hotel came over. Myles peered at the badge and realised this man was the hotel manager and therefore more superior than Darcy Spencer, so he turned his attentions to him and demanded to know what would be done.

Miss Spencer was told to round up all her staff immediately and work out what had gone on. The man had a vein throbbing at his temple and he was not impressed. He assured Myles that this would not be tolerated under any circumstances and the girl went off to do her job.

'I want someone held accountable,' Myles told the man. The more he scratched at his neck the more he knew the redness was spreading and the more it made him want someone's head to roll for this.

Myles waited in reception until the manager called him into a room, where the same girl from last night was waiting, apparently in trouble. He wondered why she'd singled him out when all he'd done was try to help her. But events took a turn he hadn't expected when the hotel manager instantly turned to the female employee and gave her her marching orders. Myles began to speak but the hotel manager, evidently intent on regaining the reputation of the hotel, was doing exactly as Myles had demanded and holding someone to account.

What Myles didn't expect after the girl fled the room, clearly upset, was for Miss Spencer to turn on him. And clearly the hotel manager hadn't expected it either.

'She wouldn't have done it if your friend had kept his hands to himself,' she cried.

'Darcy.' The hotel manager had clearly never heard an outburst of this sort from the together, well-groomed deputy front-of-house manager. 'I think Mr Cunningham was well within his rights to complain.'

'Why did she target me?' Myles addressed only Darcy. Those ice-blue eyes were difficult to look away from. 'I only tried to help her. I wasn't trying anything else.'

'She didn't target you.' Darcy looked at the floor before returning her gaze to his. 'She got the room wrong…the man she wanted to punish was in room 175 not room 157, which was your room.'

A muscle in his cheek twitched in amusement despite the prank that had been played on him, the innocent party. It was the sort of story he would probably laugh at

21

if it had happened to someone else. 'Well you're all very lucky that I didn't have a worse allergic reaction,' he said, to remind her of the seriousness of the situation.

'And what will your friend get for groping my colleague?' Darcy wanted to know. 'Bit unfair, don't you think, for him to walk away from this without any punishment?'

'Sir,' the hotel manager began, trying to deflect from Darcy's deathlike stare. 'Please accept my sincere apologies.' He began to reel off all kinds of offers – a night's accommodation in an apartment of his choice, a complimentary evening meal for two in their gourmet restaurant, a hefty discount if he were to book another party here in the future – but Myles wasn't interested in any of it. One girl had lost her job and he felt bad enough for that as it was, because his colleague had hit on her and she'd tried to pay him back. She just got it wrong. And besides, he didn't have time for all the admin these favours were going to create.

'That won't be necessary, thank you.' Myles took the handle of his suitcase and turned to leave.

It was at that moment that Brian chose to grace reception to check out and as soon as Darcy saw him, she went in for the kill.

She was feisty and Myles had to admit, he admired her for it. She went marching up to Brian and had a serious word with him about his conduct. But when Myles clocked the manager's reaction, he willed Darcy to stop. She was the face of the hotel and the way she was verbally laying into his colleague, who denied he'd done anything untoward, was attracting more than a few glances. He deserved it completely, but Myles could tell the manager wasn't thinking along those lines right now.

It all happened in seconds after that. One moment Darcy was having words with Brian, the next moment he laughed at her as though the entire thing were a joke, and then when she raised her voice and told him not to be surprised if her friend pressed charges, the hotel manager stepped in and marched her away from prying eyes.

Myles had no idea what was going to happen but it was time for him to get out of there. He'd well and truly had enough. He left the hotel and went into the small shop outside, bought a toothbrush, ducked back into the hotel to use the facilities in the foyer and got rid of the remnants of food colouring from his mouth. He checked his appearance in the mirror. His neck was still a pinkish-red but it had mostly died down and he felt sure it would be fine for the meeting this morning, so went on his way.

It was as he stood at the taxi rank out front that he heard the porter talking to one of the girls Myles recognised from earlier and when he heard the words, 'Darcy just got fired', his heart sank. That wasn't what he'd wanted to happen. Not at all. If only he hadn't been so pig-headed about someone being held accountable. Then again, this was a top hotel. He had a right to come here and not leave with memories of such an awful experience.

What a bloody mess.

The mess had happened six months ago and Myles had all but forgotten about it. Work had swallowed him up whole, he'd been headhunted and taken up a position in New York, and, now, here he was. He was waiting for an apartment on the Upper West Side to be renovated for him – the firm had arranged it – and for now he was being put up in the Inglenook Inn in Greenwich Village, where once again he'd crossed paths with Darcy Spencer.

Myles completed two loops around the reservoir and went for a third to bring him up to a decent mileage. The reservoir was magnificent even on a grey and cold December day with a low-lying mist that obscured the tops of the city buildings. He made the most of the last remnants of sunlight that made the water sparkle before it would soon be plunged into darkness when dusk fell, and he barely felt the cold he was working up such a sweat. The fresh location also took some of the pain away from pounding the pavements, and by the time he made his way back to the 86th Street station he was exhausted, but pumped up and ready to tackle the work he'd put to one side. He wondered if he would bump into Darcy again. She'd got the chef, Rupert, to deliver his sandwich earlier, probably relieved not to have to face him again. He'd cost her her job in London after all and there was no way she was going to forget that in a hurry.

As he arrived back at the Inn and climbed the steps up to the front entrance he nodded a greeting to Rupert, who was heading out. The Inn was already well dressed for Christmas and Myles did his best to take it all in his stride. The brownstone was among the many properties lit up for the season in Manhattan. Around the front door were white lights that shone against the darkened street and didn't give up when the rain or the wind tried to win, a giant garland finished with a red velvet ribbon hung on the door that opened, and the front stoop didn't escape the Christmas feel either. Garlands in green, entwined with white lights, wound round the railings all the way from the street to the door. Tasteful slender pine trees in pots guarded the entry point but at least the front of the building had escaped the gaudy flashing lights so many people loved. Myles wasn't sure his stay would've been a long one if he'd had to face those every time he returned from the office because to say he wasn't a big lover of Christmas was an understatement.

In the lounge, a communal space and where he now knew Darcy could probably be found at the desk on plenty of occasions, sprigs of holly poked out of the sides of picture frames, flames of poinsettia lit up side tables, an arrangement repeated on small tables as you reached the top of each section of the internal staircase. The tree was apparently on its way but for now there was a big fireplace with four stockings lined up, hanging from the mantelpiece, and rather than having names on them, each had a Christmas phrase: Happy Holidays; Believe; Do Not Open till December 25th; Joy. Garlands wound their way up from the foot of the bannisters to the top with tasteful white lights just pleasant enough to not give Myles a headache as he took the stairs towards his apartment, his solace away from all the merriment. All of the decorations so far had been in place since Thanksgiving, which heralded the start of the silly season for New Yorkers he was fast beginning to learn. He'd seen photographs on the website before arriving in New York but, he figured, at least whoever was in charge of the decorations hadn't gone massively over the top. There was an artificial tree in the dining room that he had to endure when he chose to have breakfast there instead of in his apartment, but usually he sat so he couldn't even see it and, instead, read the news on his iPad.

He reached the top of the brownstone and pushed open the door to his apartment. He wondered what Darcy would say to him when he next saw her. Their first encounter had ended badly, their second had ended

25

with him seeing her in next to nothing and with her stomping off as she remembered what had happened back in London.

He sighed, mainly from exhaustion but also at the thought that of all the hotels he could've walked into in Manhattan, he had to walk into hers.

# Chapter Three

*Darcy*

Darcy climbed onto the bar stool and put her cell phone next to her on the table while her friend, Isabella, brought over the drinks. She'd only be out for a couple of hours, but she liked guests, or Rupert, to be able to get hold of her whenever they needed.

'Get that into you.' Isabella had squeezed through the crowd chattering away beneath the glowing yellow globe lights that punctuated the night sky, and handed Darcy a glass of red wine. 'It's the French one, same as we had last week.'

'Thanks.' The wine took seconds to make her relax and she felt her shoulders drop.

'How's your day been?'

'Manic.'

'But you love it, right?'

Darcy smiled. She really did. 'I prepared for the new arrivals, checked them in, arranged a restaurant booking for a family of four and pointed them in the direction of Central Park, oh, and I told some other guests about the bar we found a few weeks ago for cocktails over near the Chelsea Market. They seemed happy with that. I just wish the Christmas tree had been here in time. I explained to every guest that it's on its way, but it would've been so much better to wow them from the start.'

'It'll arrive soon enough,' Isabella assured her. 'You've got plenty to keep yourself busy until then. You're an innkeeper, social events coordinator and a Manhattan map, all rolled into one.'

'I also saw a face from the past.'

Isabella sat up a little straighter. 'Oh?'

'Myles Cunningham.'

'Who's that? Should I know him?'

'He's the one I told you about.'

'I don't remember.'

'Well even I'd forgotten his name. I think I'd tried to blank it out.' Isabella looked questioningly at her as she sipped her wine. 'Remember how I lost my job in London because some guest made a huge fuss and wanted someone to be held accountable for a practical joke gone wrong?'

Isabella's eyes widened. 'Him?'

'The very same.'

'He's staying at the Inglenook Inn? I don't believe it.'

'Neither do I.'

'Talk about a small world.'

'Far too small.'

'Weren't you tempted to punch him after what happened?'

'I wasn't really in a position to do that.' She filled her friend in on the unfortunate skirt incident.

'Oh, Darcy!' Isabella had a hard time holding back the laughter. Her eyes were actually watering. 'I'm sorry, but that's so funny. It could only happen to you.'

'I was mortified.'

'Why? You've got great legs and a pretty good butt.'

With an eye roll, Darcy said, 'Punching him wouldn't accomplish anything, would it? It would only mess things up for me.' Her anger had already subsided since their run-in, which was more than could be said for her embarrassment. 'And he wasn't exactly in the wrong back there in London. Even I can admit that.'

'He got you fired.'

28

'You heard about it the day I lost the job, when I called you,' Darcy explained. 'I was livid and of course I blamed him, thinking he condoned his colleague's behaviour, but looking at it from a hotel guest's point of view, he had every right to demand someone was held accountable.'

'What happened to the other girl who lost her job? I'll bet she didn't get a reference.'

'I've no idea, she wasn't a close friend. I was in charge of them all so I think there was a certain boundary none of them wanted to cross. But I still felt I had to stick up for her. Groping is unacceptable. It happened to me a few times when I worked in the kitchens and my manager swept it under the carpet every time I mentioned it.'

'You'd think in this day and age they'd be worried about lawsuits.'

'They obviously weren't. Anyway, I got away from the hotel where it was an issue and was happy in the other positions I managed to find. That morning I was tired. We'd all worked long shifts the day before, because of the party, and I had a million and one things to do. I guess he caught me at the wrong time and when I saw another manager thinking that kind of behaviour was OK, I just flipped.'

'Do you need your cell phone there?' Isabella frowned as Darcy's hand fiddled with her device, sitting obediently beside her.

'I like to be contactable. I'm determined not to mess this up.'

'How on earth would you do that?'

'I don't think I will, but it's a huge responsibility in Sofia's absence. I've done something I'm not sure Sofia will like.' She pulled a face.

29

'Well unless you've burnt the place down, I think you'll be fine.'

'Isabella, I'm serious.'

'What did you do?'

'You know how I told you I thought Sofia needed to be a bit more proactive with the Inn, drum up more business?'

'Yes, we all think she should.' Isabella, like Dylan and Cleo, and Sofia's own daughter, Gabriella, all wanted to see the Inn succeed. But Sofia seemed happy to let it chug along and they were all afraid that one day it wouldn't be enough, that competition would make it an unviable business. Of course nobody could predict the future, but Sofia needed to give the place a fighting chance. 'All the effort you've been putting in for Christmas is a wonderful start,' Isabella assured her. 'So what have you done that isn't so great?'

'I've managed to get talking to an editor from a major magazine.' She told Isabella the name of it and her disclosure was met with an impressed look. 'The editor is coming to stay at the Inn over Christmas. She's said she'll do a write-up of her experience of Christmas at the Inglenook Inn.' Darcy put her head in her hands at the importance of it. 'It'll be a feature article in late January. She says people will still be in the winter mood, a lot of families are looking to secure bookings for the following year, so it could give the Inn an enormous boost.'

'Then I really don't see what the problem is.'

'What if I fail, Isabella? What if I can't pull Christmas off? Sofia always said she didn't want to open at that time of the year because it was when she wanted to focus on her own family, and I pushed the idea. What if this feature article ends up reporting on a terrible Christmas?'

30

'Now why on earth would it do that?'

'I don't know. I just feel out of my depth. I'm panicking.'

Isabella put her own hand on Darcy's and squeezed it tight. 'Sofia would never have left you in charge if she didn't believe in you.'

'I guess you're right. But I won't tell her about the article, not until I know it's going to be a good write-up.'

'Fair enough.' Isabella picked up her wine from the cardboard coaster. 'I'll take my Executive Assistant job any day; I don't know how you do yours with all the responsibility.'

'You have lots of responsibility too.'

Isabella shrugged. 'It's manageable though. You put in the long and erratic hours.'

'All hotel work is like that. It's not a nine-to-five job.' It was one of the things Darcy loved about working in the hotel industry. She thrived on the unpredictability – it kept her on her toes and gave her a buzz she knew she wouldn't get in a job where she was doing the same thing every day. 'And how is your new job going?'

Isabella hooked her blonde, bobbed hair behind her ears. 'Busy, but good, and I get to walk away at five or six o'clock in the evening and forget about it.'

'Is your boss still as nice as you thought she was?'

'She's no Sofia,' Isabella smiled. Through Darcy she'd come to know Sofia really well too. 'But she's a lot better than my last one. She keeps me busy, rushing to and from meetings, distributing paperwork and minutes, booking her flights or accommodation, invoicing, but on the whole I think she's one of the better ones. I'm not sure how she'd react if I ever did anything wrong – which I'm paranoid about by the way,

31

after booking a flight on the wrong day in my previous job.'

Darcy had wondered the same about Sofia, whether she would be a different person if Darcy messed up this responsibility and the Inn's reputation or turnover suffered because of it.

They chatted more about work, going right back to the mind-numbingly boring jobs they'd taken out of school – washing up in kitchens, delivering newspapers, helping at the local Dairy Queen – and Darcy talked passionately about her love of hotels. Isabella had never had the same drive and openly admitted that she wanted a steady, reliable job that wasn't necessarily exciting but that could help her pay the bills and stay in the city.

'Sherry just moved out to Brooklyn,' Isabella announced when Darcy returned from the bar with two more glasses of red wine and discreetly checked her cell phone. Sherry was Isabella's older sister and had recently got engaged to someone who had gently been trying to shoehorn her out of Manhattan to somewhere more affordable for the last six months. 'I mean, what's next – Connecticut, New Jersey?'

Darcy had no intention of leaving Manhattan either, although flipping through a travel magazine as she so often did to gain a well-rounded understanding of the overall industry, its trends, challenges and hot topics, she had seen a gorgeous inn in Vermont and it had sparked something inside of her. She'd never thought about owning her own hotel, she really wanted to ground herself in Manhattan in one of the bigger hotel chains, but being responsible for the Inglenook Inn had set off fireworks in her mind. Even chatting to Cleo and seeing how happy she was settled in Inglenook Falls with her knitting store when she hadn't wanted to leave the city at all was enough to tell Darcy that dreams could quite often morph into something else entirely, or a change could unexpectedly come your way.

'I'm sure they'll both be really happy in Brooklyn,' said Darcy. 'It's not exactly far.'

'Try telling Sherry that,' Isabella smiled. 'So anyway, how long is Mr Bigshot from London staying with you?'

Darcy wiped her elbow after realising she'd leant on a sticky patch of the table. It was warm in here and their winter coats were piled up on a stool next to them, gloves stuffed in pockets, scarves coiled beneath the coats so they wouldn't be knocked to the floor. 'He's not staying with *me*, he's staying at the Inn. And he's booked in until well after New Year's. He works for some big company in the Financial District and they're renovating an apartment for him.'

'Nice. Being spoiled like that almost makes me want to work for a big firm with all the perks.'

'He puts in a lot of hours, judging by how much he's out of his apartment. Even when he's at the Inn I know he works because he has an office set up, paperwork everywhere.'

'You seem to be taking more of an interest in him than any of your other guests.' Isabella's smile practically erupted on her face.

'Calm down, I'm not. It's just that he's the only one you've asked about. If you were talking about the O'Sullivan family I could tell you they're a party of four – parents, two sons – and they're visiting all the way from Ireland. One son likes orange juice, the other prefers apple, and they've brought with them a roll-out mat to play toy cars in their apartment. And if you asked me about the other couple I checked in today I'd tell you that they have recently become engaged and are in the

33

throes of planning their wedding in Seattle, where the bride-to-be is from, although there's some contention because the groom always wanted to marry in his home state of Colorado.'

Isabella held up a hand. 'OK, enough. I don't need their measurements as well. Although…maybe getting Mr Bigshot's would be interesting.'

'Drink your wine and be quiet,' Darcy grinned, although her mind did skip momentarily to the man staying at the Inglenook Inn and his sharp suits, strong jaw and chocolatey eyes.

Darcy's cell phone buzzed and she picked up the text from Rupert to say he was heading home from the Inn in twenty minutes, and so Darcy's cue to leave had them bundling up in their coats and weaving their way through the dimly lit bar to the front doors and onto Canal Street. She'd lit the fire in the lounge before their new guests' arrival this afternoon – it was a perfect way to welcome them to New York City – and she'd known it'd been the right thing to do when the guests had congregated beside it before they went for dinner, but what she didn't like doing was leaving it unattended, which was why she'd asked Rupert to let her know when he was leaving so she could get back and be on duty.

Wrapped up snuggly warm, their breath puffing into the cold night air, Darcy pulled on her gloves and looped a camel scarf around her neck. 'We'll catch up again soon.'

'You bet.' Isabella kissed her friend on the cheek. 'I need to make sure you're getting some time away from the Inn. All work and no play makes Darcy a dull girl.'

'Goodbye, Isabella.' Darcy smiled.

The walk blew away the rest of the cobwebs lurking and even though not a single flake of snow had fallen from the skies in Manhattan so far this winter, there was a feeling in the air that suggested it wouldn't be all that far away.

Back at the Inn, Darcy read the note from Rupert to say he'd restocked the refrigerator and left more supplies in the bigger one in the basement, so she had plenty of food to make up snacks for guests if required, and enough to put on light breakfasts if anyone requested a super-early start. She took off her coat, fired up the laptop to check the emails, but there wasn't anything from any of the guests so she went over to tend to the fire, which was still crackling away steadily.

Darcy allowed herself some time to take in the ambience she'd been a part of creating today and it made her feel proud. Since she'd begun working here she'd been looking at the Inglenook Inn from a different perspective. If she were the owner and she had the funds, she'd make a few changes for sure. She'd begun to wonder how lucrative the top floor and some of the other apartments really were. The top floor was beautiful but because of its square footage, the luxury bathroom and office space, it commanded a hefty price and wasn't always rented out. They'd got lucky with this corporate client, in Darcy's opinion. If this place were hers, she'd separate it into two, possibly three, apartments. She'd also reduce the size of the two apartments on the third floor to accommodate more separate bookings. She hadn't studied the figures much – it wasn't for her to interfere unless Sofia wanted her to – but she knew that bookings had been sparse before the festive season and Sofia wasn't all that big on advertising.

She checked her watch. Nine fifteen. She suspected the family with young kids were tucked up in their apartment, but the young couple would be out and about, taking in the sights of the city at night, a truly wondrous experience for first-timers like them. Isabella was wrong to think she'd taken more of an interest in Myles Cunningham than anyone else. She liked to get to know all of her guests. It was all part of her job.

She spent the next couple of hours planning her morning tomorrow and answering email queries about potential new bookings. She swept the hallway of the inevitable dirt that crept in every time the front door was opened to the Manhattan streets and when the fire had almost gone out in the grate, the moonlight had risen high above the clouds outside, Darcy took the stairs to her own apartment and prepared to turn in, ready to get up tomorrow and do what she loved all over again.

# Chapter Four

*Myles*

*Two weeks until Christmas*

Myles had been so busy with work that he hadn't seen much of Darcy over the last week. But after their run-in outside her apartment, it was probably a good thing. When he passed her in the hallway or came home to see her sitting at the desk, or chatting with other guests in the lounge, they were both cordial but he had the feeling it was all down to her professionalism rather than her choice.

Today, with a low-lying mist refusing to leave Manhattan alone, Myles spent lunchtime at the office talking with his brother on the phone. He generally didn't have much time to do so, but Winston had taken it upon himself to badger his younger brother with text messages, and talking to him now was the only way to shut him up.

'How are Mum and Dad?' Myles asked, already anticipating the answer.

'Still not happy about your move, still talking about you coming home sooner rather than later. And still going on about how nice it would be to see you settle down.'

Myles had been relieved he'd managed to time this move before Christmas. Christmas was something his family did insanely well. The meal was sumptuous, home-cooked, fit for a king. Every year the house was bedecked in the most exquisite decorations sourced from Liberty, Harrods, Fortnum & Mason. White lights hung in the trees lining the driveway up to the family home, a wreath on the door – always fresh, always welcoming – marked the way and the presents beneath the tree could rival those of the aristocracy. But it hadn't always been that way, and the other times were the ones that Myles couldn't help but remember. Those were the Christmases that had spoilt this time of the year for him for good.

Myles sighed. 'You'd think Dad would get it. He was a businessman and out of the country on plenty of occasions over the years.' Hard work had been ingrained in the Cunningham boys' psyche, so his dad could hardly criticise Myles for doing what he'd always been taught to do. It was what the Cunningham men did. They were businessmen above all else. And for either of his parents to criticise his personal life, well that always had been an unwelcome intrusion. Even a harmless 'Are you dating anyone right now?' was a question that had the power to see his anger levels rise.

'You know what they're like, they both worry,' said Winston, peacemaker as always.

Myles's shortcoming was that although he'd scored well on the career side of things, his personal life had yet to reach the same dizzy heights or even a height that would make him feel remotely lightheaded. And his mum, especially, had taken it upon herself to worry about him to the point where he almost felt suffocated. But where had that worry been when he was a young boy? Back then she'd been in her own world of pain, had her own way of coping, and now it was as though she was making up for it. But she couldn't turn back the clock. Nobody could. Myles sometimes wondered whether his brother had forgotten half of the stuff that went on when they were growing up, or perhaps he was just a huge believer in second chances. Myles had to hand it to his brother because he'd turned out to be the good one, a real family man setting an entirely different example for his own kids from the one they'd had growing up. And he hadn't neglected his career path either. Somehow he'd managed to get the balance just right. Winston ran his own construction firm, something out of the norm for their genealogy, where men had gone into corporate careers along the finance line, but he'd made it a roaring success.

Winston was also married with two children, whom Myles saw enough of to be called the Fun Uncle, and now they were in the background during the call demanding to know whether it was snowing in America, were all the skyscrapers five times as tall as their house in England, and was Myles ever coming back?

'How about you come home for Christmas?' Winston suggested. 'It's not too late. You could get a last-minute flight, stay with us, we'll do Christmas dinner at the parents' place and then come home here to recover. I'll even be the designated driver. I can't say fairer than that.'

He appreciated it, he really did. Winston had an insatiable energy when it came to trying to include Myles, no matter how much Myles tried to push them all away. 'You know how I feel about Christmas. I'm sorry, Winston. Another year perhaps.'

'It was all such a long time ago,' Winston tried.

It was. And yet, it was still so raw in his mind.

'I've too much work on.' Myles continued his protestations as he cradled the phone between his shoulder and his ear while simultaneously skimming over some figures he needed to translate into something meaningful before a client meeting. 'Christmas is all about the kids. You make sure yours have a great time.'

He always felt a pang of sadness when his brother asked him to do something and he didn't want to do it. And Christmas was invariably the time when he felt the guilt rise up to an almost untenable level like it was doing now.

His brother's voice softened. 'I will. I know you can't be bothered with it, but maybe one year, eh?'

Myles laughed when he heard his sister-in-law, Victoria, in the background calling him the Grinch, the name she'd jokingly called him ever since she'd first met Winston's brother on Christmas Eve at the pub, where Myles had begrudgingly gone along with them.

'Say hello to Victoria for me.' Myles checked his watch – he was out of time. 'I'd better go or I'll have nothing to show my client and all they'll get is a platter full of pastries in meeting room four.'

'Sounds all right to me.'

Myles felt instantly hungry at the thought of food, but that would have to wait until he'd formulated a mini presentation.

'Just send them a Christmas card at least,' Winston said before his brother could hang up.

Knowing exactly who he was referring to, Myles said, 'Already done. I posted one yesterday and it's as festive as you can get, they'll love it. There's an enormous hamper arriving soon too. Mum's favourite, from Fortnum & Mason, with the requisite foie gras, ham, stilton, caviar, champagne.' He stopped at the mention of the alcohol. He wondered whether Winston would berate him for it, but sensed his brother wanted to keep him on side right now. Since ordering the hamper that came with champagne, Myles wondered whether he should've done it. To some it was a nice gesture, but to his mum it was like waving a red flag at her and he just hoped she wouldn't charge.

'Well done, I knew you'd make a fuss somehow,' was all Winston said. 'Mum will love being spoiled.'

If Winston were here now, Myles would meet him at the nearest bar after work and buy him the biggest beer he could find. His brother, always by his side, never stopped trying to bring him back into this family.

After he hung up, Myles stared out the window across the Manhattan skyline. It was peaceful up here, nowhere near the mayhem at street level. Myles sometimes wondered why he didn't resent his older brother more for his all-round contentment, but it was because they got on so famously, always had. Only two years separated them and they'd grown up together, messing around down at the allotment with their grandad, running wild around the fields at the back of their house in the school holidays. And whenever it had snowed in winter, they'd always built an igloo in the garden if the snow was plentiful enough and then they'd used it as their hideout until the weather melted their creation and it was back to reality. Myles should've known then that Winston would go into the construction industry. He'd bossed Myles around until they'd laid the foundations of the igloo, supervised the entire build. But they'd worked as a tight little unit, and Myles saw the same thing now with Winston and Victoria, who complemented one another. He ran the business, she ran the household; he coached the football team at weekends, she was on the Parent Teacher Association at the kids' school. It was the way they worked, a husband and wife team, something their parents had never really been. Myles often wondered how he and his brother had turned out so different, his own feet firmly following the path of his

41

career, never straying for a moment. He'd had relationships along the way, a lot of women saw the attraction in a man who would be reliable and who could provide for them and a family, but somehow he'd never gelled with any of those women. He'd wondered whether it was them or him. Or was it his past experience of family holding him back?

He got to work on the figures and gathered everything up ready to meet the client. His daydreams only continued as far as meeting room four, where he switched back to corporate mode, shook hands with the people he was hoping to impress, and began his spiel about the company and how this venture could work in both of their favour.

*

New York was freezing! Myles was sure the temperature had dropped ten degrees since he'd arrived at the office that morning.

He took the subway and got off a stop earlier to grab a bite to eat at a Mexican place he'd found on his first day here. It was a no-frills establishment but service was speedy, the food was good and filling, and he could sit on his own without feeling too out of the ordinary.

The wind whipped around, hurting his ears as he walked the few blocks back to the Inn. The air promised snow but he wasn't used to this weather and had no idea whether they'd get a light dusting or a serious snowstorm, or dump as he'd heard New Yorkers refer to it. He was hoping for the light dusting if anything, because his days of wanting to build an igloo were long gone. He wanted to be able to navigate the streets, get to work on time and home at a reasonable hour.

He pushed his key into the lock of the brownstone with its sign and curly writing out front announcing that it was an inn. He liked the informality of this place, the fact it felt like coming back to his own separate apartment in many ways.

'Good evening,' he said to a young couple who were making their way outside as he wiped his shoes on the mat.

The young man replied with a more casual, 'Hey there', something Myles was still getting used to. At the office his colleagues were of all nationalities, many American but lots from overseas. Myles remembered his dad's British accent had taken a few dips and dives along the way as he worked for a multinational company, although now he was as British as they came and you'd never know he'd spent a second out of his birthplace.

When he passed by the lounge room, to the left of the wooden-floored corridor, there she was. Darcy was crouched down in front of the fire, positioning logs just so, and he paused, watching her.

When she turned to pick up the box of firelighters beside her she saw him and stood up, straightened her skirt and brushed the front as though some of the residue from the fireplace might have found its way onto her clothes. 'Good evening,' she said, very formally.

'Good to see you, Darcy.'

She smiled. 'Will you be needing dinner this evening? The chef is here for another hour, or I can order a takeout for you if you'd prefer.'

Very professional. 'No, thank you, I've just eaten.'

She tidied the newspapers in the stand on the table to one side of the lounge. She'd left the fire for now, clearly deciding it would be rude to literally turn her back on her guest.

'I went to Casa Alessandra.' He decided to try and make conversation to make his stay as pleasant as possible, even though he'd thought she would've thawed by now. Maybe that was what made him do it – the frustration that she was being so aloof. He wasn't used to being ignored and he was still annoyed that his meeting today hadn't gone as well as he'd hoped for.

'Lovely,' she said. And with everything in the room tidy, she returned to the fireplace.

'Do you need a hand?'

'No, thank you.'

'I feel we got off on the wrong foot.'

She tore off a piece of firelighter and buried it beneath the logs and kindling, then put another on the opposite side and another in the centre. She adjusted the damper at the front of the grate to open. She collected up the firelighter box, pushed the wrapped remains inside and turned to him. 'It was a long time ago.'

'I was angry.'

'What was done to you was unforgivable.'

She was saying it all with a straight face and hardly the looks she'd been giving him ever since she realised who he was that night. He hoped it wasn't the calm before the storm. Was her anger lying dormant and at some point it would rise to the surface, taking him by surprise?

'You didn't do anything wrong,' he responded, 'but you still paid the price.'

'I should've been more polite to you at the time,' she answered diplomatically. 'It was my job and I didn't do it well that day.' She put an end to the conversation by picking up a box of matches. 'It's turned cold outside, but you're welcome to enjoy the fire this evening.'

He looked at the armchairs and the sofa positioned to look out through the slightly curved bay window. Once the fire was going it'd be a wonderful place to relax with a drink, but when she spoke again he knew he'd rather squirrel himself away upstairs on the top floor, lie on his bed for time out, or sit at his desk and gaze up through the skylight at the night surrounding them.

'The Christmas tree will be here tomorrow.'

'That's great.' He said the words but didn't mean them. Christmas was something that got in the way as far as he was concerned. Along with the bad memories, it was merely commercialism gone wild and although he understood big multinational companies cashing in on the season, all it meant to him was that the office would be quieter and perhaps he could get on top of the backlog of work before everyone came down to earth again in the new year.

'We're a bit late with it this year,' she carried on, 'but I'm assured it will arrive after nine tomorrow, so by the time you come home from work I should have it sorted.'

Her smile was so genuine he wondered what her Christmases had been like growing up. He wouldn't mind betting her parents had made it a fun time. There was no way anyone could appear to love it as much as Darcy if they weren't that way inclined. If she'd grown up with the experiences of the big day in his family she might have a different take on the whole affair.

'Will you be joining us here for Christmas dinner?' she asked him. 'It's just that you haven't booked in to do so yet, and I don't want you to miss out.'

When this place was booked he'd seen an invite in amongst the paraphernalia they'd sent via email that his secretary had printed out. He'd put it to the bottom of the pile and forgotten about it. 'I hope to, yes.' He'd be happy to take the meal up to his apartment and treat it like any other day, or rustle something up in the kitchenette in his apartment, but he was trying to make peace. For reasons he wasn't even sure of himself, he didn't want to seem like a complete arsehole in front of her.

'Should I write your name down?'

He nodded. 'Thanks, I appreciate it. Are many others coming?' He tried to keep her talking. She seemed to want to end the conversation now the formalities were out of the way.

Darcy got back to the fireplace. She struck the long match along the side of the box, poked it between the logs and instantly a small flame glowed. She lit the other parts of the firelighter that had been dispersed and then pulled the glass screen down in front. 'So far we have the six other guests staying here plus another lady from the Upper East side, who'll join us nearer to Christmas.' She smiled and for a brief moment she must have forgotten it was him and her expression almost matched the glow from the fire that was taking hold.

She was an attractive girl. He'd thought the same in London, and he found himself wanting to know more about her. 'Will you be joining us, or on waitressing duty, or will you be elsewhere?' His questions were a way to find out more about her, whether she had a significant other who lived here or somewhere else in New York City. But he wished he could turn his curiosity off because it was like prising information from a business associate who played their cards very close to their chest.

'I'll be here,' was the only answer she gave.

'May I ask you a question?' Perhaps small talk was the best way to get to know her. He'd never bothered so much with a woman before. They were either interested or they weren't. But something about Darcy was different.

'Of course.'

'Why is this place called the Inglenook Inn? The fireplace is quite something, but it's not a classic inglenook. I was just wondering how the name came about.'

'The owner, Sofia, went through a hard time.' She restacked some of the kindling she didn't need just yet onto the shelf to the right of the fireplace. 'She found comfort with friends out in a town called Inglenook Falls. The friendship group was very supportive when Sofia took on the venture of this inn. She'd originally planned to call it something else entirely but then changed the name to be the Inglenook Inn, to say thank you I suppose.'

His gaze held hers and he wondered was she one of those people, those friends, who had been involved? He could imagine she probably was – it seemed the sort of thing she'd do. 'In England an inglenook is huge; you can sit in it it's so big.' As soon as the words were out he knew he sounded like an idiot, like he was trying to show off somehow. But she didn't take it the wrong way.

'I remember. There was a pub on the street where I rented a flat and it had the most impressive inglenook fireplace.' For a moment she let herself forget who he was. 'I loved Sunday drinks sitting beside it through the winter months.' But she was distracted when someone else came through the front entrance to the brownstone.

The cold nipped at his ankles beneath his suit trousers, socks and polished shoes, and it was his cue to go upstairs to his apartment.

47

He worked some more at the desk equipped with everything he needed, but as figures began to swim in front of his eyes and he'd drained the bottle of beer from the fridge, he had a moment where he wondered whether he'd try talking to her again. He went downstairs, but when he heard other guests chatting away in the lounge he went out for a wander instead.

He had the feeling he'd missed his opportunity with Darcy Spencer, or perhaps there'd never really been one in the first place.

# Chapter Five

*Darcy*

*Thirteen days until Christmas*

The open fire was a huge hit with the O'Sullivans, who had just returned to the Inn and come in from the cold. Last night Darcy had wondered whether Myles Cunningham was going to sit and enjoy it like they were doing now. Part of her had hoped he would; the other part of her was so uncomfortable around him that she was relieved when he disappeared up to the top floor.

'It's really coming down out there,' Darcy sympathised as the parents tried to warm up. They'd taken off their coats but still looked bedraggled and in need of respite. The rain had started a few minutes ago and was already hammering against the window panes. 'How was dinner?'

'It was wonderful,' the mum, Adele, replied, but Darcy could tell she was about five minutes away from collapsing with utter exhaustion. Manhattan was bigger than you realised and while the phrase 'it's only a few blocks away' conjured up a pleasant, meandering walk, Darcy knew that to out-of-towners those few blocks could be torturous if you were already tired, if the weather was as bad as it was now, and if you had kids in tow. The children weren't very old either and the way they were whining, Darcy suspected this guest had reached the end of her tether.

'This fire is a godsend.' Adele's eyes lit up momentarily until she forced herself back into mummy mode. The kids looked like they'd had enough instruction for one day and were fractious. 'Come on, kids, let's go and get into some dry clothes, tuck you up for the night.'

When both boys dialled the whining up a notch, Darcy whispered to Adele before crouching down so she was at the boys' eye level. 'How about you all get changed, then come down to the fire and I'll make you each a cup of hot cocoa.' The parents' shoulders relaxed but not as much as when Darcy added, 'If you're good' – she looked at each child in turn – 'I'll even make some s'mores.'

'What are they?' the youngest wanted to know.

'They're a big treat with chocolate and marshmallows.'

It was all it took. Eyes wide, they were perfectly compliant when it came to their parents' instructions and the mum mouthed a thank you to Darcy as they took the stairs.

This is what Darcy loved: going that extra mile for guests to lift their experience from good to fabulous. The mum had leapt at her suggestion, willing to try anything when Darcy sought her approval before making her offer. They'd expected to come back to their accommodation and collapse into bed, and in a bigger establishment they may have gone into a restaurant or ordered room service, selecting cocoa from the menu. But what Darcy was learning more and more now she'd worked somewhere smaller were the little tweaks you could offer guests.

Darcy went about preparing the ingredients she'd need. Rupert was finishing up and she assured him she'd take it from here. He went off home and she took out the Graham crackers, a block of chocolate, a packet of marshmallows and some wooden skewers, plates, cups and cocoa powder. She brought a pan of milk up to temperature and whisked through the cocoa powder, and when it was hot she switched off the heat and put a lid over the pan so it was ready when the family returned downstairs. She took everything through to the lounge on an oval platter just as the two boys came downstairs with their dad, Troy.

'Now, which one of you is Saul and which one is Jarrod?' Darcy asked as Troy settled himself into the sofa opposite the fire.

The littlest blond boy announced he was Saul and at the same time the taller of the two said Jarrod.

'Well please, call me Darcy.' She held up two skewers. 'Take one each.' The boys' eyes lit up as they stretched out their hands to lay claim to the thin pieces of wood. 'S'mores are a favourite of mine, and very American.'

They were full of energy, eager to get going with the proceedings.

'I ate a lot in my childhood.' She whispered so their dad didn't overhear. 'They're terrible for your teeth.'

Both boys sniggered conspiratorially.

Darcy grinned. She was having fun making this a Christmas vacation they'd surely remember. 'Now, see those marshmallows, you need to put one on the end of the skewer, then lay that down here.' She pointed to the clean plates and stood supervising.

'I appreciate this.' Troy, his eyes open now his wife had come to join them, watched on as Darcy had the boys line up halves of Graham crackers and place a square of chocolate on top of one half each.

'Mum, can we make these again when we go home?' the boys asked Adele.

'Oh, I don't know about that.'

'Pleeeeeease!' they chorused.

Darcy carried on instructing the boys on how to toast the marshmallows and when they understood the task she lifted the glass in front of the fire to expose the flames. 'I made these every Christmas as a little girl. It was my dad's favourite thing to do. My dad wasn't allowed too many, Mom said he'd be bigger than Santa and he'd have no teeth if he did, but it never put me off.' The boys' giggles filled the room. The only year Darcy had ever missed the festive tradition of s'mores was when she'd had braces and they were at the top of the list of what not to eat, along with all the other treats teenagers loved. Sometimes she swore the dentist made half the stuff up to turn them all into health nuts until their teeth were straight. 'Now, we all know how important it is to clean our teeth, don't we?' She looked at each boy in turn, pulling Jarrod back from the fire and explaining he needed to straighten his arm and rotate the stick so that the outside of the marshmallow could turn slowly golden.

'We know,' the boys said, probably worried that if they didn't say it, they wouldn't be allowed the delectable treats.

'Like this?' Saul rotated his skewer, the concentration written across his brow.

'That's exactly right. You know, I think that's nearly done.' She moved over to his brother. 'Yours too. Now, carefully take them over to your plates.' They did as told. 'Now lay the marshmallow on top of the square of chocolate sitting on the Graham cracker. That's it. Now, put the other half on top.' She watched them as they intently did as asked. 'Push it down gently but firm enough to hold the marshmallow in place, and at the same time pull the skewer.'

52

'Can we eat them?' Jarrod's smile matched Saul's.

'Count to sixty to give them a chance to cool and for the chocolate to melt, and then you're good to go,' she beamed. And when she turned around, there, leaning against the doorframe to the lounge, was Myles Cunningham, who looked like he'd been watching them for quite a while.

'Is it time for hot cocoa?' She addressed Adele and Troy, leaving Myles to his own devices as he moved towards the table near the bar to peruse the newspapers. She wondered if he'd be brave enough to sit in here with a family around. It didn't seem his sort of thing. He seemed more of a fine-dining, peace-and-quiet type gentleman. Even at the party in London he hadn't seemed to let go with his colleagues. Perhaps it wasn't something he ever allowed himself to do.

'That would be lovely,' Troy answered. 'Cocoa all round, I think. I'm not sure the kids will sleep after their sugar load, but what the heck – we're on holiday.' He earned himself a kiss from his wife, who looked twenty times more relaxed than she had when they'd returned to the Inn earlier.

Darcy knew she couldn't be rude so asked Myles, 'Can I interest you in a cocoa, Mr Cunningham?' Funny, she called him Myles in her head but tried to address him formally out loud even though he insisted she didn't.

'It's Myles, and no thanks, but I would be interested in seeing what other drinks you have.'

'Are you sure? Cocoa and s'mores are on the house, all part of the festive fun.' Her smile almost had him, she could tell.

'I don't think my stomach could handle one of those things. They look lethal.'

'I ate them all the time as a kid,' she confessed, 'but they're definitely a sugar hit.' She retrieved a menu from the front desk, handed it to him and excused herself. 'I'll give you a chance to make your choice and you can let me know when I'm back. Drinks are charged to the room or you can pay cash straight away if you'd prefer.' She had a sneaky suspicion all of his expenses would be covered by his company.

'Adding on the room is fine.' His eyes still hadn't moved from hers to the menu.

Darcy escaped to the kitchen. Myles certainly wasn't lacking in appeal. With those melting-chocolate eyes and dark hair cropped neatly, and the charisma carried on his refined British accent, he'd almost reeled her in. But her previous encounter with him couldn't be forgotten.

Darcy made four cups of hot cocoa, adding an extra splash of ice-cold milk to the boys' mugs. If she knew anything about little kids it was that they liked to eat and drink anything tasty at full speed ahead – she'd once seen Gabriella's son Kyle eating cake like the entire thing would disappear if he didn't do it quickly enough – and she hated to think Saul and Jarrod would burn their mouths.

'Here we go.' She returned to the lounge to find Adele hugging her boys, one at each side, and Troy and Myles deep in conversation, sharing a laugh.

Darcy handed the cocoa round, reminding the boys to blow across the top and cool the liquid down before they drank it. Adele suggested more s'mores another night as the men continued to talk between themselves and Darcy pulled the glass front down over the flames of the fire again for safety. She often did so unless it was later in the evening and only adults were around. The glass was so clean it didn't lessen the effect when it was in place, and, now, the glow filtered through the room along with the low lighting from the tall lamp in the corner. She'd left the curtains open onto the street. It was nice for guests to look out and see the personality of the neighbourhood, part of the big city, and anyone who passed by could be inquisitive about this little inn that was becoming more and more special to Darcy.

'Can I get you anything?' Carrying plates, she addressed Myles, who had left Troy to it and picked up a leaflet about nearby attractions from the collection on the table set among the newspapers. She doubted this man had done much sightseeing at all in his time here. It was a pity – there was so much to discover. New York was far too special to waste your time cooped up in an office day and night.

'I'll have a bourbon, neat, no ice please.'

'Of course.' She took the plates through to the kitchen before returning to the bar in the lounge. It was a modest size, on the opposite corner to the front desk, so tucked away, but there were two stools at the front of the mahogany top on which drinks were served. She found a glass, lifted the tongs for ice before she remembered he'd requested none to be added, and poured a single measure into the vessel.

'Thank you.' He sipped the liquid and it seemed to instantly relax him.

'Busy day today?'

'A busy afternoon,' he confirmed, 'and not a good one.'

'I'm sorry to hear that.' Darcy used a cloth to wipe around the bottle where a drip had made its way down the outside and replaced it on the shelf behind. She tried to treat Myles as any other guest. It would make his stay here more comfortable for the both of them.

'Let's just say my meeting this afternoon could've gone better.'

Darcy was used to strangers telling her their woes. For some reason, the hotel environment became a bit of a confession box for some guests, a sounding board for others. She leaned against the bar. With her other guests in the comfort of the sofa and armchairs at the other end of the room as they sipped their hot cocoa, she had time to listen. 'What happened?'

'My client wasn't happy with the information I presented them with. It happens, but I was sure this one was in the bag.'

She nodded, smiled. She wondered whether it was only that that was stressing him out. The tension in his neck was visible, the way he held his drink and stared into it whenever he looked away from her. But it wasn't for her to pry.

'My family are bothering me too.' It looked like she didn't need to ask many more questions. The information was spilling out now he'd begun. 'Across the miles, can you believe?' He swigged more of his bourbon.

'How can they possibly be doing that?'

'My parents do it well, believe me. Sometimes it's subtle.' Another gulp. 'There's always been a pressure.'

'In your career?' She had his attention and she added, 'Lucky guess.'

His drink was almost gone and Darcy poured him another at his nod of approval. He'd better slow down a bit or he'd have family, plus work, and a hangover to face in the morning.

'It was a good guess. But it's my personal life and their incessant need to obsess about it that gets me down. The only thing they nag me about with regards to my career is that I work so far away now. They want me back on English turf. What gets me is that my dad was a businessman until he retired, he travelled extensively – lord knows we didn't see him much – so when he's telling me America and England are worlds apart, it seems hypocritical.'

'Maybe he just wants you close by,' she suggested, even though she didn't know enough about the situation to give him advice. 'Parents get more like that as they get older. My family were all for me travelling around and seeing the world, there was no hurry to come back, but the way my parents have been since I returned, I can tell how happy they are.'

'You're lucky.'

There was more to this than Darcy could work out right now. 'Perhaps your parents miss you.'

He looked up and when he'd held her gaze longer than was comfortable, Darcy was relieved the O'Sullivan family had started to make a move. She wanted to be nice to all her guests, but there was a fine line between politeness and intrusion and she didn't want to cross it.

She waved away efforts from Troy and Adele to clear the cups and wipe up a small spill on the little round table the boys had knelt at for their cocoas. She said goodnight, took the crockery out to the kitchen and came back to wipe down the area. The floor would need a clean too: there were crumbs on the rug from the Graham crackers, debris from shoes had come off near the sofa. She grabbed a broom from the closet in the hall and swept up. She picked up most of the crumbs from the rug by hand – the more thorough hoovering could wait until the cleaner came in the morning. She was rostered on three times each week to come in and do the bulk of the housework – washing floors, dusting, cleaning the bathrooms in each apartment – and it was Darcy's responsibility to stay on top of the rest.

Keeping things shipshape was even more essential when such a major publication was going to give them valuable coverage. Sofia always held back when it came to putting the Inn in the limelight, but you couldn't afford to be in the shadows in this game and already Darcy had upped the amount they added to their Twitter feed and Facebook page, and had started an Inglenook Instagram account for potential customers on there. She couldn't wait to share more pictures of the Inn beneath a blanket of snow when the time came. Those pictures would capture the essence of the place and raise its profile to a new level.

'Am I keeping you?' Myles wanted to know after she'd returned the broom to the closet, swept up the pile of dirt with a dustpan and brush and deposited it in the bin down the hall.

'I'm here as long as you need me.' She felt her cheeks colour. What she meant was she would stay up until he no longer needed her to get him drinks. Strictly the bar wasn't open after midnight, but she knew Sofia made an exception for some guests. She told Darcy it was one of the little things that boosted her reputation from a nice little inn to a damn fine establishment. They'd laughed over the description, but already Darcy knew there was a great deal of truth behind the words.

'I think I'll take this and sit in front of the fire.' Myles moved from his stool and took his drink over to the curved window, looking out at the street. 'The rain has stopped.'

'I don't mind the rain. It's soothing.'

'When you're tucked up inside,' he smiled, as he turned to face her before going back to looking out the window.

'You're right.' Darcy decided not to add any more kindling to the fire. It was crackling away well enough already and added a beautiful orange glow to the sand-coloured walls. Myles looked content in this light, or maybe it was the two bourbons in quick succession that took his troubles away. She busied herself at the desk tidying away invoices and receipts. She turned the computer off and went out to the kitchen, where she put all the dirty crockery into the dishwasher and started the cycle, ensured the ovens were off and the back door locked, and then returned to the lounge. Myles was in the same place she'd left him.

'Can I get you anything else?' she asked.

'I wonder if it'll snow.' He was completely distracted.

She joined him at the window. 'I hope so. New York in the snow is something else; you'll think it's magical.'

'The fire is wonderful.' He turned his attention to the flames flickering away.

Darcy sat on the edge of the armchair opposite. 'We're lucky to have this at the Inn. If we wanted to put a fireplace in now we wouldn't be allowed to, but it's already there so we're good as long as we use special firewood that is less smoky when it burns.'

He was smiling at her as she spoke. 'It's a lovely touch.' He looked around him, up at the high ceilings lurking above, the bookcases lining the walls. 'This is a special place.'

'Nicer than your bigger hotels, isn't it?' she probed.

'Definitely. I haven't been here long but it's easy to forget I'm not coming back to an apartment. It's much more personal.' When she pushed her hands against her knees and went to stand, he stopped her, with the words, 'Stay a while longer.'

If it was any other guest – the young couple in number two, or one of the O'Sullivans – she wouldn't think twice. But they didn't make her insides flutter when they looked at her, make her conscious of everything she said, remind her of their assertion of authority that had cost her a job she loved.

'So, you're excited about the Christmas tree arriving.' He said it before she'd even sat down and so as not to be rude she found herself staying put.

'I am. We're so late this year, a mix up with the ordering of the tree, but I can't wait to get it ready. The boys upstairs will love it.'

A muscle in his jaw twitched. 'I'm sure they will.'

'The family have asked for a tree to be delivered to their room too.'

'You do that?'

'Sure.' She smiled. 'We have boxes and boxes of decorations as we know guests don't want to miss out.'

'Ah yes, that's right. I remember seeing it on the website.' He let a small smile escape. 'There was a little tick box if I wanted a tree to be arranged and set up.'

'You didn't tick it.' He seemed surprised she knew. 'It's my job to know everything about my guests.'

'Everything?'

'Enough so they feel welcome,' she clarified. 'But not so much they feel like they're on trial.'

He laughed properly this time. 'That's good to know.'

'You can change your mind. I'm sure we can source a tree from somewhere. It seems a shame to have that enormous apartment and leave it without a bit of festive cheer.'

He smiled and said nothing until he asked, 'Will you see your family this year?'

'I'll be working,' she said.

'Sounds familiar.'

'Do you have siblings?' She didn't want him drawing any comparisons between them.

'A brother, Winston.'

'Does he work in a similar industry to you?'

Myles shook his head. 'No, he's in the construction business. He's made quite a success of it. He's the son who can do no wrong, with the job, a family, and all living under the non-existent British sun.'

He may have smiled but she detected a grain of truth in what he was saying. She wondered if resentment ran deep. 'Do you get on?'

'Famously. Always have. As kids we were best mates and we've stayed that way.' He was definite. So no resentment, but something was amiss in the family. She'd got used to reading people in her line of work. Some people opened up to her – some so much she knew things she'd rather not – but others were content to have someone there for a while to listen to their woes but never revealed too much about themselves.

'You must miss him.'

'Yes and no. I think I'm too busy to think about it much. He wanted me to come home for Christmas, but to be honest, I would rather give the family shindig a miss.'

'You have a big family Christmas?'

'Every year.' It didn't sound like a good thing. 'If you saw it you'd think you'd walked into a magazine spread of the perfect family Christmas.'

She didn't probe any more. Hopefully this year at the Inn they'd make it one of his better Christmases.

'Do you run this place full time?' he asked.

She shook her head. 'This is temporary. Sofia would usually be here, but she's with her daughter in Switzerland.'

'Would you like it to be a more permanent arrangement?'

'I haven't thought about it too much, but financially I don't think Sofia could afford to employ anyone else.' She shouldn't be sharing this. 'I'm sorry, forget I said anything.'

He held up his hands. 'It won't go any further, don't worry. But I'm a businessman, I get it. And one thing I do know is that sometimes when you least expect it, things can turn around completely.'

She wouldn't mind betting he also knew things could go the other way too, and fall apart. She hoped Sofia would take steps to stop that happening before it was too late, and had her fingers crossed the editor of the magazine doing the write-up in the New Year could go some way to propelling them into a different bracket.

'So what's Christmas like for you? Do you have siblings? Have a big family gathering?' He interrupted her thoughts and, thankfully, made her relax so her forehead wasn't all creased up in a frown.

'I have a brother, Tate, who lives out in Connecticut near my parents, and I have a sister, Sarah, who moved to San Francisco with her husband last year.'

'Do you all get along?'

'We do. Sarah doesn't always make it home for Christmas, so usually it's Tate and I whenever we're around – which isn't always, given the nature of my work – and my parents host Christmas at their place.' She leaned against the mantel, the warmth of the fire caressing her legs through her tights. She felt about ready to take off her shoes and put her feet up on the sofa, relax and let the busy day wash off of her. 'It involves a lot of hugging when we arrive because we usually haven't seen each other for ages. Mom and Dad are always in funny Santa aprons the second we get there and they'll both be busy in the kitchen, perfecting the Christmas dinner. There's always way too much food so we'll have leftovers for days after.'

'It sounds like a real family Christmas.'

'It is.' On the surface it was easy to think he'd had the same after he'd described his own experiences, but he'd said enough to tell her that wasn't the case. Still, her heart warmed at the memory of sharing Christmas with her family, although she realised she was revealing far more than she usually did, and to a man she'd previously not felt much of a connection with.

'What sort of food do you have?' He asked the question as though he couldn't wait to lose himself in someone else's memories.

'We usually have the ridiculously big turkey with all the trimmings. Dad insists on the oversized bird because he and Mom both like to make different things with it after Christmas. On Boxing Day we usually have a turkey salad for lunch because everyone is still so full from the day before. But then at dinner time everyone has forgotten about that so Dad makes my favourite.'

'What's that?' He seemed genuinely interested.

She bit her lip at the guilty treat. 'He gets a round loaf of sourdough, slices off the top and hollows it out but keeps the insides of the bread, which he chops into pieces. He fills the empty centre of the sourdough with a mixture of cheeses, onion, garlic – and, of course, turkey – and then tops it with more cheese plus chives and puts it in the oven. It comes out all golden and we sit close

63

around the table dunking in pieces of bread, scooping up the insides.'

Myles let out a long breath. 'You're making me really hungry.'

'I'm making myself hungry too,' she laughed. 'If you ever get the chance to make it, I can give you the recipe. I look forward to it every year. And Dad has promised that the day after Boxing Day he'll bring it to me if I have to work.'

'He sounds like a good man.'

'He really is. He had some health problems a few years ago and we thought that was it.' Her eyes swam as she recalled her dad being taken into the hospital after falling over. 'They found a tumour on his brain but thankfully they removed every last piece of it. After that day he cut way back on work hours, learned to cook at evening classes and when he eventually retired he'd found his true vocation. In the kitchen.'

'So he cooks now?'

'When Mom lets him. She enjoys it too. Last year they went on a culinary tour of Italy. Next year they're planning on Indonesia.'

Darcy drew in a breath. She'd shared more with him than she had with most other men she met. Her fleeting relationships when she was travelling around the world hadn't warranted many heavy conversations about family and holiday arrangements. She shifted the focus back to him. 'Does your mom cook, or both your parents?'

He swigged the last of his bourbon and set the glass on the coffee table. 'I don't think Dad could even make a couple of slices of toast without having to call for help.'

'I don't suppose cooking is everyone's idea of fun.'

'I enjoy it.'

'You do?' She failed to hide her surprise.

'I rarely get the time, but one year my mum was sick and I took over the entire Christmas lunch – turkey and everything.'

'Wow, I'm impressed.'

'You should be. I even made my own stuffing.'

She smiled. This man kept surprising her, and recently it was in a good way.

'You looked like you knew what you were doing with those s'mores earlier on,' Myles commented, but then pulled a face. 'Is that the right word?'

'You got it right. And they were a real favourite in our house, so I must confess I have prior experience. Every year when I was little we'd have them on Christmas Eve, Tate, Sarah, and me fighting for the best toasting position in front of the fire. I always ended up feeling quite sick.' She wondered what his traditions were. 'What about you and your brother? What did you do on Christmas Eve?'

'Early to bed, early to rise for us boys.'

'Oh come on, you must've done something.'

'We always left a mince pie for Santa and a glass of bourbon.' He pulled a face, realising he was drinking the same thing.

She nodded, a little embarrassed that she kept forgetting he was a guest rather than a friend. Despite their history, he was easy to talk to. She tended to the fire as Myles finished his drink. It was almost eleven o'clock so she switched the damper to encourage the flames to lessen. It would stay warm for ages even when only the last embers remained. Sometimes Darcy wished she could sit here all night and watch it, doze off listening to the crackles.

'It's getting late, I've kept you,' he said, as though he too had realised he was just another guest. 'I'll say goodnight.' He looked tired in the same way he had earlier, like he was missing something or someone.

'Goodnight, Myles.'

After he left she turned on the small lamp at the desk. She'd give the fire an hour to settle until its last remains glowed in the hearth. She opened the bottom drawer of the filing cabinet and took out her knitting as it finally came to the end of her working day.

She wasn't fast yet, nothing like her nanna had been, with her knitting needles going clickety-clack, clickety-clack, and she was nowhere near the speed of her friend Cleo at the Little Knitting Box. But after talking through the pattern with Cleo and selecting a snuggly soft brown yarn from her store in Inglenook Falls, Darcy had made a start and already this sweater for Kyle was actually starting to look like more than a few rows of yarn that could turn out to be anything. She'd have to show Cleo when she came into the city with Dylan. She'd invited them both for Christmas Eve and she really hoped they could make it. It would mean a lot to Darcy to show her friends that she was doing a good job here at the Inglenook Inn.

As she knitted, Darcy thought about their guest on the top floor. With every mention of Christmas she found it harder to gauge what Myles thought. He definitely had family issues, something Darcy was so glad she didn't have. Gabriella had had her share when her parents divorced, Cleo too with a stepmother it took her a while to warm to, but Darcy and Isabella seemed to have solid backgrounds with only the merest hint of angst in their teen and early adult years. It was certainly something to be grateful for.

When Myles had asked her about the tree arriving in the morning, she'd seen a twinkle in his eye, one that suggested perhaps he was open to the season but felt that on his own it was barely worth the fuss.

But fuss was what Darcy liked to do when it came to going the extra mile for her guests.

She put down her knitting and booted up the computer again. She hoped she hadn't misread his signals, because she had an idea. This man was stressed, working hard, and facing Christmas in an apartment all alone.

It only took a few clicks and she was done.

She settled back down by the fire and carried on knitting. She'd chosen to be mature, rise above her history with Myles Cunningham, and here was her chance to go above and beyond her requirements as a hotel manager. Because that was what it was all about – making the customer happy. Her guest was an Englishman in New York, but this year, he was going to have a wonderful Christmas. She'd make sure of it.

# Chapter Six

*Myles*

*Twelve days until Christmas*

Myles was glad he'd stopped at the two neat bourbons last night, or his head wouldn't be at all clear this morning. It was foggy anyway but he knew it had more to do with Darcy than it did the alcohol. Most women who crossed his path he either got involved with or he didn't. They rarely hung around in his mind long enough to bother him.

There was a time when Myles hadn't been able to touch alcohol, but once he'd left home and his mum finally got her act together, he'd gradually been able to enjoy a drink or two. He never had too many though; he couldn't stand the thought of ending up anything like his mum had in those darker days. Seeing her completely wasted was the stuff of nightmares, and not something he ever intended to replicate. Many a time, mates had tried to cajole him into late-night drinking sessions and he managed them by seeming to go along with what they wanted but ensuring he drank very slowly. By the time he stopped drinking, they'd always been too wasted to notice he wasn't downing the drinks at the rate they were.

His client meeting hadn't gone well at all yesterday but Myles made up for it that morning. He impressed an existing client with a PowerPoint presentation that left them in no doubt of his expertise, he had a meeting with his manager that went well, and the seven deals he had on the go at the same time were all ticking over as expected. He looked at pricing tables for a loan for a client, he negotiated which banks would lead the transactions for another and the fees they intended to charge, and he read over a credit agreement before taking an afternoon meeting with one of his firm's top clients.

'Myles, do you have a moment?' His manager, Neil, poked his head around the door long after most people had left the office for the day.

'Sure, boss. Come in.' He entered the figure he'd calculated into a spreadsheet, clicked save and turned his chair back to face the front of his desk. 'What can I do for you?'

'How are you settling in?'

'Really well.'

'And the Inn is good?'

'It's excellent, thank you.' His boss reminded him of his father both in looks and his no-nonsense approach. Both of them had the same air of authority that came naturally, the hair that was more grey than silver, and the expensive suits and accessories. He had on an Alpina Startimer Pilot watch with a brown leather strap and blue dial. Myles should know. His dad had been wearing the same watch since his mum gave it as a Christmas gift last year.

'My wife put me onto it. I shall let her know she did good.'

'Thank you, sir.' Myles smiled, wondering what this chat was about. He was excelling in his role so he was confident it wasn't any kind of reproof.

'So, the Christmas party.' Ah, now they were getting somewhere. 'I do expect a full attendance.'

'Not a problem. I'll be there.'

'Glad to hear it.'

'I'm looking forward to seeing The Plaza.'

Neil grinned. 'I've had it booked for quite some time – it'll be a night to remember. It'll be a chance for you to really get to know your co-workers, partners, clients.'

Myles didn't need much convincing. Since he'd arrived in Manhattan he'd done little else apart from work, eat, sleep and run, so a night out sounded just what he needed.

'We have some important clients coming along this time.' Neil elaborated and Myles took all the information in, soaking up what he needed to. Neil also talked about a potential new client, a firm that would be represented by its CEO and General Manager. He regurgitated facts about other clients and firms they already had on their books.

Myles had done his research before starting this job and he knew the information already. He'd spent his flight over here reading up on the history of the company, many evenings at the Inn finding out about the firm's range of clients, and he rarely switched off. So where was this going?

'I'm keen to impress and get this new client on board,' said Neil.

'I'll be on my best behaviour.' Myles's answer didn't seem to have the desired effect and his boss, being the man Myles already knew he was, came straight to the point.

'I've known these people for a while. They're well respected. They'll all be bringing their wives. You know the way it is. Wives go off in their little huddle and put the world to rights, we men kick back with a cigar and a whiskey and talk business.'

'Right.' Was he asking if Myles smoked? Or whether he drank whiskey? The latter he could manage and if he needed to have the odd cigar to chew the fat with potential clients, so be it. It wasn't his favourite pastime but he could do it as a one-off.

'It's old-fashioned, I know,' his boss went on. Still Myles wasn't really sure what he was getting at. 'These affairs are usually more balanced if the wives come along.'

'Can't magic one of those up, I'm afraid.' Myles fidgeted in his seat. His eyes were sore from looking at the screen for too long and, as darkness had descended over Manhattan, he was ready to get out of here, but his boss was prolonging his escape.

'How about you ask Rhonda,' Neil suggested.

'My secretary, Rhonda? I suppose I could, but is it really necessary? I mean, if I was asked I'd have to say I was single.'

'These clients slipped through the net last time, Myles. I really want to secure their trust. I'm not saying you absolutely have to bring someone, but last time we landed a client of their stature and size it was following a friendship struck up between the wives, one that landed the women in Martha's Vineyard, costing me more money than I care to think about,' he guffawed, 'but here at the firm I believe business and pleasure can be mixed to make for really good prospects.'

Myles had experienced this before. Five years ago his sister-in-law had set him up with a friend of hers to attend a business function. His date had impressed everyone he worked with, apart from him. Not that she wasn't pleasant company, a half-decent conversationalist and reasonably attractive. It's just that he didn't want to get involved. Not until he was really sure about someone. When you'd grown up in a family like his you saw what marriage could do to people, what it could do

71

to kids. Myles had spent the whole evening becoming more and more uncomfortable as he realised she was looking for a lot more than he could offer. And when the evening was over and he had to say he wasn't looking for a relationship, he knew he'd hurt her. He hadn't wanted to do that, she didn't deserve it. But taking Rhonda or anyone else to this Christmas function was going to be like history repeating itself. And besides, he liked Rhonda in a purely platonic way. Thirteen years his junior, she had a pleasant manner and was a damn fine secretary, and he didn't want to ruin that.

'I'll find someone to bring along,' said Myles. It wasn't a suggestion from Neil but a requirement and he wanted to secure this client as much as his boss did, especially if they'd slipped through the net last time. This would be another chance to prove himself and he was always up for the challenge.

'Great.' His boss stood, satisfied with the outcome. 'Talking of other halves, I'd better get home or my wife will be sending out the search party.'

After Neil left, Myles turned his chair to face his computer but when the figures swam in front of his eyes he admitted defeat, tidied the papers on his desk and left everything ready to face again in the morning.

*

Outside, on the stoop of the Inglenook Inn, Myles passed the family who were staying in the apartment on the floor below his. They bustled past and out the door and he nodded a friendly hello. He'd wondered whether they were going to be too noisy during their stay, but so far they were model guests. He hadn't heard a sound apart from the usual street noise and he was usually so exhausted that he slept soundly whatever was going on around him.

He wiped his feet on the mat and shut the heavy door behind him. Already he could smell the scent from the fireplace and knew it would be lit, hypnotic in its presence. The thought comforted him until he got a waft of a different smell mingled with the woodsmoke: pine. And it conjured up memories he'd rather forget. He wondered, would it be too impolite to walk right past the lounge and totally ignore it? If he didn't see it at all over the festive period it would be fine by him. Bad enough there was already a tree in the dining room in his opinion.

He set down his briefcase, took off his coat – unnecessary now he was wrapped in the warmth of the brownstone – and from the hallway could see Darcy busying herself at the desk, typing on the computer. He watched for a moment, surprised at how different she looked with her hair falling about her shoulders. Soft waves shimmered in the light of the desk lamp and she took on a softer appearance now she looked less businesslike. She was standing as though she'd been in the middle of something else and he wondered how many hours she put in running the Inn. Probably more than even he did, but he supposed they both loved their jobs. His mum had never worked, not that he would've minded. Perhaps it would've stopped her becoming so lost along the way and things could've turned out very differently. She'd always been there for her boys physically but that was as far as it went. And when they reached their teen years and didn't long for her company as much, he hadn't missed the regret on her face at what had gone before.

The doors to the lounge were permanently open in a doorway that was much wider than you'd expect of a brownstone, and they were all the more welcoming now the tree was in position. He could see how it would draw guests to the communal area, perhaps lure people in from the street to enquire about bookings. Darcy had a good head on her shoulders. He expected her hotel career would go far.

He smiled at Darcy when she looked up, then turned his gaze to the tree, psyching himself up to show at least some enthusiasm. 'It's huge!'

She smiled and came round to the front of the desk. 'I'm glad you like it.' She went over to the tree, which was yet to be decorated, and he noticed she'd already begun stringing lights from the top all the way down to the bottom. The wires were still protruding and she crouched down beneath the tree to push in the pieces that were on the floor so it looked neat.

She tried to reverse out gracefully but stopped when her hair got caught on one of the lower branches. He watched her attempt to free herself but she couldn't do it without the benefit of being able to see where the tangles were.

'Here, let me.' He bent down and gradually pulled each silky strand from the needled branch, the air a mixture of pine and a more pleasant zesty shampoo.

'Thanks.' She brushed at her hair with her hand. He loved that his touch had made her uneasy enough that she couldn't look at him. She seemed so in control most of the time, but the gesture showed she was as human as everyone else. 'Now all I need to do is decorate it.' She pushed the plug into the socket and the white lights dazzled him momentarily.

'Is your chef still here?' asked Myles, feeling the need to escape.

She'd obviously become lost in the task of decorating a Christmas tree – only for a split second, but her expression told him enough to know she was snapping back to hostess mode. 'He isn't, but I can make you a simple snack if you'd like.'

'Thanks, just a basic ham, cheese and tomato sandwich would be really good. And I'll eat in my apartment this evening.'

'Sure.' She shifted a big box of decorations aside so nobody would trip over it. 'Coming right up.' And off she went to the kitchen.

The smile she'd given him was brighter than those lights she'd turned on and it was a little unnerving as he made his way up the stairs. He wasn't going to do any work this evening but he needed to gather his thoughts about the idea that had struck him on his walk from the subway station to the Inn. Darcy wasn't too much younger than him and she was bound to have friends who would be happy to go to a work function with him. If he explained the predicament he was in, that he needed a platonic escort, hopefully Darcy could help him out. She seemed an astute businesswoman, and the incentive for anyone coming along would be a top-notch menu, an all-you-can-drink liquor supply – none of it cheap – and an evening at The Plaza.

Myles let himself into his apartment but the second he did, he knew something was different. There was a smell. Not shower gel from his morning routine, not polish from the cleaner who sneaked in and out so seamlessly he would never have known had it not been for the bed being so professionally made, and it was only when he took another step so his view wasn't obscured by the small piece of wall that jutted out with coat hooks lined up in a row that he found the source.

'What the hell's this?' He glared at the Christmas tree standing there in all its glory, its towering height and majesty filling the space. A symbol of Christmas, white lights fading in and out as though mocking him and his reaction, fading to nothing but then coming back to remind him that they were very much there. An angel gloated from the top of the tree, crafted ornaments in wood, silver and white danced between candy canes dangling from branches, and there was a card tied on with a piece of silver ribbon like a decoration.

Myles stalked over to the tree, snatched the card from the branch so hard that pine needles scattered in fear all over the floor. He tore open the envelope and pulled out a card with a picture of Central Park on the front. The park was covered in snow, a winter wonderland, and when he opened it the handwritten message said, 'May all your Christmas wishes come true.' It was signed 'Darcy, The Inglenook Inn'.

The frown was still on his face when a knock came from the other side of the door. Exhausted and deflated, he opened it to see Darcy herself, beaming in delight and clearly waiting for him to return the reaction. Instead he reached out, took the tray with the sandwich, muttered a thank you and said a terse goodnight.

She put a hand against the door before he had the chance to shut it properly. 'Is everything OK?'

He glared at her. 'I don't need you jumping in and trying to be some kind of Cinderella.' His tone didn't hide his feelings. He was mad. Mad as hell.

'Cinderella?'

'All this.' He cast his eye around the apartment, targeting the tree and everything littering its branches. 'I didn't tick the box, remember. So I don't need you fussing around me like Cinderella, clearing up after me, making sure everything is shiny in my world.'

She looked taken aback and he knew he'd gone too far. But rather than try to sort it out and perhaps reason with her that he'd had a long day and didn't intend to be so rude, he did what he did best and avoided trying to rectify the situation.

With a swift kick he shut the door a lot more firmly than he'd intended.

He wished it was just as easy to shut the door on the past.

# Chapter Seven

*Darcy*

*Eleven days until Christmas*

Darcy found the café in Midtown Manhattan, on Avenue of the Americas, where she'd arranged to meet Isabella. She took off her chenille gloves, unlooped her scarf from round her neck and hung her coat on the back of her chair so it could dry. A winter drizzle lurked in the air outside with low grey clouds suspended and blocking out the tops of buildings.

Last night she'd been so stunned at Myles's behaviour that she hadn't been able to knock on his door again and talk to him. She hadn't expected quite that reaction from the person paying an absolute fortune to stay in the Inn's most expensive apartment – not that he was actually paying the bill personally – but she'd at least expected a smile, a thank you, a small gesture to show his appreciation. She'd returned downstairs and tried to focus on paperwork. She'd chatted with other guests as they came and went. She took photographs of the finished tree, the Norway spruce that filled up the lounge with the joys of the season.

Shame she couldn't bestow some of that joy upon their guest on the top floor.

She'd finished her evening without seeing or hearing from Myles again. She'd sat behind the desk and carried on with her knitting, determined to send this to Gabriella across the miles as soon as she could, and then, when it seemed most guests were settled, she'd switched the damper on the fire, let it die down and gone to bed.

'Sorry I'm late.' Isabella bustled into the café now. 'My boss runs a tight ship but I've got forty-five minutes.'

Darcy hugged her friend and sat back down opposite her while Isabella took off all the accessories required for a New York winter: gloves, hat, scarf, coat. 'Have you been shopping already?' She eyed the bags at Isabella's feet.

'That's why I'm a bit late,' she grinned. 'I figured if I grab one or two things each lunchtime, my shopping will be done in no time.'

'Good idea.'

The waitress came over and they ordered their coffees.

Isabella rummaged in one of the bags. 'You know you were wondering what to buy for Cleo and Dylan's little boy?'

'I desperately need help with that,' Darcy confessed. Over time she'd built a solid friendship with Cleo and Dylan and without any nieces or nephews of her own yet, Darcy enjoyed buying for their kids. It was almost an excuse to go back to her own childhood and think about what had made this time of the year so magical, except that didn't help when she needed to buy a gift for the opposite sex. 'I don't know the inner workings of a boy's mind.' Or a man's come to that. She couldn't figure out Myles at all. When she'd first realised their paths had crossed once before, she'd hated him. But then she'd warmed to him. Now, she was back to disliking him intensely. Maybe that was the way it would always be.

'Ta-da!' Isabella pulled out a box that rattled with pieces. 'I got this from the Lego store on Fifth.'

Darcy took the box. 'Now why didn't I think of that?' She shook her head. 'I'll email Cleo later to see what Jacob has in his collection already and then I'm there. Thank you. I might see what I can get Ruby too. Girls love Lego as well, don't they?'

'Hey, we are all equals here.'

Darcy rolled her eyes. 'Didn't say we weren't.'

'There's a definite age when all girls are interested in is make-up.'

'Good point. That may suit Ruby more.' She handed the box containing a Scorpion character and a Spider-Man character back to her friend as Isabella told her these could do serious battle in a boy's imagination. She'd obviously absorbed some of the sales speak today.

'Have you done the rest of your shopping?'

'All done. When Sofia gave me this enormous responsibility, I knew I wouldn't have much time to shop. The kids' presents are the only ones I haven't sorted, because I was stuck for ideas.'

'Well, if you like, I'm going to the Inglenook Falls Christmas markets in a few days. I promised my gran we'd go, it's kind of our thing. I can deliver the presents to the Little Knitting Box if that's easier for you.'

Darcy's shoulders sagged in relief. 'Oh, would you? That would be great. Right, I'll shop later today or tomorrow, I'll wrap and I'll get the gifts to you. You're a life-saver. I'll make it to the markets next year, I hope.'

'How's the knitting project going?' Isabella thanked the waitress for the coffees and habitually scraped off the top of her cappuccino froth with a spoon.

'I'm doing a little bit each night, when I'm not too exhausted.' Darcy stirred her caramel macchiato, her thoughts disappearing into the whirls of coffee.

'Running the Inn is that bad?'

Darcy looked up and her frown turned into a smile. 'Not at all. I'm still loving it, but it's 24/7. And I'm really nervous about the magazine editor checking in.'

Isabella dismissed her worries. 'Don't be. You've got this.'

'I hope so.'

'And is Mr fire-all-your-staff-because-they're-terrible upstairs behaving himself?'

Yesterday she would've smiled and said yes. 'He's an ungrateful pig.'

'Darcy!'

'Well he is.'

'What happened?'

'I tried to bring a little bit of Christmas cheer, that's all.' She explained the story, how she'd ordered a real tree for him, something to make that huge apartment festive and make his stay even better. But Isabella was shaking her head. 'What's wrong with that?'

'Oh, Darcy, not everyone loves Christmas as much as you do.'

'It's not just me. It's the rest of New York City.'

'Not necessarily; he could be Jewish.'

'He's not Jewish.' She picked up her cup and took a long drag of the sweetened liquid. 'And even if he doesn't like it, he doesn't have to be so rude. He admired the one downstairs.'

'Maybe he was just being polite. He didn't have to be rude, I agree, but you don't know what's going on for him personally.'

Darcy put her face in her hands. 'I've messed up haven't I?'

'You were trying to be nice. You were going the extra mile.'

'But in doing so I've made it worse. We were being civil at least.'

'I wouldn't mind betting there's more to this than rudeness, Darcy. He obviously has a history that you don't know and, being a man, he's not likely to be forthcoming with any explanation. Not that he needs to – you're a stranger.'

'You really missed your vocation you know.'

Once upon a time, Isabella had been the go-to girl at school if anyone had a problem: bad breakups, parent troubles, struggling with homework. Isabella had an uncanny knack of advising and helping people grasp the positive side. She'd toyed with the idea of becoming a psychologist, particularly around the time she got glasses for reading and said they made her look really intelligent, but she'd given up on the idea when she realised how much extra study it would be.

'I'll stick with amateur psychology for my friends I think,' said Isabella. 'Have you seen the man since?'

'No. He didn't come into the lounge this morning. He must've had breakfast in his apartment. You know, he called me Cinderella.'

Isabella nearly spluttered her coffee across the table. When she'd regained her composure she said, 'I'll bet that made you angry.'

Her friend knew her too well. 'Nobody has called me that since Lachie was on the scene.'

'I suppose you should be grateful he didn't call you an ugly sister.' Isabella's comment did what it was supposed to do and raised a giggle from Darcy. 'That's better. Don't let him get you down. It sounds as though the comments were all made in the heat of the moment. He's a guest who you won't get rid of easily so it might be a good idea to make peace with him. Take the tree away, you can't say fairer than that. And stop cleaning out the fireplace – that should put an end to the Cinderella comments.' She grinned.

'I love that fireplace. It's part of the Inn's character.'

'I know.' Isabella's face gave away the fact she had more to say. 'I'm not sure whether I should tell you this, but I heard from Michelle.'

'How is she?' Michelle was from high school and Isabella had been on the hockey team with her. But Michelle was also best friends with the enemy. 'Lachie is engaged. To one of the ugly sisters.' She attempted to inject a little humour.

Darcy had never thought she'd mind, but she felt the colour go from her cheeks, a shiver run through her body. Lachie was the only guy she'd ever been remotely serious about and he'd broken her heart. It was hard to let that go.

Lachie and Darcy had met at school and he'd liked her for ages, asked her out, and within a week – with no arm-twisting from his camp – she'd emerged from her well-established gothic phase and lost the dyed black hair, the black fingernails and thickly applied eyeliner, as well as the tatty black or dark grey clothes, and become a more feminine version of herself. The night she met him at the Shake Shack for burgers he almost looked straight past her and from that day he'd said it was as though someone had waved a magic wand and she'd transformed. He'd called her his Cinderella from that moment on.

She'd taken the nickname as a compliment and it had been meant that way. They'd enjoyed long summers lazing in his parents' garden, cosy winters together where they'd ice-skated in Central Park or been to Times Square on New Year's to watch the ball drop. They'd graduated high school with bright futures, they'd travelled to Toronto and Vancouver together, making plans for the years ahead. Darcy had been in a happy bubble that rose further and further into the sky every day, until it burst one day when she caught Lachie going to second base with someone else. That someone else was Charlotte, one of the attractive twins who had been in their class at school. Isabella had dubbed her one of the ugly sisters, given Lachie's nickname for Darcy.

Lachie had said he was sorry, he'd begged for another chance, he'd insisted it wasn't serious, but when Darcy saw him in a jewellery store a few weeks later just before Christmas buying a beautiful bracelet and it didn't appear when she ripped the wrapping from her own gift, he admitted he was torn. He didn't know who he loved. Darcy made it easy for him. She dumped him, on Christmas Day.

'At least he made cheating on me worth his while,' said Darcy. 'He obviously was in love with her. I hope they'll be very happy. I do,' she insisted.

'It doesn't make it any nicer for you to hear though.' Isabella watched her friend with concern and then shook her head. 'He ruined dating for you. I hope he knows that.'

'And I hope he doesn't! I don't want him thinking he has that kind of power.'

'OK, sorry.'

'And I've had plenty of dates after Lachie, don't you worry.'

'You know what I mean.'

Surprisingly enough, Lachie didn't ruin Christmas for Darcy, but she did revert back to her gothic phase – although it wasn't the same once Isabella had moved on and grown out of it. But Darcy was so upset, so angry, she couldn't see the point of conforming, of fitting in, of trying so hard with anything. The breakup with Lachie happened in her early twenties around the same time her auntie had been through a devastating divorce from her uncle and Darcy had seen first-hand want it meant to depend on someone who took themselves out of the equation. It had the power to leave you broken, unable to pick up the pieces, and she'd decided from then on that it would never happen to her. She moved quickly on from her goth phase to a very definite feminist phase, which lasted until well after college, when she finally found her groove and settled into the person she still was today. And the first Christmas without Lachie, she'd decorated the tree, joined in with every festivity, and had been determined to make it the happiest Christmas ever, grateful for what she did have rather than dwelling on what she didn't.

'He was an ass,' said Isabella firmly.

Darcy grinned. 'He *was* an ass.' And so was Myles, the man who had called her Cinderella more recently. He was an ass because he'd made her remember the four years that had been her world with her ex and then the devastating breakup that had left its mark. Darcy knew full well that despite her protestations, the Lachie-effect as it had become known between her and her friends had been like a cloud hovering above her everywhere she went, and she didn't seem able to escape it. Isabella had always said it would take a special someone to make her move on, but right now, Darcy couldn't ever see it happening.

'So, back to the man of the moment,' said Isabella.

'And who might that be?'

'Mr top-floor of course!'

'Oh, him.'

'Yes, him. Why do you think he called you Cinderella really? Do you think that's who he wants you to be? Do you think he wants to be all macho and rescue you from a life of hard work or poverty?'

'Isabella, you're doing your amateur psychology thingy again. Don't.' Her look suggested she had no intention of stopping so Darcy relented. 'He thinks I've fussed around him. He said I wanted to add shine to his world or some other bullshit.'

'Do you? Do you want to add a shine to his world?' Isabella's eyebrows did a playful twitch and Darcy couldn't help but grin. It was light relief compared to thinking about the Lachie-effect.

'Let's change the subject.' Darcy warmed her hands on her coffee cup when a chill made right for her as a customer left the café. 'How are your Christmas plans going? Are you seeing Jake?' Isabella had been dating Jake for quite a while so Christmas plans were about to get complicated.

'I'm seeing my parents on the day itself, then on Boxing Day I'll go over to Jake's house. Next year we said we might try to spend the day together but I'm not sure how either family will take it. Mine like to have me home, his like to have him at their place.'

'You might have to do two Christmas dinners.'

'No chance.' Isabella pulled a face. 'It took me most of this year to lose the weight from last year's Christmas dinner and New Year's celebrations.'

'I'll be too busy to worry about that this year.'

'Your mom must be disappointed.'

'She is, but she understands.'

'Is your top guest joining you for Christmas dinner?'

'You can't move on from him, can you?' But she smiled when she said it. 'He did ask me to put his name on the list, but who knows.' Maybe he'd change his mind after their confrontation.

'Do you want him to?'

'Don't get any ideas.'

'I'm not.'

'When your voice goes all high-pitched like that, it means you are. But I can tell you now, Myles Cunningham and I have absolutely *nothing* in common.'

Isabella stayed quiet and tipped her cup back to get the remains of her coffee before shrugging on her coat, scarf and gloves. 'Whatever you say.'

Darcy talked to her friend's retreating back as she buttoned up her own coat and they stepped out onto the busy sidewalk. Her breath made white puffs against the cold as she spoke. 'All I want from this guest is a bit of politeness and his best behaviour when this editor comes to stay. The last thing I need is media coverage that paints the Inn in a bad light.'

Myles Cunningham staying at the Inglenook Inn couldn't have happened at a worse time. This editor worked for a publication with a circulation of thousands and Darcy felt sure she had a nose for a good story. If there was angst between the hotel manager and a guest, it would add a lot of colour to the piece, and Darcy had no intention of letting that happen.

*

Darcy didn't dare spend too much time inside Myles's apartment later that day for fear of retribution. But once the cleaner had been, it was her job to keep guests comfortable, see to it that all the little touches were added.

Myles had already accused her of fussing but she pushed the name Cinderella from her mind as much as she could and replenished kitchen supplies, ensured there were enough pods for the coffee machine, put a handful of chocolates in a small basket beside the bed, and added a bowl of fresh fruit. She checked the bedroom and the bed had already been made, the pillows lined up as they should be, the velvet runner perfectly straight. She checked the sills. Even if you didn't open the windows, the Inn had a way of accumulating some of the New York dust that came with living in the hub of a city. She put a fresh soap tablet in the bathroom, changed towels in there and in the kitchen, and tidied the desk by putting the two stray pens into the pot beside a writing pad.

She wondered when the best time to remove the tree would be and as she picked up her tidy box of cloths, supplies and other implements, she heard a key in the door.

Her heart thudded inside her chest. This wasn't going to go down well.

'I was just leaving.' Head down, she went to move past Myles as he set his briefcase down and hung up his coat.

'I overreacted,' he said before she got all the way out of the door. 'I apologise.'

His voice made her stop in her tracks. She needed to maintain professionalism. It was the only way to keep things civil. 'It was a presumptuous move on my behalf,' she explained. 'So I should apologise to you. I didn't mean any harm. I will remove the tree at your convenience.'

'Darcy.' He put a hand on her arm but removed it quickly enough when she looked at it. 'I'd had a bad day, Christmas isn't my thing, and I lost it. I'm very sorry.'

'Apology accepted, Mr Cunningham.'

'Would you stop calling me that?'

She said nothing. 'I'll leave you to it.' There was his hand again, on her arm, the heat of his skin penetrating the sleeve of her shirt.

'Darcy, please.'

She met his gaze and nodded that they were OK. She ran through a list of what she'd done in the room, the food supplies she'd left. 'I can take the tree away now if it suits. I'll sweep up too. You'll never know it was there.'

'That won't be necessary.' He looked like a little lost boy and no longer could she be angry at his comment. Isabella was right. There was more going on than they could ever understand. And what right did she have to the information? None. He was a guest. That was it.

'Well, let me know if you change your mind.' She turned to leave but spotted one of her business cards she must've either dropped or knocked down from the side table by the entrance door. She picked it up and was about to pocket it when he put out a hand to take it from her.

'That's mine.' He looked embarrassed, something she hadn't seen from this usually strong, confident businessman.

But she'd seen enough on that card to know why his demeanour had changed. It wasn't a business card for the Inglenook Inn with a silhouetted brownstone and the curly writing and contact details, but a card from an escort agency.

'It's not what you think,' he assured her.

Tidy box in one hand, she smiled and said, 'What you do in your own time is your business.' It certainly wasn't any of hers.

'Darcy.' He tried to stop her walking away again but she was too far for him to use the power of touch.

'It's none of my business. Good day, Mr Cunningham.'

'It's Myles,' she heard as she walked away. And she would've felt guilty at being so aloof if she hadn't thought harder about that business card, wondering whether she needed to raise the issue with Sofia. If Myles was bringing women of any type of disrepute back to the Inn, surely that was a disaster for business.

And that wasn't the reputation they wanted across Manhattan. Not at all.

# Chapter Eight

## *Myles*

In his early twenties Myles had gone to see a counsellor. When he realised his brother had managed to put the past behind him, succeed in his career, get married and raise two very happy children, Myles recognised that he may need some help moving forwards. But the sessions hadn't lasted. He'd had two, then missed one because of work, then another, and another, and then he'd begun to make excuses not to turn up, until slowly, over the years, his discomfort around his family particularly at this time of the year had become such a big part of him that, now, he had no idea how to move past it.

After Darcy left him to it and dismissed any plea that the escort-agency card wasn't what she thought it was, he put the business card on the side table and slumped onto the sofa, staring into the tree. It still had the strong scent of pine, its branches a verdant green, ornaments that had been carefully chosen and were coordinated in silver, white, and a blue that reminded him of Darcy because it was the same colour as her eyes. Those eyes that appeared to trust him one minute and the next, had no idea where he was coming from. But really, he couldn't expect anything else, could he?

He'd given up on his idea of asking Darcy if she had a friend he could take to the Christmas party, because after their run-in he felt sure what her reaction would've been. So he'd thought of an alternative plan, and the escort agency sounded both legitimate and respectable. It wasn't a seedy, pay-for-a-full-service type thing, it was a fee-charging, reputable place where he could find someone to take to the party with no strings attached.

When he pulled himself together, Myles did what he did best and lost himself in work. He'd had client meetings all morning and here he could get much more done. There were no interruptions in the corridor as he went to get a coffee, nobody running things by him when they needed a push to get going on a project. He cocooned himself in his work frame of mind, fielding calls, juggling paperwork, and by early evening he'd made progress. But his stomach told him who was boss and when it gave an almighty growl he knew it was time to get away from his desk.

He changed into jeans and a jumper – or sweater as he had to get used to saying in the USA – and he grabbed a jacket after checking the weather app on his phone. The temperature had plummeted about ten degrees since lunchtime and he whistled. It was going to be his first winter here and he suspected they'd see snow before too long.

He picked up his keys and momentarily paused at the escort card lurking beneath. Should he make the call now? Get it over with? He wondered how it worked. Did you get assigned someone depending on your budget? Did you ask for a certain type of women, view mugshots?

Laughing to himself, he left his apartment and ventured down the stairs. This was alien to him, but he needed to keep his boss happy. He was already settling into life in Manhattan, a life that ran at an even faster pace than in London. But it was an addictive pace, a mayhem that made sense to him, or maybe it was the way he was wired.

When he reached the foot of the stairs in the entrance-floor hallway he adjusted the garland on the bannister that had tried to wind its way loose, so it was tucked in neatly, and paused before he went into the lounge and leaned against the door jamb before he could be seen. Never mind the twinkling lights, the wreaths, the holly and the pine-scented tree that stretched all the way up to the ceiling. The fire was crackling away in the hearth; seeing it relaxed him instantly – he could leave the world behind as he peered into those orange flames – and already he felt a desire creep up on him to request a drink and sit on the sofa by the window.

'We don't have anyone booked into the apartment at all after Mr Cunningham leaves.'

At the sound of his name on Darcy's lips, Myles hovered, still unseen.

'The other apartments are at partial capacity but it's patchy. We need to do something to really get the Inglenook Inn out in the open. I don't want you to worry though, I've been following up on advertising possibilities, the website is coming up in every possible search engine, and with every guest and every review our reputation builds that little bit more. I promise you, Sofia, I'm doing the best I can.'

It pained him that he'd snapped at her, called her Cinderella, moaned about the touch of niceness she'd tried to add. He could tell she was worried and he wouldn't mind betting his sniping had made things worse.

He went out of the brownstone quietly. He turned up the collar of his jacket as the cold bit at the tips of his ears. There was a fine layer of frost glistening in the passing tail lights of vehicles. It lingered on car wing mirrors, the tops of lamp-posts where the glow gave away all the city's secrets, on the stoops of the brownstones standing in a row, reminding you to be careful making your way down to street level.

Myles walked from the Inn to Washington Square Park. He followed the streets past New York University. He passed restaurant after restaurant, eager owners more than happy to jostle him inside, but each time held up a hand as though he was on a tight timeframe and had someone to meet. He passed a diner, a shop that looked as though it sold junk although he was sure they'd claim it was hardware or bric-a-brac. He finally turned left as he reached Canal Street and, battling the crowds, made his way along until he saw something he wanted. Not in the mood for a sit-down meal, especially not alone, he found a Chinese restaurant serving classic dim sum that he could take away after he'd finished a big bowl of wonton soup that warmed him right through.

By the time he reached the Inn, Darcy was hefting a bag of something inside the front door. He took the steps towards the warmth of the hall that grabbed him in off the street. 'What's that?' He stepped inside and rubbed his hands together, blowing into his palms to heat them up. He wasn't even ready to take his coat off yet.

Darcy shut the main door behind him. 'It's a de-icing product. The streets are starting to get worse, the sidewalk too. I slipped when I went across to the café on a patch I hadn't expected. I'll get up early in case I need to clear some with a shovel, but I'd hate one of my guests to fall. Just when you think winter isn't coming, it shows up to take you by surprise.'

He'd been caught up watching her talk and hadn't realised he was staring. She was more conversational than she'd been earlier and he wondered whether it was because this situation wasn't about them in any way.

'It's good of you to think of us. I don't do a graceful fall.'

'I'll try to remember that.' She put the bag to one side, dusted her hands and straightened the black cropped suit jacket that fitted neatly over a sky-blue blouse, fitted trousers and, of course, the heels that she rarely seemed to go without. He tried to ignore thoughts of toned calves and the long legs he'd seen that time she'd been without a skirt, because those were the thoughts that would get him into trouble.

'About earlier.' He followed her into the lounge and checked whether there was an audience in the form of another guest. There wasn't, thankfully. There was no way he was going to let anyone else know his desperation and need to contact an escort agency.

'There's no need to mention it.'

'I feel I need to. It really isn't what you think.' He detected a smirk that wasn't allowed to escape behind her professional conduct. 'You see, I'm a bit stuck.'

'Really, Mr Cunningham. No need to explain any further.'

'Myles.' Exasperated, he said, 'Stop calling me Mr Cunningham because it makes me feel even more of an ass – that's what you guys in America say isn't it? – than I already do.'

'OK. Myles.'

'Thank you. And I feel I do need to explain.' He didn't want her thinking he was using the Inn for anything untoward. 'My boss, he's having a Christmas party, and he wants me to bring someone.'

'An escort?'

This was all coming out wrong. 'The client, or potential client, he's hoping to impress is a traditional man. Everyone seems to be married these days and

95

apparently the wives get together, the men discuss business and it all works in some weird harmonious parallel universe.'

Darcy pushed the top on a pen at the desk as they talked, he one side, she on the other. 'I take it you don't believe in all that.'

'I don't believe it's necessary for a business deal, no. But I will concede that I get where he's coming from. Whenever I've been to functions alone it's hard to talk business when wives or girlfriends are there. Or boyfriends,' he added, for fear of retribution. Plenty of his colleagues were women after all. 'Other halves are usually happy enough but it does facilitate the process when they can talk amongst themselves.' God, he sounded like he was quoting from a corporate ethics manual. 'What I'm trying to say is that I need someone who is familiar with the corporate world, who makes a good impression and who can hold a conversation with whoever comes along.'

'It sounds as though an escort is exactly what you need then.' She said it without joking and he was impressed. If he were in her position he'd probably make more of a joke out of it, but her business etiquette, as always, shone through. 'Have you found someone suitable?'

'I haven't called them yet.'

He stopped talking about it when Rupert came in, looking agitated. The man may have had an English-sounding name but he couldn't be more American if he tried. He had the same accent as one of Myles's colleagues, a Texan with a habit of chewing tobacco and a drawl that dragged out long, lazy vowels.

Darcy excused herself and followed Rupert out to the kitchen. Myles hung around a bit longer and was about to head up to his apartment when Darcy reappeared, looking as flustered as her chef had as though he'd passed on whatever he was stressing about.

'Everything OK?' Myles asked.

'Yes, everything is fine.' Distracted, she used a key to open a drawer in the desk but he couldn't see what she was looking for. Whatever it was, she didn't find it because she stood up empty-handed.

'I'll leave you to it,' he said, picking up his briefcase.

She mumbled something and he took himself up to his apartment. But the beers in the fridge didn't appeal; being on his own was less attractive than it usually was. He picked up the card for the escort agency again, toyed with it in his hand and picked up the phone.

Less than twenty seconds later when the call was answered, he hung up. He rested his forehead against the wall. 'What are you thinking?' he said out loud. He couldn't do it. Although this agency said it was upmarket and implied it was company and intellectual conversation he would be paying for, he wasn't stupid. He knew men used these types of agency for sex, and as much as he was going through a dry spell, he wasn't interested in one night with a woman, especially for money.

He leaned his back against the wall and had a sudden desire for a glass of bourbon again. Or was it rather that he wanted to recreate the evening he'd spent in the lounge, by the fire, talking to Darcy as though they were friends?

Restless, he left his apartment and went back downstairs. There was a low hum of music – definitely Christmas music – but he didn't mind it too much. He sat on the sofa in the lounge and looked out onto the street. Greenwich Village was a much better location than being put up in the Financial District in one of those modern residences with no personality. Here, it was real Manhattan life and he felt connected to it.

He hadn't been sitting there long when Darcy came through, looking as frazzled as before. She was with Rupert still. She handed him a bundle of cash and he patted her on the shoulder in an everything-will-be-OK-you'll-see gesture.

'Good evening, Myles.' Her formality and smile were back in place the second she saw him.

The family that was staying in one of the other apartments chose that moment to bustle through the front entrance and the kids told Darcy all about their day. She acted as though the only thing on her mind at that very moment was their well-being and antics. He loved the way she had the power to make people feel as though they were the centre of the universe and that nothing else mattered. He wondered if anyone ever exchanged the favour and made her feel that way.

The kids told her how they'd looked at some of the Christmas window displays and, whatever else she'd been in the middle of, Darcy listened to them extol the virtues of the window at Macy's with the North Pole and Santa's Communication Station, then a big shop of Fifth Avenue that had had giant lollipops and cotton candy in the window as well as a ten-story-high light show. Myles watched the family, the kids' voices laced with delight, fascination and exhaustion that was slowly beginning to creep up on them.

When the parents had ushered their offspring upstairs and they had all bid goodnight to one another as though somehow by staying under the same roof they were an extension of family, Myles ordered a drink. He took off his sweater, a cable knit that wasn't needed when you were this close to the fire. He wondered if Darcy would join him but when it looked like she had no intention of doing so, he picked up the newspaper and lost himself in the pages of the *New York Times*.

The young couple staying in the other apartment came through the front entrance just after Darcy served him his bourbon and a gush of icy air rushed in to remind guests of the season. Myles peered out of the curved window, not that he could see much now the moon had taken the sun's place, but it was curative with the passing lights of cars, people bobbing past the window as they dashed here and there, the day coming to a close yet the night still young.

Darcy went into hostess mode and passed on some details of the carriage rides through Central Park. The couple – who he'd established were called Vanessa and Zach – had booked one for the following day and Darcy took out a photocopied map of the city before using a pen to trace the route from the Inn to the meeting point.

'We left our cell phones at home for the holidays,' Zach announced proudly, hugging Vanessa to him. 'Our families know we're having some much-needed down time.'

'That's a good idea,' Darcy smiled. 'You'll have a proper vacation without anyone bothering you.'

When the couple went on their way Myles wondered if anyone would ever look at him in the way Vanessa looked at Zach, as though he was the person they wanted to tell all their secrets too, the last person they wanted to see at the end of the day, the first face they wanted to greet in the morning. He had an overwhelming urge to snigger. He wasn't sure a woman from an escort agency would ever be giving him that much of an extensive service.

'Can I get you another?' Darcy caught him gazing out onto the street, noticing couples walking by, families huddled together.

'The city that never sleeps,' he smiled, turning back into the room and towards the fireplace.

'It sure is.'

'I thought London was busy but this is something else. Did you miss it while you were away travelling?'

As he'd expected, she seemed reluctant to launch into conversation of a personal nature but offered, 'Very much, it's why I always knew I'd come back.' She reached out to take his empty glass and he confirmed he'd like another.

'Join me?' he asked with a smile he hoped would be enough to persuade her.

'I'm working.'

'Come on. The lovebirds have gone upstairs and I doubt you'll see them again, and the family looked beat to me. I'll bet the kids are in their pyjamas already and tucked up in bed.'

'I'd better not.'

'Come on, I'm not asking you to get so drunk you can't stand up. Just one drink, keep me company.' Boy, did he sound desperate? He didn't mean to, but something about this girl made him want to keep trying, encouraged him to keep bashing his head up against that proverbial wall.

When she came back he smiled because she'd relented and in one hand she had a bourbon, and in the other a gin and tonic for herself. The ice in her glass clinked against the sides as she sat down on the armchair adjacent to the sofa. He figured it would've been weird if she'd joined him on the two-seater, a little bit intimate for a platonic nightcap.

'Bad day?' he asked when her shoulders relaxed after her first sip.

'Something like that.'

'Anything I can help with?'

She smiled across at him although he sensed her smile hid an exhaustion, an apprehension she wasn't sharing. 'No, nothing anyone can help with.'

He leaned forward, forearms on his thighs, glass poised between his palms. 'Are you sure about that? It's just that you look as deflated as I do when I lose a deal with a major client.'

'The Inn isn't doing as well as I'd hoped, that's all.'

Good. She was talking. 'Financially?'

She cast a glance around to ensure the other guests were tucked away safely in their rooms and not about to walk up behind her. Her eyes sparkled from the glow of the fire and the white fairy lights coming from the bannisters out in the hallway. 'Sofia started this place from scratch. It used to be her home. She went through a nasty divorce but turned her life around by starting up an inn.' She looked around her, at the high ceilings that would be imposing if there wasn't this incredible warmth about the place. 'She's done a brilliant job.'

'But…'

'There's no but.'

'Oh, there's a but.'

She grinned. 'I barely know you but I can't keep much from you, can I?'

'Blame my business acumen. I'm used to reading people in my line of work as I'm sure you are.'

'She doesn't have a handle on the marketing she needs to do for this place,' Darcy admitted. 'There are so many other hotels, big and boutique, there's Airbnb now so that's another competitor, owners are renting out their investment properties via other websites. Sofia needs to turn things around and really think about how to maximise profitability. Take the top floor, for example.' She took a generous swig of gin.

'Where I'm staying?' The bourbon slipped welcomingly down his throat. He was at ease with Darcy, this conversation, this shared interest in business.

'It's a stunning apartment, right?'

'It's the best.'

'It's not rented out very much.'

'That surprises me.'

Darcy shook her head. 'It doesn't surprise me. At the price we're charging customers could go to one of the major hotel chains, with a pool, spa, a cordon-bleu restaurant. This place isn't catering for those people. I'm actually surprised you came here really.'

Myles nodded. 'It was partly my doing. I was asked where I wanted to stay while the apartment was renovated for me to live in. I said I preferred a boutique hotel or an apartment, somewhere I could come and go and that wasn't too busy. Apparently my boss's wife recommended this place, so your word-of-mouth advertising is working.'

'That's comforting to know. But, again, there aren't enough bookings throughout the year. I've been spending a lot of my time between tasks looking into what Sofia could do to change that.'

'And what did you have in mind?'

'She could go the corporate-rental route. So she could market to companies who bring people in from overseas. People like yourself.'

'That's a good idea. What else?' He liked that she was talking. He didn't want that to stop.

'Alternatively, she could easily separate the top floor into two apartments. It would be an initial outlay but she might find the affordability generates way more bookings.'

'You've got a lot of ideas.' Darcy had relaxed into her armchair and Myles mirrored her by leaning back against the sofa.

'It's hard to persuade Sofia to do much at all. I think part of her is scared whatever she does may backfire and she'll be worse off. It took a lot of courage to get this far. She really had a terrible time.'

'It sounds like you're close.'

'We are. Gabriella, her daughter, is my best friend. We were always in and out of each other's houses growing up and so Sofia is like a second mom to me. Seeing her go through that divorce was horrid, but seeing her come out the other side was the best thing.'

'You really want this place to work for her, don't you?'

Darcy nodded, toying with the sprig of mint leftover in her now empty glass. 'She went to Switzerland to help her daughter but she told me that now she's there, she's glad she's away. She's never opened the Inn at Christmas until now, and she only did it because I was so insistent it was a good idea.'

'I'm surprised,' he said. 'Christmas in New York is something a lot of people dream about and the premium prices aren't something to ignore.'

Darcy got up and changed the lights on the Christmas tree from rapid twinkling to a constant white glow that brought out the colours of the ornaments. 'She's always closed up shop, saying she couldn't neglect her family. I know where she's coming from. Gabriella went through her parents' breakup and Sofia is keen to make up for it in any way she can.'

'Does Gabriella need her to?'

Darcy shook her head. 'Gabriella is one of the most rounded people I know. She emerged from that divorce strong and together and she was there for her mom. But Sofia has so much guilt, and she's letting it blinker her view of what the Inn needs. I'd hate for her neglect to become her downfall. What I'm hoping is that she returns from Switzerland and I can talk to her, help her see that she needs to evolve and shake things up.'

'Have another,' Myles prompted, noting her empty glass between slender fingers.

'You know, I think I will.' But she didn't top her glass up until she'd lingered in the hallway for a minute or two to ensure guests were ensconced in their apartments. Not that it mattered. He felt sure her professionalism would return in an instant if any of them emerged.

With another gin and tonic, she took a seat and his heart skipped a beat when she crossed her legs, because he couldn't ignore how attracted to her he was, both on the outside and by the personality he was slowly getting to know.

'You need to do a PowerPoint presentation.' He lifted his eyebrows at her.

'For what?'

'To show Sofia what you want to say, about the Inn.'

'Oh, I don't think that's necessary.'

'You know, when my niece and nephew were desperate for a puppy they got tired of begging my brother and his wife. So, one day, they – now I may have helped out a bit – prepared a PowerPoint presentation on all the reasons why they should be allowed to get a dog.'

'That's hilarious.'

He held up a hand. 'Hilarious, but it worked. They'd cited reasons such as the puppy teaching them to care for another being, teaching them responsibility, encouraging them to get outdoors even when the weather was miserable. They had it all worked out. You know, I think Winston and Victoria caved in because they were so impressed with all the effort their kids had gone to.'

'So they have a puppy now?'

He took out his phone and scrolled through his photos. He handed it to Darcy. 'Meet Sally, the labradoodle.'

'She's gorgeous.'

He took his phone back. 'I just think that rather than telling Sofia what you think she should do, in snatched pieces of conversation, you need to back it all up with hard evidence. Present the facts in an easy-to-comprehend format and she might just see exactly what needs to be done. She'll understand a way forward.'

'I would hate to see this place close.'

'It's not that bad is it?'

Concern etched across her brow. 'It will be if she doesn't rethink things soon and bring those customers in.'

'Is that what this Christmas is about?'

'It came at the right time. This is my chance to start by showing her, with photographs, figures, testimonials to back it up, that Christmas is a time she not only *should* open but *needs* to open.'

Darcy fixed herself another drink while Myles was still on his second. He hadn't had to prompt her this time, but she was relaxing as they talked more about the Inn. They covered suggestions and plans for how it could be advertised, about what to include in her presentation to Sofia. He discussed with her ways to get corporate customers on board. Much in the same way as he did with his clients, Sofia would need to earn their trust and ensure they could see what was in it for them.

'I think the key with Sofia,' he said, 'is to know exactly what you're talking about, cover every aspect you think she'll question.' He probed some more. 'Is that what was going on earlier?'

'What do you mean?'

'When the chef came through to get you.'

'Ah,' she remembered. 'He went to the store and the credit card got rejected. I didn't even have any money in the cash box to give him. I had to use some of my savings. I've spoken with Sofia, who was more than embarrassed and promised to have some money transferred to the business account, but the way she was talking, I'm not sure she's got an endless supply. I just hope we don't have any mishaps through Christmas. We've ordered and paid for a turkey, sorted decorations and the liquor, but there's still the day-to-day food we'll need, particularly when the snow starts and everyone is hunkered down inside.'

She seemed to check herself and held her glass aloft, the mint leaves wedged between ice cubes. 'This has loosened my tongue far too much.'

'Don't worry, it won't go any further, I promise.'

'I appreciate it.' A look passed between them. He wondered whether this side of Darcy rarely showed, the side that dropped the business woman façade and showed her vulnerability. 'You know, I like to manage things on my own, and even calling Sofia was a struggle. I have to pull this off.'

'Christmas?'

She nodded. 'Sofia doubted holding the main meal here would be popular, let alone profitable, but already the bookings have more than covered the costs, and I know the liquor consumption will go up so that'll generate more money. And then there's my secret weapon.'

'Oh, and what's that?' He wondered what else she had hidden up her sleeve.

'I have a very prestigious guest staying from Christmas Eve through the festivities. She works for a major publication and has promised me a huge feature in the New Year. She says a lot of people brood in the aftermath of Christmas and they want to make bookings for something to look forward to. She says the article will run and their reach for the magazine is huge.' She used her hands to illustrate the point. 'This could see bookings for next year, and to know that the season from Thanksgiving through to January is solid would be an enormous boost.'

'I have every faith you can do it.'

'Really?' She put a hand against her chest. 'You know, I think I can too.' Her smile disappeared. 'When Sofia's husband left her, she almost hit rock-bottom. He was the provider, the man, the one who earned the money. She was lost. It's a blessing he left her this house and she managed to do something with it.'

'It worked out for her in the end,' he confirmed.

'I'm never getting into that position.' The drinks certainly had made her a lot more talkative.

'And what position is that?' She was swaying slightly and he wouldn't mind betting she hadn't eaten enough to soak up the gin and tonics she'd drunk in quick succession.

'Relying on someone else.'

'A man?'

'Don't get me wrong, I'm not gay.' She laughed and he couldn't help but smile. This was a Darcy he'd never seen before and she was as fun as her conversation was stimulating. 'It's just that I never want to be one of those women.'

'One of what women?'

'The ones who need a man!' She went behind the bar area, took out a bottle of water and downed almost all of it, pulling herself together with every sip. 'It's easily done. Women have a career, they marry, have kids, and then the job goes out the window. There's nothing wrong with that. I get it. I just don't ever want to be dependent on a man or anyone else for that matter.'

'I don't think you ever would be, Darcy. You seem as though you've got a good sense for business.'

'You know, I'm going to do what you said. I'll make a PowerPoint.'

'I'm glad to hear it.' The last swig of bourbon warmed him right through and she didn't ask whether he wanted another, just took the glass, refilled it, got another drink for herself and carried on their conversation.

'So what about you?' She handed him his drink. 'Have you called the agency yet?'

He squirmed a little inside. So sure of himself until she'd brought up his potential dalliance with someone whose services he'd had to pay for. 'Almost.'

'Come on, live a little. You never know, you could meet the woman of your dreams.'

He almost thought she meant it until she laughed. 'Don't joke. My boss has made it clear I should take a date. And if I don't find one, he'll be sorting me out with someone and that brings with it complications, expectations, things I don't need.'

'And how much do these escorts charge? You know, for a basic service.' Her voice wobbled in amusement.

'Glad you think it's funny. They're not cheap. It'll definitely cost but it's not the money I'm bothered about.'

'How much are we talking? Ballpark.' When he gave her the cost she whistled through her teeth. 'You'll pay that for one night of company?'

'I'm looking at it as a strategic move,' he countered. 'A way to impress the boss, the client and get business moving longer term.'

'I'd have thought a man like you would have women lining up to go.'

He watched her. 'I think you and I are very alike you know.'

'How so?' She moved forwards – just an inch, but enough that he could smell the floral scent he often caught wafts of on the air. It was subtle, sophisticated, and very Darcy.

'We both work hard, we're both independent and know what we want.'

Darcy jumped up and went to the desk and the moment was over, but he smiled when he saw what she was doing. She took out a pair of glasses and perched them on the end of her nose. Myles began to laugh. She looked like a school-ma'am except way hotter. She pulled out an A4 pad of paper and a big black marker and stood in front of the fire, then kicked off her heels.

This time it was Myles who turned to check they weren't being watched. He suspected she rarely let her guard down and it was refreshing. He sensed she needed to do it, and at gone midnight they were pretty safe.

She propped the pad on the mantelpiece. 'Let's go through the pros and cons.' Darcy drew a straight line down the centre of the page, top to bottom. 'Pro?'

'I think she would be.' He laughed hard and she joined in before shushing him.

'Pro et contra, Mr Cunningham.'

He kept his voice low against the peace of the brownstone. 'If you're going all Latin on me, then I didn't listen much in that class at school. Hated it.'

She pulled a face, reprimanding him, and pushed her glasses up her nose a little so they didn't fall off. 'Pros and cons list. We'll start with the pros of hiring an escort.' Her pen was poised.

'No strings,' he called out.

'Excellent.' She scribbled it at the top of the left-hand column.

'Intelligent conversation.'

She looked down her glasses at him. 'Really?'

'I'm assured of it. Well, as much as I can believe from the website. I haven't spoken to them yet.'

Darcy jotted intelligent conversation beneath the words no strings. 'What else?'

'She wouldn't be demanding when it was time to talk business. She could talk to the other wives, whilst being discreet.'

'Excellent point, fabulous.' Darcy scribbled away and he couldn't help notice her buttocks having a little wobble beneath her skirt. Not in a bad way; firm but tantalising.

He really needed to stop with the bourbon. Perhaps have a cold shower before bed. And if Darcy knew he was thinking these kinds of things he doubted she'd stand for it anyway.

110

'You could potentially find someone for life,' she suggested, but he shook his head before she wrote it down.

They both thought for a moment.

'You could get laid,' she suggested. He spluttered on the bourbon in his glass. 'What? It's a genuine one for the pro list.'

He couldn't wipe the smile off his face. 'OK, write it down.'

She penned S-E-X in huge letters.

'I think we should move on to the cons now,' he concluded.

She unbuttoned her suit jacket and shrugged it off, another layer of her formality gone. 'Hot,' she said as though that explained it. She most certainly was. Her cheeks had pinked up from the heat of the fire and the drinks she was getting into.

His lips twisted as he thought and he blew out his cheeks. 'Laughing stock. Put that on the cons list, because if anyone finds out I'll look like a total loser.'

Grinning, she wrote LOSER as big as the word S-E-X. 'What else?'

'Money.'

'Perfect.'

'She could be boring and I'll wish I'd taken my grandma.'

That one had her laughing as she wrote Granny on the right-hand side of the paper. 'Anything else?'

He sighed. 'Darcy…'

'Mmm…' She was tapping the pen against her bottom lip, trying to think of something else.

He leaned forwards again. 'Darcy.'

'Go on, I'm waiting.' Pen was poised.

'Would you go with me to my Christmas party?' When she swung round to face him he added, 'You don't need to answer now. Think about it.' He'd caught her off guard.

'I'm not sure, Myles.'

Should he have asked? In this moment, there was nobody else he'd rather take than her. He liked how independent she was, how she knew what she wanted, how she'd stood up to him that first time in the hotel in London. He liked that she had a work ethic to rival his own.

'One moment please.' Her school-ma'am approach was back as she looked down her nose through her glasses at him. She turned to the list propped up on the mantelpiece and his eyes followed her stocking-covered legs from her ankles up to the material of her skirt before he focused on the list too.

She put a thick line through S-E-X. 'I'll be your escort,' she said. 'Should I cross out the no strings too?'

'Why don't we just wait and see?'

A noise on the stairs had Darcy pushing her feet into her heels and shaking herself to look professional. 'Everything OK?' she asked whoever had appeared at the door.

'I'm sorry to bother you so late.' It was Vanessa. 'The shower in our bathroom is leaking. I didn't notice it earlier but there's an enormous puddle on the floor. I'd hate for it to seep through the ceiling.'

Darcy was straight into business mode, even this late at night, and he had to admire her; she looked stone-cold sober. 'I'll get some old towels and come to mop the water up for now, which should keep it at bay until morning, when the plumber can take a look. He's pretty good at coming out straight away. Don't worry too much, we'll get this sorted. And please accept a full complimentary breakfast in the morning.'

Vanessa brightened. 'Thank you so much.'

When she disappeared off up the stairs again Darcy sighed deeply. She adjusted the damper on the fire. 'Duty calls,' she told Myles.

'It's OK.' He stood, took his glass over to the bar and left it on the darkened wood. Darcy was already bending down to turn off the tree lights and even Myles had to admit the room lost something when they were off. He'd got used to the pine smell by now, the gentle flicker of lights and his distorted face reflected in the odd decoration as he walked by. 'I'll say goodnight.'

'Goodnight, Myles.'

He turned to add something about the fact he'd asked her out on a date, but she'd already bustled off to the door that led down to the basement, presumably to find those old towels she'd mentioned.

He just hoped she remembered this in the morning, all of this. She'd let her guard down and, without thinking, so had he. And he couldn't help wondering whether this was the start of something real.

# Chapter Nine

*Darcy*

*Ten days until Christmas*

'Follow me, it's this way.' Darcy smiled at Vince, the plumber, who had replied to her text message at six o'clock this morning, a rude awakening for Darcy after a few gin and tonics in swift succession and very little water to soak them up. She thought she'd represented sobriety very well last night when Vanessa came downstairs to tell her about the leak.

Vanessa and Zach were ensconced in the hotel dining room enjoying eggs sunny-side up and waffles with maple syrup as Darcy dealt with the shower disaster. But after a swift evaluation, Vince confirmed it was the silicone sealant joint between the shower tray and the shower screen at fault. It had created quite a puddle last night but today Darcy was relieved to hear it wasn't a problem with the shower walls or anything that would mean the cause needed substantial investigation. Basically, anything that was expensive would not be welcome, but this she could deal with.

She left Vince to it and went downstairs. She'd switched the lights on for the garlands on the bannisters first thing, as she always did, so they lit the path to the ground floor. Her next task was to clean out the fire grate. She liked to do it as soon as she was up and about, then lay another fire ready to start when the moment was right. If she knew all the guests were going to be out during the day she often held off or timed it for their return.

She hadn't seen Myles yet and wondered how things would be between them after last night. Her mouth had gone very dry as she'd tried to give him an answer to his question, but she'd never felt so pleased at being asked on a date. Not since Lachie. Isabella was right. She had taken a lot of interest in her guest on the top floor and although she knew it wasn't strictly professional, she couldn't help the way she felt. The feelings had crept up on her and she'd gone from hating him for making demands in the London hotel that had led to her being fired to seeing him last night with his guard down. He was a different man entirely when he smiled and his right cheek dimpled ever so slightly, betraying the boy he once must have been. She didn't know this man, but her heart skipped at the thought of getting to know him more.

Darcy had a moment of panic that if something happened between her and Myles she'd get a reputation as the hotelier who liked to put it about. She froze, pan and brush in her hands, kneeling by the fire. Would customers think they could order extra perks, perhaps tick a box but instead of saying Christmas tree in room it would ask if they required Darcy's special service?

She shook away the crazy thought, cleared out the grate, and when she'd washed her hands she took out the pad of paper from the drawer she'd stashed it in last night before going to bed. She grinned as she looked at the words, her scribblings, the moment she'd bonded with Myles Cunningham.

'All done.' Vince was in the doorway, box of tricks in hand.

'That was quick.'

'Very easy to do.'

'How much do I owe you?' The dreaded question. There was the callout fee, any materials he'd used. She had enough in her personal account to cover a small charge but hoped it was exactly that.'

Vince shifted from foot to foot.

Oh no, was it that much?

'Sofia said she'd pay the last invoice and never did.' He shrugged his shoulders, pulled a face as though he was feeling terrible about having to ask for money owed.

'Vince, I'm so sorry. I never knew.'

Now he looked more embarrassed. 'I figured I wouldn't chase it until Sofia came back, but now I'm here...'

'Absolutely no need to explain, Vince.' Darcy took out her own personal chequebook. 'I'll settle up the entire bill.' She didn't want to risk writing a business cheque in case Sofia hadn't transferred the funds yet. It wouldn't be fair to Vince and it would be embarrassing on their part too.

When Vince told her the total amount, which included repairing the leaking faucet in the kitchen and unclogging a bathroom drain, both on separate callouts, she tried not to wince. She wrote him a cheque, added a tip, and when he went on his way she went to the computer to catch up with Sofia. She wasn't available for FaceTime so Darcy sent an email asking whether the cash had gone into the account. Tired of prevaricating, she also asked whether Rupert's wages were covered and if Jill, the cleaner, would definitely be paid this side of Christmas. Her personal funds could only go so far and she didn't want to be in the position where she had to go to anyone else for money.

Darcy took logs from the basket and arranged them in the grate and when the fire was laid she took a call from

Holly, the editor who was coming to stay. Holly confirmed her reservation, the Christmas dinner she'd opted for, and said she was looking forward to her visit. But all it did was remind Darcy that this year had to be a success or she'd be worrying about the future of the Inglenook Inn. And the thought of it closing simply didn't bear thinking about.

By the time Darcy got to lunchtime and Rupert held the fort if anyone wanted a light lunch, snack or drink, Darcy escaped into the chill of Manhattan. Since she'd been back in New York she realised how much she'd craved the defined seasons. Winter was cold, magical, snowy and white, autumn was a plethora of reds, greens, golds and the time of pumpkin carving and wrapping up warm but still finding out those sunglasses. Summer was sweltering in the city and the heat wavered on the top of the tarmac streets, crowds congregated in Central Park for their alfresco lunch break, and with spring came the promise of a fresh season, the time to start anew. Now, blades of grass huddled around trees on the sidewalks but were no longer green, accepting their seasonal white coating of frost. Snow was forecast tonight although they'd been predicting it for the last week and, while it had certainly cooled down, they were yet to see a single flake fall from the sky.

She walked from Greenwich Village to Washington Square Arch to meet Isabella, and ensconced in a restaurant she was looking forward to a proper catch up.

'I've got a couple of hours,' Darcy announced, handing her coat to the maître d'.

Isabella grinned as they took their seats at the table at the far end of the room. 'Don't tell my sister I'm having a long lunch though. She's been trying to drag me along

117

to home-furnishing stores to choose things for her new place.'

As they talked some more about her sister Sherry and the apartment she'd bought in Brooklyn, Darcy wondered when she'd be able to get on the property ladder. Given her love of Manhattan, she doubted it would be anytime soon.

'So come on, I want to hear more about the Inn,' Isabella prompted after they'd chosen from the menu and covered the topics of siblings, parents and Christmas-shopping progress.

'I nearly forgot.' Darcy reached into her bag and took out two presents. 'If you could take these to Cleo's store in Inglenook Falls it would be fantastic.'

'Of course.' She reached across and at the rattling sound from one of the presents, she asked, 'Did you get the Lego?'

'Lego for Jacob, but I went for make-up for Ruby. I hope Dylan doesn't mind.'

'She's a girl, she'll love it, and he'll love that she loves it.' She put the gifts into her own bag. 'Come on then, how's the Inn? Still standing?'

'Of course! And the tree is up now so it's lovely in the lounge.'

'Uh-huh.' She sipped from her glass of water.

'Sofia has been a bit behind paying bills though, so I've emailed her. She can't ignore it any longer.'

'You need to sit her down when she gets back to New York and tell her all your thoughts on the place. She probably doesn't really think about them when you mention changing the room specifications, or making Christmas a big feature, etcetera etcetera. Sit her down, tell her what's what. You're good at that. Well you are.' She shrugged as the waiter set down her fettuccine

118

Alfredo and Darcy's sea scallops with sweetcorn and rosemary-roasted potatoes. 'Why are you smiling?'

'It's just that I asked someone else's advice last night and was told much the same. I was told I have to present the facts to get Sofia to fully comprehend what's going on.' She cut through a scallop and savoured the seafood burst as she took a bite. Hand in front of her mouth, she asked, 'Now why are *you* smiling?'

'The advice wouldn't have come from a certain businessman, would it?'

The colour in Darcy's cheeks gave her away. 'Why do you say that?'

'Just a feeling I had, that's all.' She only stopped grinning because she had to focus on getting the fettuccine into her mouth without it splattering anywhere.

'Well it was just a friendly chat.' Apart from the bit where he asked her out on a date that was. 'And he was helpful. He suggested I put everything together in a formal presentation. We went through several possibilities; it was good to talk with someone who…what? Would you stop looking at me like that!'

'Well usually you'd have a glass of wine with a special catch-up lunch, but I'm assuming you had a few glasses last night when you had your talk with Mr Upstairs.'

'Oh my god! Are you psychic?'

'Just a hunch. Not like you, to drink on the job.'

'It was well after hours and everyone else was in bed. And stop calling him Mr Upstairs, or Mr Top Floor. His name is Myles, and you know I like the personal touch with my guests.' Of course, her remark caused Isabella to collapse into fits of laughter. 'That came out wrong.

You know exactly what I mean. Now if we could change the subject, I'd appreciate it.'

Talk changed to Jake. Things were getting serious. They'd discussed sharing a place together and already Darcy could tell Isabella was hoping it would lead to a more serious commitment.

'I'm really pleased for you, Isabella. You deserve to be happy.'

'His brother's coming into town next week.'

'For Christmas?'

'Just for a couple of days. He's moving back from Chicago.'

'Wait, I hope you're not thinking what I think you're thinking. You know I don't do blind dates. I don't have the time, energy or inclination.' It was almost like getting an escort when you thought about it, except it didn't cost you anything.

'Oh come on, we've got tickets to see the Christmas Spectacular at Radio City Hall, it'll be a blast.'

'I'm sure it will, but I'm still not interested.'

'He's gorgeous you know. Come on, Darcy. When was the last time you had a date?'

She thought about it. 'In London.'

'My point exactly.'

'I've been busy since I got back.'

'It's no excuse.'

'Oh be quiet and finish your pasta. Then we can order coffees. I'll just text Rupert to make sure everything is OK back at the Inn.' She sent off a quick message and he replied soon enough to say everything was running smoothly. Her shoulders sagged with relief when he added that Sofia had confirmed the money was safely in the business account and they could go on as usual. She'd also transferred an amount to Darcy's account to cover the bills she had to pay for and had apologised profusely for the inconvenience. Darcy could only imagine how guilty she felt. It wasn't how she'd intended to make her feel but Sofia did need to make some changes when she came home.

They finished their meal and after they'd ordered a coffee each, Darcy admitted, 'I actually have a date.'

'Get out!'

'I do.'

'Who with?'

Darcy pulled a face.

'Myles? No way!'

'Yes, but he only asked me because he's stuck for someone to go with him to a work Christmas party.'

'Rubbish. I'll bet he asked you for more reasons than that. Well I never.'

Darcy hadn't forgotten that he'd said 'we'll see' when she offered to cross out the 'no strings attached' comment in the pro list they'd come up with. She didn't go into all those details with Isabella but she did explain that Myles had been considering hiring an escort.

'He sounds a bit naive. Surely there are sexual favours with those.'

'He says not, but I think he had his doubts, which I suspect is why he ended up asking me to go with him. Oh god, you don't think he'll try to pay me do you?'

Isabella's eyes widened. 'I don't know. How did you leave things?'

'We kind of didn't. As soon as he'd asked me, there was a plumbing emergency upstairs and I was back to work.'

'So you don't know any details, like when the party is, or where?'

'Nothing.' Darcy realised how lame this date actually sounded. In fact, it sounded like a non-date, as though she'd dreamt it all up. 'I haven't bumped into him yet.' She wondered how she'd handle it when she did.

Isabella thanked the waiter when he set her coffee down in front of her and Darcy did the same. 'I think I need to drop by the Inn, vet him myself.'

Darcy paused, stirring her caramel macchiato with a spoon. 'Don't you dare.'

'Why not? We used to do it in school. If one of us was ever asked on a date, the other had to see them first and give their honest opinion before we could agree.'

'We're not sixteen any more, Issy.'

'Then don't call me Issy.' She grinned. Darcy had adopted the name she'd called her friend right up until Isabella had insisted it was no longer shortened. She was a respectable member of the workforce now and she claimed her full name gave her superiority. 'Please let me see him. He sounds incredibly hot.'

'Why would you think that? I haven't described him to you and I haven't exactly been complimentary about him either.'

'That's what's given me the impression. He's got under your skin, that's how I know there's something about him. So what time can I stop by?'

'He's a guest at the Inn, I'm not his keeper. He's a businessman with unpredictable hours.' She sighed and relented. 'He comes back by sevenish, sometimes earlier, and then he's usually around after nine o'clock when he comes down for a nightcap.'

'I'll bet he does,' she winked cheekily.

They finished their coffees and Darcy put up with the joking about Myles, Isabella's speculation about what he'd be like in bed if things ever progressed further.

122

One thing was for certain as they left the restaurant and ventured back beneath the bruised black clouds threatening rain. She had no idea where she stood with Myles Cunningham.

# Chapter Ten

*Myles*

*Nine days until Christmas*

Myles ran along the High Line early, before crowds of tourists plagued the place. He'd learnt his lesson soon after arriving in New York when he tried to run along there in the middle of the day. It'd been a case of him versus the selfie stick, same on the Brooklyn Bridge. Now, unless he was running somewhere with wide-open spaces, he made it a rule to go earlier.

He hadn't seen Darcy at all yesterday but as his breath met the cold air and his feet pounded Manhattan's celebrated pedestrian park that was once a railway, he knew he'd have to face her sooner rather than later. Doing so had become almost as terrifying a prospect as phoning the number on the escort-agency card. He'd never got nervous asking a woman out on a date before. He'd taken it all in his stride.

He reached the end of the route and slowed to walking as he made his way through the Chelsea Market. He checked his training watch, impressed he'd beaten his last time here. Two areas of his life were flying: work and his running performance. He wondered if he'd ever be lucky enough to add in the personal element and score the trifecta.

He walked back to the Inn hoping he could sneak inside and shower before he bumped into Darcy but when he saw her dark hair cascading around her shoulders as she adjusted the wreath out front on the entrance door he knew he'd have to face her now.

'Hey,' she said in her American accent that was returning more by the day as she lost the touches of accents and phrases she'd picked up around the world and slipped back into her native tongue.

He trudged up the steps of the brownstone as she held the door open for him. The rain of yesterday had stopped and it was as though the air stood still, waiting for the snow that had been promised on all the news channels for the last few days. 'I wouldn't get too close,' he warned as she shut the door. 'I've been running.'

'I can see that.' Her hair covered her face enough so he couldn't tell whether she was smiling as she grabbed a broom to sweep the hallway.

'I hope it snows soon,' he said, desperate to make regular conversation. 'I'm looking forward to Manhattan in the snow.'

'It's beautiful,' she confirmed, her brush gliding past his feet. She propped the broom against the wall and took out a dustpan and brush from the closet in the hallway. 'I love it, but I hate the aftermath.'

He smiled in acknowledgement. 'Ah yes, the filth and the black slush when it melts; the part we all like to forget about.'

Was she even going to mention the other night? Perhaps she'd put it down to too much to drink, a stress reliever at the time but something that offered nothing more than confusion now.

The dirt all cleared away, she asked, 'Did you want to order breakfast? Rupert is still here.'

Usually he had a bowl of cereal in his apartment before dashing out of the door for work. He looked at his watch. Strictly he didn't have time, but he needed to psyche himself up to talk about the date he'd suggested, and he was never going to do that unless he spent more time near her. He ordered poached eggs with toast and a side of mushrooms and said he'd be down after his shower.

Myles used his time beneath the warm jets to go over in his head what he was going to say to Darcy. This was worse than when he was meeting an important client. Where was the confidence he usually had no problem administering in social situations?

Downstairs in the dining room at the rear of the brownstone, with balcony doors that would open in the warmer months but were now blocked with a Christmas tree, he sat at a table by the wall. Rupert brought out his breakfast and they chatted about countries they'd visited, New York's approaching winter and what it was really like in February when the cold felt like nothing else, and by the time he'd finished and he still hadn't seen Darcy, Myles knew he had to make the bold move and just talk to her.

He found her in the lounge, where it looked like she was concentrating hard on something at the computer. She looked up when she became aware of him lurking.

'Darcy, I wanted to touch base with you about the other night.'

Her smile reached her eyes and he hoped she was smiling with him not laughing at him. 'Touch base? Now that sounds formal.' She came round to his side and perched on the desk, her proximity making him flustered.

'The question I asked you. Now, I totally understand if you woke up and realised what a colossal mistake it would be to go with me to the work Christmas party.'

'I don't think that.'

'The thing is, I really need someone…hang on…' He paused. 'Do you mean you're still happy to go?'

126

She shrugged. 'You didn't give me any specifics, which makes it hard for me to commit.'

He gave her the date and the time. 'It's at The Plaza.' He didn't miss the look on her face. 'It's a big deal, yes.'

'I've never been to The Plaza before, not apart from the food court downstairs.' She adjusted her suit jacket although it was already sitting straight, the tailored lines complementing her figure by falling across her curves in all the right places.

'Then it'll be a first for both of us,' he said, holding her gaze.

She moved to the other side of the desk. 'Let me double-check my diary.' Her nails drummed against the computer keyboard and then she looked up. 'It appears that date is fine. I'll need to check with Rupert that he can cover if I need him to, and I'll have to take my cell phone in case of emergencies.'

He tried not to smile so much it scared her away, because he couldn't believe his luck. She'd said yes! 'So it's a date?'

'I guess so. Just one thing…what's the dress code?'

'We'll be in the Grand Ballroom.' He didn't miss the sharp intake of breath. 'I'll be in a tux.'

'I'd better get something sorted then.'

He was sure whatever she wore, she'd look fabulous. Suddenly he felt relieved he'd had the bourbon that night and that he'd been able to persuade her to relax and take a moment for herself. He was looking forward to the party, something he never would've been able to do had he opted to take his secretary or, god forbid, an escort. Now, he was taking someone because he actually wanted to, and it felt good.

Watching her now, awkward with their personal conversation, her confidence not quite as resounding as it usually was, he felt bad about calling her Cinderella the day she'd attempted to introduce some of the Christmas spirit into his apartment. It hadn't been fair on her at all, and he would never stop being sorry that he'd reacted that way.

'If you need help with the dress…' he began, sensing she was fretting about the formality of the occasion.

'I think I'm quite capable of choosing something.'

'I meant, if you need help buying it. Dresses for these sorts of functions don't come cheap.'

She held up a hand. 'I'll stop you right there. I'm happy to buy something, I don't need you to do it for me.'

'Accept a dress as a gift,' he suggested. 'It's cheaper than paying for an escort.' As soon as the words were out of his mouth he wished he hadn't said them. 'I didn't mean it that way.'

'I'd better get on.' She indicated the desk behind her.

'Me too.' Perhaps he should leave before he ruined it completely.

He turned and only breathed a sigh of relief when he was the other side of the entrance door to the brownstone. Something about this girl made his brain turn to mush and his words come out in the worst possible way. The only exception to the rule had been the other night and it had ended all too quickly. He hoped they'd be able to get back to the easiness of conversation and enjoyment of one another's company when it came to the night at The Plaza.

He pulled his scarf tighter round his neck, headed for the subway, and put his personal life out of his mind for now as he got back to what he knew how to do best. Work.

*

Myles lost himself in a client account for the rest of the day. His projections went down well, they signed agreements and over lunch they discussed strategy. He caught up with paperwork in the afternoon, attended four meetings, and by the time he switched off his computer and night fell all around the office surrounding his floor-to-ceiling windows with a thick black cloak punctuated by stars and city lights, he was exhausted.

He almost ignored the phone when it rang but for some reason picked it up as one arm pushed into his coat.

'Winston, how's it going? Two phone calls, I am honoured.'

His brother saw the funny side. 'Yeah, don't get used to it. It's just the season.'

'What can I do for you?'

His brother's voice didn't come across straight away, as though he was thinking carefully about what he needed to say. 'It's Mum.'

'She's OK, isn't she?'

'Yes. Well, I think so. You see, I think she might be drinking again.'

His brother knew Myles's time was precious, so he knew better than to tiptoe around a point. Myles sat down again. 'What makes you think that?'

'Dad's worried about her. She's really low and refuses to go and see a doctor or anyone else for that matter.'

'That doesn't necessarily mean she's drinking, Winston.' The vestiges of childhood memories pounded his mind, trying to creep their way back in. He'd got well versed at blocking them out. During their years as young boys, Winston and Myles had had to contend with their mum being absent emotionally, their dad being away physically. Perhaps that was what had brought them so close together as brothers.

'I've said that to Dad,' said Winston, his voice laced with concern. 'I think he's just terrified it'll happen again.'

Myles couldn't imagine his father being terrified of anything. 'Have you spoken to Mum?'

'I haven't asked her outright. How can I? But I've chatted with her as normal and she seems the same to me.'

Myles didn't need to hear that his move to New York had probably made her blame herself for her failings. He hadn't done it to spite her, and he'd never admit this to Winston, but part of him was glad she was starting to question herself. It was something she should've done years ago.

'I haven't been up to see her yet,' Winston confessed. 'The kids' school is crazy busy with nativity plays, end-of-year parties, you know the sort of thing. I just hope Dad isn't right about this one.'

Myles suspected part of Winston's fear was that his kids would see Grandma the way they used to see her, half-cut, stumbling or falling asleep, or sometimes worse, acting up and being as silly as a five-year-old, dancing and singing, and, worst of all, ruining the entire Christmas dinner on the one day where family problems seemed to become so much more of a strain.

'Are you there?' Winston was still on the other end of the phone while Myles had lost himself looking out of the window at the few stars peppering the sky. He wondered how many other families had issues like theirs at this time of year. How many problems hid behind the smiles you saw on the streets of New York, or behind the doors of elegant brownstones?

It was a long time since Myles had had a happy Christmas, and if Winston was right, escaping to the other side of the world wasn't going to do much good either. He'd have to add another December 25th to the long list of Christmases where he'd wished the whole season would just go far, far away.

# Chapter Eleven

*Darcy*

*Eight days until Christmas*

Darcy didn't really have time for a shopping expedition, but she had nothing suitable for a night at The Plaza in her wardrobe either, so later today she was meeting Isabella for project find-a-dress. For now, she had to get on with looking after the Inn. She could see exactly how Sofia was able to neglect advertising and the bigger picture when there were so many little things to do.

The streets were icy every morning it seemed and Darcy's day began by using a shovel to scrape the worst off the brownstone stoop, before using a de-icing product. She spent no end of time sweeping the hallway. Another guest had checked in last night and, although only staying for two nights, had required a lot of the extras, which of course meant an extra weight on the already toppling workload. This guest wanted an evening meal, drinks early evening, a taxi arranged, three days' worth of clothes washed and pressed, a full breakfast this morning and directions to a few landmarks before moving on to the next destination.

Darcy had spent a while yesterday preparing for the PowerPoint presentation for when Sofia returned. She tried to pre-empt likely questions and although she had no idea of her role once Sofia was back, she didn't mind. This was what she enjoyed: the responsibility, the tantalising smell of success under her control. It felt good too. She loved the air of independence she felt, even as she continued with the mundane chores of cleaning down some of the woodwork in the hallway that had gathered dust. She vacuumed the big rug in front of the fire. She polished the mirror above the mantelpiece, she cleared the kitchen when Rupert had to rush off, she turned down beds, she replenished towels and she restocked cupboards and refrigerators in each apartment.

Darcy longed to get out her knitting needles and lose herself in the task for an hour, but she had no time for that and once she'd had lunch it was time to meet Isabella and sort out something to wear. At least being so busy had stopped her stressing about what to say to Myles when she next saw him, or how conscious she was that she was choosing a dress to wear on a date with him. If she let herself think about it too much she'd panic. What if she was a big dull dud and had no conversation skills in front of the people he worked with? Running an inn and welcoming guests was one thing, but the corporate world was another entirely, especially at The Plaza's Grand Ballroom.

Isabella was waiting on the street corner that afternoon, puffing out white circles into the air as though she was a little kid, when Darcy arrived to meet her on Fifth Avenue.

'You ready to do this?' Isabella certainly seemed raring to go. 'How long have we got?'

'You mean how long have *I* got? I'm assuming you have all day.'

'Yep, it's a Saturday and I'm as free as a bird.'

'I've got between two and three hours. I've got my cell phone in case anyone at the Inn needs me, but I did most of the chores this morning, everything else will have to wait.'

'That's the spirit. This is your first date in a long time. It's important. And it'll be good to see you in a nice dress, see a bit of flesh. You're always so done up in those suits.' She hooked an arm through Darcy's.

'Hey, I've got one of those suits on now. Under my coat.'

'And you look fabulous in them, but they're work suits; this is a totally different outfit we're about to shop for.'

As they walked she told Darcy, 'I dropped the gifts with Cleo in Inglenook Falls.'

'Thanks so much for doing that. How is she? How's Dylan?'

'I didn't see Dylan but Cleo is really well. She said to tell you that you must make it to the markets next year because she's bagged an even bigger stall.'

'Already? That's great. The knitting business must be booming. Which is more than can be said for my own knitting project.'

'Not managed to finish that sweater yet?'

'Not unless Gabriella wants her son dressed in something that currently looks more like a scarf.'

'You'll finish it, you just have other priorities right now.'

'Talking of which…' She nodded to the welcoming front doors of Saks Fifth Avenue. 'It's time to get started.'

Inside, the warmth of the store a welcome relief, Isabella was already taking out dresses and assessing them. 'What look are you going for?'

'I think classic is the way to go.' Darcy found a black dress, knee-length, plain. 'This sort of thing. It's simple, elegant—'

'Boring.'

'Isabella.' She put the dress back, deflated.

'I'm sorry, I'm not trying to make this miserable for you, but you need to think outside the square. That dress was nice, but you could've worn it for work – am I right?'

Darcy thought about it. 'Then it'll be worth spending the money.'

'Darcy, sometimes I want to shake you. This is shopping, for you, for an occasion that is special.'

'It's a first date. I'm not marrying the guy.'

'You're going to The Plaza! To a function in the Grand Ballroom!'

Darcy had texted Isabella the second she knew more details of where Myles wanted to take her. 'Well I don't want anything too showy. I like understated.'

Darcy tried on five dresses, but none appealed. They ended up in the shoe department but found nothing there either. They left the big department store and zigzagged in and out of clothing stores, shoe emporiums, designer stores where either the price tag dazzled them or the lack of a price tag made them casually leave knowing it would be way too expensive. Darcy had given Isabella her budget from the start, and it was generous but not ridiculous.

Isabella dragged her into another designer boutique, giggling away at the price tickets. 'These are crazy prices,' she whispered.

'Come on, we'd better go somewhere a little more in our league.' But Darcy had to admit it was another world in here, the clothing so immaculate she didn't dare touch any of it. 'He offered to buy me something you know.'

Isabella, distracted by a trouser suit marked on sale, said, 'Who did?'

'Myles. He offered to buy me a dress.'

135

Isabella gasped. 'You're like Demi Moore in *Indecent Proposal*.' They weaved past sales assistants and out of the door. 'Would you sleep with him for a million bucks?'

'Isabella!' Darcy nudged her friend.

'So does he look like Robert Redford?'

Darcy shook her head. 'No, better.'

'Girl, you're in deeper than you know.'

'Come on.' Darcy refocused. 'I really need some help, but we need to aim for more realistic stores than that one.'

They went into store after store. Darcy tried on a one-shoulder bow dress in royal blue but hated the colour and the style. She tried on a herringbone embroidered fit and flare dress in another store, a backless number somewhere else, but nothing felt right.

It felt as though they were never going to find anything.

They stepped out of yet another store and when Isabella declared hunger they grabbed a hot dog each from a stall on the next block.

'I'd better not have too many of these if I want to fit into any dress.' Darcy savoured the onions and slather of mustard as she popped the last piece into her mouth. 'My hands are freezing.' She quickly replaced her gloves. It was the season for hats already. Isabella had a navy one with a fawn pom-pom on top, and Darcy had one to match – another purchase from Cleo's store in Inglenook Falls – except hers was a pale pink knitted version with the same faux-fur pom-pom.

Isabella wiped her mouth, found the nearest trash can and deposited her napkin in there. 'You know, it's so cold I think it's going to snow soon.' She hunched up her shoulders and put her own gloves back on.

'I hope it does.' Darcy beamed. 'I love winter. The smell of it in the air. Even autumn was something I really noticed this year.' They continued their walk along Fifth Avenue, waiting for the pedestrian signal to walk.

'Since you went off travelling you mean?'

'Yes. Australia was nearly always warm and when it wasn't, it was far from the cold we get here. And London, well, London was damp and we had a bit of a snow flurry but nothing like a Manhattan winter where the snow comes down and everything around you falls silent. It's like there's magic in the air.'

Isabella sighed. 'Come on, you. This isn't helping us choose a dress. Clothes first, winter talk later.'

Next up was Armani, despite Darcy's protests that it was too expensive. The warmth was glorious and the gorgeous clothes held their interest until Isabella started going on about Myles again. 'If you'd let him buy you something you could shop in here.'

'Not going to happen.'

'You could've had those Manolo Blahnik satin heels from Saks,' Isabella went on.

Darcy had had enough and waited by the door until her friend had finished. They stepped out onto the sidewalk.

'I'm sorry, Darcy,' said Isabella as they waited to cross the street at the next block. 'You know me. I get carried away in my own fairy-tale imagination.'

Darcy nudged her friend, her breath making white puffs in the air as she spoke. 'I know you only want the best for me.'

'I do.'

137

They crossed when the sign changed. 'It's just you know I've always liked to be completely independent. I hate the idea that I'll be reliant on someone else.'

'But you're not.'

'I know I'm not now. I don't think I ever could be.'

Darcy let herself be persuaded to grab a hot chocolate to take away and they strolled further down Fifth Avenue drinking their beverages and chatting. 'I've seen too many women hurt by people they depend on.'

'You mean men.'

'OK, men.'

'But what about all those people you see who end up happy?' Isabella batted back.

'I've never admitted this to anyone else, but I think I'm scared of not having control over my own destiny.'

'That sounds dramatic.'

'Lachie is ancient history, but after what he did, I realised how much safer I felt doing my own thing, following my own path. If we'd stayed together, he never would've been happy with me travelling you know.'

'You guys talked about it?'

'Not at great length, but a few things he said told me he wanted a more traditional, stable home life.'

'Then it's better you guys broke up when you did,' said Isabella, before adding, 'but sometimes you need to see that it's OK to not always be in complete control. You might find you enjoy having someone to share things with. You know, I think this date could be your turning point.'

'Well don't go getting too excited about it. It's one date, that's all. It may all come to nothing. I've only had a couple of brief conversations with the man, so it's early days.' But secretly, even though she wasn't sure she wanted to admit it to herself, she really hoped it could develop into something more.

They finished their drinks and left the sidewalk for the warmth of an upmarket yet not over-the-top-pricey clothing store.

'I'm sick of trying on dresses.' Darcy was flagging already from taking all her layers off, putting them on again, then repeating it over and over at each store they reached.

'This is gorgeous.' Ignoring her, Isabella took out a purple ruffle dress. 'But it's the wrong colour.'

The shop assistant didn't miss a thing. 'It comes in a black also. What size do you need?'

Isabella directed the assistant to Darcy, who told her the size, and moments later there she was again in the fitting room removing her hat, scarf, coat, suit jacket, shirt. She looked at the black dress on its hanger, the smooth material, and she felt a leap of excitement at the event she was choosing this outfit for. The price was reasonable too: expensive but not ridiculously so.

'Come on, I'm dying out here. Give me a look.' Isabella's impatient request carried through the fitting-room area.

'Just a minute.' Darcy pushed her arms into the material. She gently wriggled it over her chest and zipped it up. She stared at her reflection. 'I'll be out in a sec,' she called, because she wanted to get used to a less-formal-looking Darcy before her friend voiced an opinion.

The dress, a classic black, was sleeveless to show the olive skin of her arms and had a ruffle on one shoulder, but it was simple, understated. The material at the neck sat in a flattering line across her collar bone, so she wouldn't need a necklace, and the dress finished above her knee.

'Wow.' Isabella appeared in the changing room. 'You look good in that. Your legs. I need those legs. Mine are good up to the knee, but beyond that they need to be covered.'

Darcy giggled at her friend's assessment. 'Your legs are just fine.'

'Give me a twirl.' Darcy did as instructed. 'It's gorgeous. And I know you say it's classic, but as well as that, it's dramatic.' She stood next to her friend as they looked in the mirror. 'See, at the bottom the ruffles give it an uneven hemline at the sides. And it's perfectly nipped at the waist to flatter your figure. What colour shoes are you thinking?'

Darcy turned so she could see the back of the dress in the mirror. There were a couple of ruffles at the bottom of the skirt and the beauty of the black material was that you couldn't see too much detail straight off but when the dress moved with you, it did so in an elegant way.

'You could go with black,' said Isabella, unsure.

'I have black heels.'

'Sparkly would be better,' Isabella beamed. 'Silver, teamed with a silver clutch. Do you have sparkly earrings? Perhaps studs would be best – classic and stylish.'

'I have something,' Darcy smiled.

'Wait there.' Isabella left her friend admiring her reflection but was back within less than a minute. She thrust a garment through the curtain. 'Try this bolero jacket. You'll need something to go from the Inn to The Plaza, and this is perfect.'

Darcy took the garment and put one arm in, then the other. It was snuggly warm, a faux-fur black bolero that

didn't detract from the shape of the dress. 'It's perfect.'
She smiled. 'All we need now are shoes and a purse.'

Isabella grinned back at her. 'I knew I'd get you
enthusiastic about this somehow.'

When she was changed and the dress back on its
hanger, Darcy took it out to the assistant, handed over
her credit card, and, bundled up against the winter blast,
she left the store one happy customer.

It didn't take long to find a shoe store that had a great
range, and Darcy had only tried on two pairs before she
found the ones she wanted, a sleek pair of glittering
silver stilettos that were surprisingly comfortable to
wear. 'These are perfect,' Darcy declared.

'As good as some of those we saw earlier?'

'Better. And hundreds of dollars cheaper.' She
slipped her feet out of them, decided, and paid.

Next up was purse shopping. They needed to match it
to the shoes and in the store next door they found the
perfect silver clutch that glittered when it caught the
light.

'Just one coffee,' Isabella begged when they were
done.

'I really have to get back to the Inn,' Darcy insisted.

'Then I'll come to you. You can give me odd jobs to
do if you like. I don't mind helping out.'

Darcy couldn't hold her laughter in. 'You only want
to gawp at Myles Cunningham, I'm not silly.'

'I'm your friend; it's important I make an assessment
of him.'

Darcy linked her arm through Isabella's, in a
thoroughly good mood now she had something to wear
on her date. 'Fine, come on then.'

'Yes!'

'And thanks so much for today. I couldn't have done it on my own.'

'You wait. My sister is getting married next year and I'm going to make you come with me to find a bridesmaid dress. I need to find something suitable so I can guide her away from anything frilly or pastel. Pastels make me look ill.'

*

True to her word, Isabella helped Darcy out back at the Inn. She swept the hallway while Darcy answered the phone and started the fire going in the grate. While Darcy gave directions for the O'Sullivan family to find Battery Park, Isabella neatened up the newspapers on the table and wiped down the side tables.

'For some reason,' Isabella began, 'doing this is a lot nicer than cleaning my own place.'

'I think this place is even worse at the moment because of the glitter that comes with Christmas decorations.' Darcy grimaced.

'Ah, that's why, it's like sweeping up fairy dust,' Isabella grinned. She tugged on her coat and took the broom from the closet in the hallway. 'I'll sweep the stoop.'

Darcy almost called after her that it was probably icy already given the plummeting temperatures outside, and that it was so dark she wouldn't be able to see a thing. But with the time bang on six thirty, Darcy knew full well Isabella had an ulterior motive for doing all of this. She was trying to hang around long enough to see Myles, and by hovering outside she'd most likely get her wish.

Her suspicions were confirmed moments later when she heard Isabella chatting animatedly and a male voice carried through the door as her friend returned inside.

'It's freezing out there.' Isabella had a coat on but her hands were bare.

Serves you right for being so nosy, Darcy thought, but didn't give away her amusement.

'It's a bit icy for sweeping,' said Myles, but Isabella dismissed the concern saying it was the first impressions that counted with guests. Darcy suspected Myles was onto Isabella as much as she was.

'These came for you.' Darcy handed him a couple of envelopes that had come in the mail today. Not many guests had mail delivered but he was here a lot longer than most, so she guessed it was inevitable.

'Thank you.' He reached out and took the mail, his skin briefly making contact with Darcy's.

Isabella, the broom propped under one hand, was looking from Myles to Darcy and back again as though trying to read their faces.

'Is there any chance of an evening meal tonight?' Myles asked. Darcy wondered if he'd be more conversational if Isabella wasn't lurking in the background.

'Of course.' Darcy left her friend pretending to straighten the garlands on the stairs beside them and found the menu. She handed it to Myles, who had one foot on the bottom step, ready to go up, take off his coat, dump his briefcase. He didn't take long to choose the lasagne with salad, said he'd eat in the dining room this evening, and Darcy went off to confirm with Rupert.

'Stop looking at me like that.' When she came back from the kitchen, Isabella was still leaning on the broom handle, fit to burst with comments.

'Like what?' Isabella did her best to look innocent.

Darcy returned to the lounge and added another log to the fire. It didn't take long for the flames to envelope it and roar away, heating the room to its optimum. Dating a guest wasn't something she'd planned, and she hoped it wasn't going to compromise her professionalism here at the Inn.

She turned to her friend. 'Am I mad? Mixing business with pleasure is bound to be a recipe for disaster.'

'Darcy,' Isabella smiled, 'he's gorgeous. Do me a favour. Give yourself a break and just go with it.'

# Chapter Twelve

*Myles*

Myles opened his mail and shook his head at the Christmas card from his parents. The piece of mail that tried to show everyone they were a normal family when they had a long way to go to achieve that status.

By the time he went downstairs to eat dinner, Darcy's friend had gone. He'd known she was assessing him on Darcy's behalf and he hadn't minded one bit. Sometimes he wished men had the same camaraderie rather than remaining tight-lipped, revealing nothing about their feelings.

Darcy smiled at him as he passed by to go to the dining room. She was on the phone, and each time he saw her, he expected her to say she'd changed her mind about accompanying him to the Christmas party. She was professional, serious, independent, and he sensed she didn't like mixing business with pleasure. He didn't do it much himself, but this was different. He wondered what he'd have done if Darcy had said no. Would he have called the escort agency? Would he have let someone else set him up?

He tucked into the lasagne, which was the perfect food for this kind of weather. He'd have to make it out for a run in the morning or he wouldn't fit into his tux for The Plaza.

'Is everything all right for you, sir?' Rupert approached the table.

'Please call me Myles. It took ages to persuade Darcy to, but I much prefer it.'

'Very well. Myles it is.' Rupert smiled. 'Can I get you a glass of wine? The dessert menu?'

'I'll pass thanks, but the lasagne was great.'

Rupert thanked him for the compliment and took his plate away. If the man was tired after so many shifts at the Inn, he didn't show it.

Disappointed he didn't see more of Darcy, Myles decided he was going to have to rectify that and went upstairs to pick up the gift he'd bought. He'd wanted to buy Darcy something special to show his appreciation for her coming to this party with him, for agreeing to go on a date, for taking a chance on him. There were plenty of flowers dotted around the Inn – a vase of what looked like lilies on the table just outside his apartment entrance, another arrangement of deep red blooms on the next floor down as you rounded the stairwell, although he was no expert on varieties of anything, having never had his own garden to play with or the time to do so – so he'd passed that idea by.

'Hey, Darcy.' He'd already adopted the American 'hey' around work and the Inn, and he attempted to sound more confident than he really felt now he was in front of her as she sat at the desk, brow creased in concentration.

'Hello, Myles. How was your dinner?'

'It was wonderful, thank you. You have a superb chef.'

'We do. And I hear the lasagne is the best. The O'Sullivan family all seemed to think so.'

He smiled. 'It's usually a crowd-pleaser. Not something I've ever made myself. I imagine it takes a while.'

Silence hovered between them until she asked, 'Can I get you anything else?'

'I'll take a bourbon if I may.'

'Sure.' She seemed glad of something to do and went to the bar area to fix the drink.

'Don't you get tired of never switching off?' He looked at the time, already nine o'clock.

'I could ask you the same.'

'I'm here now, I'm switched off.' That wasn't strictly true. His mind had pinged back and forth between work things at dinner as much as personal stuff.

'Well, I don't have the luxury today. I've been out shopping for the majority of the afternoon.'

'Buy anything nice?'

She turned to face him and allowed a trace of excitement to show on her face. 'I have a dress, shoes and a purse for the party. Let's just hope I leave before midnight or the sequins and heels might turn into my boring work clothes again.'

He wasn't sure how to react to the hint of a Cinderella reference but she seemed to be making the remarks in good spirits. He took the gift from his pocket. 'I hope these go with the outfit.'

She looked at it, the box wrapped in silver paper with a white bow. 'For me?'

'It's a small gift to say thank you for agreeing to go with me. Thank you for saving me from hiring someone, which would be so demeaning if I'm completely honest. And…well it's also to say that I'm looking forward to it.'

She took the box.

'Open it, go on,' he urged.

She looked around, uneasy at the intimate gesture in her workplace. She tugged at the end of the bow and it unravelled so she could pull off the paper and reveal the box inside. She opened it up.

'I hope they're suitable. I went for diamonds, they go with everything.'

She looked at him, the gift ensconced in her palm. She looked at the earrings sparkling back at her cheekily. But then she shut the box. 'I can't accept them.' She handed it to him.

'Why not? It's a gift, from me to you.'

'I already have earrings I can wear.'

'You don't like them?' His heart sank. The earrings were classic, beautiful, not at all over the top. Just like Darcy.

'It's not that.' She walked over to the fire. She lifted the glass panel and used the poker to jostle what was inside. The flames obeyed and flickered higher. 'You really don't get it, do you?' She didn't look happy now.

'I really don't.' He kept hold of the little box containing the earrings he'd carefully chosen with Darcy in mind. 'You'll have to explain it to me.'

'Excuse me.' The phone rang and she answered it.

Myles turned and walked over to the window. He looked out at the row of brownstones opposite, their own Christmas decorations battling each other over who could be the brightest, the shiniest, the talk of Manhattan. From what he could gather she was talking to another guest due to arrive tonight, directing them from the Washington Square Arch, an ideal landmark if you were ever lost trying to find the Inn.

'Another guest?' he asked the second he knew her call had come to an end. He thought he'd adopt the nothing-wrong-here approach and see how it went down.

'Yes, checking in tonight.' She looked at her watch. 'I've given him directions. He's only a few blocks away, so won't be long.'

He wondered if the intended implication was that he shouldn't be hanging around, but he wanted to clear this up. 'I didn't mean to offend you. It's the last thing I wanted to do.'

'I appreciate the gesture, but it's really unnecessary.'

He sighed. 'Don't you accept gifts from boyfriends?' He felt a prize idiot for referring to himself in that way. It made him sound as though he was back in school, fumbling for the right words to ask a girl to the dance.

'That's just it.' Her voice softened. 'We haven't been out on a date yet.' Coyly, she added, 'At least wait until the third or fourth date to shower me with diamonds.'

Appreciating the lighter atmosphere, he offered her the box again. 'Please, take them.'

'They look like they're expensive.'

This was a woman who couldn't be bought. Whoever ended up with her would have to earn his place and her respect. 'They were. And you know what happens if you return earrings?'

She shook her head.

'They refuse to exchange or refund. Hygiene reasons apparently.'

'Actually, I have heard that somewhere.' She held his gaze.

He pushed the box forwards again. 'So…'

'Myles Cunningham.' She shook her head but this time reached out for the box and her smile matched what he'd hoped to see when she laid eyes on the three-dimensional diamonds that captured the delicate symmetry of sunflowers. 'They're beautiful, really.'

'Try them on.'

When there was a knock on the front door she said, 'You'll have to wait until our date.' And with that she was off to greet the new guest.

Myles left her to it. He'd come down and done what he'd aimed to do, which was give her the gift and put her at ease, make sure she was looking forward to their date as much as he was.

He made it to the next floor, rounded the staircase as tiny lights twinkled from the garlands showered in a glittery frost finish, but before he reached the foot of the next staircase, the voice of the latest guest to check in at the Inn had him stopping in his tracks.

It couldn't be, could it?

# Chapter Thirteen

*Darcy*

*Seven days until Christmas*

Darcy struggled when her alarm went off to start another day. She loved what she did, loved the newly appointed role at the helm of the Inn, but she wasn't immune to the morning blues, especially after a fitful night's sleep.

Darcy wasn't used to her feelings yo-yoing up and down at their own will. First the gift from Myles had taken her by surprise, and as soon as she'd made peace with that and accepted it as a nice gesture from someone she would like to get to know better – if she could forget her misgivings about relationships and dependence – her new guest had shown up and toppled the world on its axis. At least that's what it had done for Myles, and he was back to being the same man she'd always assumed he was: aloof and unreachable, with a harder side that she hadn't seen for a while.

Her latest guest had been a last-minute booking, secured with a credit card in the name of Martha King. As it turned out, the man's wife had booked the accommodation for him and his surname wasn't King, but Cunningham – a name that was, by now, familiar.

Myles's father had travelled all the way over from England to talk to his son and when the two men met in the hallway last night Darcy could've cut the tension with the knife Rupert had sharpened that morning as she'd stood talking to her chef about what needed to be added to the list of groceries to replenish the apartments upstairs.

Darcy savoured the solitude of Sofia's apartment a while longer. She loved it here, cocooned in her own four walls. Sofia was a minimalist, or at least that's what she would have you believe – she claimed it was the way she needed to be if she wanted guests to stay here. She only had this small section of the Manhattan brownstone now, with a modest kitchen, a nice sized bedroom, a newly fitted bathroom and a lounge area with a small dining table and two sofas sitting at right angles. Heavy drapes framed all the windows but when pulled back they let the light of the day spill into the room whenever the seasons allowed.

Darcy cradled a hot mug of tea and perched on the window seat in the bedroom. She drew her legs up, leaned against the wall and sipped the steaming liquid. The city hadn't gone to sleep last night but rather dozed as fitfully as she had, with the odd siren, the odd yell from someone out either too late or far too early, and the sound of trucks getting around before the rush hour commenced, delivering to local delis, stores, restaurants, and keeping the city operating as though those things never really happened. She'd seen a programme about it once, about how the city operated, and it was true. You did forget everything that went on behind the scenes. Only the finished product mattered. Standing in Grand Central Terminal you never considered the computer systems on a level beneath you that kept trains on time and screens updated; sitting in a restaurant you didn't think about the buyers out at the markets in the early hours while everyone else was tucked up in bed, ensuring only the freshest and best produce made it to their tables.

Darcy had always wanted to be a part of the service industry and she'd loved her studies as well as her travel.

And now, the Inn was giving her everything she wanted, and when situations arose she felt ready to adapt to them and change accordingly. Last night had been the perfect example.

'I apologise,' her latest guest had said when she took his credit card and realised the difference in surnames. 'My wife booked the accommodation, but here's my card to secure the room for any additional charges.'

Darcy was back to being the host. None of this was her business. But the tension hovered in the air as Myles appeared in the lounge doorway, hands deep in his pockets, waiting for this man who Darcy could only assume was his father.

The man was very polite. He'd insisted on being called Ian – much like Myles had insisted on his Christian name being used when they first met – and he said thank you for the offer of food but he'd already eaten. Myles had waited in the wings the entire time and Darcy had been at odds over what to do. Usually she would take new guests up to their rooms, show them in, list the supplies they'd included for their stay.

In the end she'd decided to continue as though nothing was out of the ordinary. It could possibly give Myles some breathing space, both men the time to think before they spoke. 'Mr Cunningham…sorry, Ian.' She smiled at this man who had every ounce of his son's charm. 'Let me show you to your apartment.' She picked up his small suitcase from where it stood in the hallway.

'No, no, no.' Ian grabbed it right back. 'I couldn't possibly allow a lady to carry this. I'll manage.'

'There are a few stairs.'

'Are you saying I'm too old?' He pretended to look put out but she shared the joke, smiled, and then at Myles's discomfort got on with the job intended. She showed Ian upstairs but Myles didn't follow. She ran through the basics: the kitchen area, where the smoke alarm was, the leaflets of attractions in the city, the complimentary food items, how the safe worked.

Eventually she left him to it and as she passed Myles on the stairwell she put a hand to his arm. He looked at it touching his sleeve and nodded that he was OK. Both men had gone up to the top floor and she hadn't heard from them again.

From her position on the window seat now, Darcy wiped the back of her hand across the glass. It was still dark but she could see with the help of the glow from the streetlamps that the roofs opposite were tipped with frost, the odd light was dotted at a window on the same level as hers, a couple more on the levels above, but most of the city's residents were probably still tucked up in bed. She sipped her tea and wondered how long the men had talked for last night. What had been said? Were both her guests still here this morning or had there been a huge fight she'd not heard? Her understanding from Myles was that Christmas hadn't exactly been a happy affair in his household, which suggested there were other problems besides.

Darcy finished her tea as the brownstone woke up around her. The pipes creaked and groaned as they prepared for another day, warming from their low-set temperature to something that would offer more come the time people were forced to shed their covers and brave the world. The streets outside became noisier and with the time still not yet seven she had a shower before the sun dared to show its face.

Darcy hadn't been in the lounge for long when Isabella stopped in on her way to work that morning.

'His dad? Wow.' Isabella had come baring bagels and coffees for both of them.

'I don't know what's gone on between them, but the tension.' She raised her eyebrows as she sipped her caramel macchiato and led Isabella through to the kitchen. The hot liquid trickled welcomingly down through her insides. 'This is so good. I had a cup of tea this morning but this is so much better.'

'Of course it is. Tea was for England, coffee is for New York.'

'Where's yours?' Darcy took out a knife and the butter from the refrigerator.

'It's damn cold outside, I drank it on my way over.' Isabella buttered both bagels, Darcy found two plates and they leaned against the countertop to enjoy them.

Darcy bit into the bagel, shutting her eyes at the winter taste, the melted butter and the sweetness of the raisins. 'Thanks for this.'

'You're welcome.'

'I'm really hoping it snows soon.' Darcy looked out of the kitchen window to see what the weather was doing, but there was no sign yet.

'No, don't let it come down before I finish work. I've got three more days. Then it can dump the biggest load on the entire city and I can stay in my jammies all day.'

'But who will bring me bagels and coffee?'

'I'm sure you can think of someone,' Isabella grinned.

Rupert appeared and they finished their bagels, chatted with him and then went back through to the lounge.

'I'd better go soon.' Isabella checked her watch. 'I'm lucky to be getting away with a late start today as my boss wants me to stay behind tonight, take minutes at some meeting or other.'

Darcy loved how Isabella pretended to brush off her job as though it was an annoyance. She knew her friend too well. She'd put in one hundred and ten per cent in that office, but whenever she was out of it, she was as relaxed as she could be. Darcy wished she could be more like that sometimes.

'Keep me posted on Myles,' Isabella whispered as she plucked her coat from the hook in the hallway. 'The party at The Plaza is still on, right?'

'I'm sure it is.' She hooked a finger in a come-here motion and when Isabella followed her to the desk in the lounge, she unlocked the top drawer and took out the earrings she'd put in there for safe keeping. She'd done it discreetly when Ian Cunningham was slotting his credit card back into his wallet.

Isabella whistled through her front teeth. 'Darcy.' She couldn't stop staring at the earrings. 'Where…' She covered her mouth with her hand. 'From Myles?'

Darcy nodded and flipped the box shut, stowed it in the drawer again. 'It's too much, isn't it? I mean, we haven't even been on a date yet. I'm not used to this.'

'Darcy, go with it. You haven't dated for a long time. I know how independent you are, how dedicated you are to your work. But I'm here to tell you that sometimes it's OK to let someone else be a part of all that.' She squeezed her friend's hand. 'It'll all work out, I can feel it.'

'I tried to give them back,' she confessed.

'What did he say?'

'He told me the store won't accept returns or give refunds for earrings.'

'He has a point, they don't. Have you tried them on?' she asked in the next breath, her coat now on and gloves poised at the ready.

'Not yet.'

'They'll go perfectly with your clutch and shoes. You're going to look amazing. Oh, promise me you'll get plenty of photos.'

'I'll get one, how does that sound?'

'Like it's not enough.' She smiled. 'Now I'd better go but I'll see you soon.'

'Thanks for the breakfast.'

After her friend left Darcy had plenty to do. Unfortunately one of the O'Sullivan children had come down with a heavy cold but she'd managed to find a hot water bottle amongst the bits and pieces in a cupboard in the basement. She even went to the pharmacy for Adele when her husband took their other son out for the day and she didn't want to leave her child. All Darcy was doing now was keeping everything crossed that the head cold didn't turn out to be the flu, because the last thing they needed was an outbreak over the holiday season. It could get the Inn into the media for all the wrong reasons.

Vanessa and Zach came in chatting away about the Empire State Building, which had been fantastic apart from the low-lying mist hanging around Manhattan obscuring their view. Darcy appreciated the positive spin and was glad to see they were making the most of their vacation.

Just after lunch Myles turned up, puffed after a run.

'Not working today?' She bent her head down to push another tiny bulb onto a twinkle light on the bannister. She'd noticed it wasn't working this morning but it was easy enough to replace.

157

'I'll go in later,' he answered.

Ah, a man of few words. She inspected the rest of the lights, found another that needed replacing and took a second new bulb from the small cardboard box she'd placed on the stairs. 'Am I in your way?' She shuffled close to the bannister so he could come up the stairs.

'Not at all.'

He didn't seem to want to talk, or go past. Darcy decided the best thing she could do was to carry on and let him do whatever he needed to do in his own time.

She took the box of bulbs back down to the basement and with one load of laundry finished, she took out the clean set of sheets, bundled in a load of towels and set the wash to go again. She put the sheets into the dryer, set the timer and headed back up the stairs.

He was still there, hovering, letting himself recover after his exertion. 'Snow's forecast tonight,' he offered, following her when she walked past and into the lounge.

'You'll love your first New York snow. The whole city stops.' She opened the mail that had sat patiently in a pile on the edge of the desk ready to be dealt with.

'That would be nice.'

She sensed this man needed his world to stop, if only for a time. 'Well, it doesn't really stop, but it makes everyone take pause. It's beautiful, everything is muffled and white. Then people kind of realise they can't actually stop, life has to go on.'

'Back on the treadmill,' he muttered, looking out of the window now as though willing those flakes to fall from the sky.

A creak on the stairs implied someone was about to join them and Adele poked her head around the door as she rounded the bottom of the bannisters.

158

'How's Saul?' Darcy put down the mail. Myles was staring at the Christmas tree, not talking, barely moving. But if Adele noticed anything odd, she was kind enough not to mention it.

'He's watching TV and feeling a bit better after some soup.'

'Rupert is an expert at chicken soup,' Darcy smiled. 'And chicken soup always helps when you have a cold.'

Mrs O'Sullivan crossed the fingers on both hands. 'Let's pray it goes as quickly as it came and that the rest of us don't get it. I really want to thank you for all your help.'

'It was my pleasure, and do please let me know if there's anything else you need.'

'I think I have everything. A lifetime's supply of tissues should do it.'

When Adele left, Myles looked relaxed, as though the simple exchange had made him forget everything else around him. 'What did you do?'

'I only went to the pharmacy for her.' She shrugged and picked up the mail again. 'No biggie.'

'Rubbish. It's those little touches that'll make the Inn stand out in the crowd.'

She was conscious of him watching her. 'I hope so.'

She opened a couple of bills that made her wince but their due date wasn't for another few weeks so they had time on their hands, and she opened a Christmas card from her parents and put it up on the desk. She'd put it in her apartment later. And when Myles still hadn't gone upstairs she wondered whether he really did want to talk but just didn't know how to start the conversation.

She joined him by the window. He was far too much of an English gentleman to sit down all sweaty after a run, which she appreciated. Sofia had once told her about a guest who'd run in Central Park each day and every time he returned to the Inn dripping with sweat at the height of summer in Manhattan, when it's so hot you can barely breathe on some days, he'd order a juice, sit down with the newspaper in the lounge and stay there for an hour. 'All I kept thinking about was my poor sofa,' Sofia had told Darcy and Gabriella. She'd upgraded the furniture soon after, bought leather sofas so they were easy to wipe down, but they hadn't had another guest like that as far as Darcy knew.

Standing next to Myles, he didn't smell bad. He had on running skins that clung to every defined part of his legs, a long-sleeved top that showed off biceps worthy of someone who had a physical job rather than his position on Wall Street, and was holding a dark blue hat that he'd peeled off the second he came through the hallway. The beads of sweat that had clung to him at first had dried now and he smelled kind of sweet but not unpleasant.

'So,' she began. They were standing side by side, looking out across the street. A man wobbled past on a bicycle singing at the top of his voice and although Darcy wasn't looking at Myles, she knew he was smiling. 'Your dad's here.'

'My dad's here.'

'I had no idea who he was.'

'His secretary always booked his business trips. Obviously my mum did it this time. I think she has an account in her maiden name.' He seemed to snap out of his train of thought. 'I'll be working from my apartment for a few hours this afternoon.'

'Would you like me to send up a late lunch?' Darcy switched back into hostess mode rather than trying to be a friend. The surface of this man seemed as brittle as the

160

first layer of ice on a lake in the winter, and with too much weight, it would break.

The door to the brownstone opened and a gush of icy air rushed into the lounge, prompting Darcy to think about lighting the fire soon. She'd checked the wood supplies that morning and ordered more to arrive in the New Year. They were getting through a lot and it wasn't cheap to order the special wood with low moisture content and low emissions.

When Darcy saw Myles's dad standing in the doorway to the lounge she greeted him and then went over to her desk, leaving both men to it. But rather than stay and talk, Myles simply left the room and Ian hovered awkwardly.

Darcy offered him a menu for the lunch options. 'Our chef is still here and soup of the day is chicken, which I can highly recommend. It comes with a lovely crusty bread roll too.'

Ian smiled at her, his warmth reaching eyes that showed fear. He looked like a man with a lot on his mind. His long, black woollen coat was so clean it looked new, he had on tailored pants even though he was unlikely to go near an office during his stay, and his grey hair was trimmed neatly so it sat just above his collar. A rich, chocolate scarf completed the ensemble and Darcy wondered if he ever looked any different, or any more relaxed.

Ian had his lunch in the dining room while Darcy got the fire going and when he was finished he came in to sit beside it. He requested a bourbon and without a newspaper in front of him or an electronic device to distract him, he just sat there as the Inn operated around him. And when he was done with his whiskey, he got up, nodded over at Darcy and went on his way.

She knew he was about to brave things with his son.

# Chapter Fourteen

*Myles*

'We didn't get far last night, son.' Ian sat at the dining table next to the kitchen countertop in Myles's apartment. He'd taken off his coat and hung it on a hook along with his scarf, and Myles sat opposite him as though they were at a board meeting rather than two members of the same family at a special time of the year.

'I don't understand all the fuss,' Myles argued. 'I'm in New York because it was a strategic career move for me.' But even as he spoke, Myles knew that wasn't why his dad was here. He wasn't sitting across from him now to reprimand him for leaving the country, but Myles didn't want to hear the words, he didn't want to acknowledge his mum hadn't changed and had found solace in the bottle, yet again. He didn't want to talk about the problems that had hovered among them for far too long.

'Your mother…'

Myles stood. He couldn't do this. This conversation was never going to reach a satisfying conclusion, a solution, like he could find in a business meeting when clients and the business aligned and identified a way forwards. This family had been in trouble since his childhood and it was going to take a lot more glue than a few words exchanged across a wooden table.

He walked over to the window, reached out a hand and traced it down the ice-cold glass. Hard to believe it was around zero degrees outside when it was so warm in here.

'Martha isn't coping.' His dad spoke softly, out of character for a man so authoritative and used to commanding respect.

Myles felt his insides curdle in sympathy. But it didn't last long. 'Winston seems to think she's drinking again.' The lack of denial from his dad confirmed it.

When they'd been through this before, many years ago, his father was hardly ever there. The boys had got through the days with each other to lean on. It was amazing they'd come out as unscathed as they actually had. This would be the first time Ian Cunningham had really had to deal with his wife's problems, because they were well established last time, before he even realised. He'd worked away so much, building a life, giving her the big house and a gardener, a cleaner, the life he thought they all deserved.

Myles looked up as far as he could at the Manhattan sky. You couldn't see much, not right now. Clouds thickened overhead in the small space available to see between the rows of brownstones. When he'd first arrived in the city he'd been to the Top of the Rock, and up to the highest level you could go at the Empire State Building. He'd thought of the sky as limitless, fresh and full of possibilities. And that was his father's problem. He'd always looked one level above and never really thought about what was going on in his world right at eye level.

'Why is she drinking again?' Myles demanded without taking his gaze away from the outside.

'Son, would you please look at me.'

'I can't, Dad. I'll talk to you, but looking out the window stops me from being so angry.'

'I can understand you're upset.'

Myles clenched his fists tight, released them, still looking outside. 'This isn't a counselling session. I also have a lot of work to do so please get to the point.'

He heard his dad sigh, another out-of-character mannerism he'd rarely heard growing up. It seemed to be something that had come with retirement. As though he'd finally been allowed to take a breath and let it out slowly, as if at last he could focus on everything as a whole rather than the tiny parts of their lives that should slot together easily.

Myles heard the kettle go on but still he didn't move. And when a brew appeared in his father's hand at the side of him, the steam wafting towards his face, he began to laugh.

'What's funny?' his dad asked.

'The English think all problems can be dealt with by making a cup of tea.' He slurped the top of the hot liquid. 'Thank you.'

Ian nodded.

He felt a sense of calm wash through him as he drank. 'They don't drink a lot of tea over here.'

'I remember it well,' said Ian, still beside him at the window.

Myles wondered if all New Yorkers looked outside as they were doing. He'd certainly done it a lot since he'd arrived. It helped him think. It was either that or look at the inside walls which he knew would slowly drive him crazy.

His dad reminisced about his own work life, the offices he'd been to, the cities he'd visited all over the world. It was a topic Myles and he were both comfortable with and Myles knew he was doing it as a distraction from the real reason he was here.

'I'm surprised you have a tree,' said Ian, turning to look at it.

'It was put here for me and I guess I've kind of got used to it.'

'It's a nice touch. The Inn will have a lot of custom if they add extras like that.'

'You should tell Darcy, she'll appreciate hearing that.'

'She's very young. Does she own the place?'

Myles cradled the remaining half cup of tea between his palms. 'She's managing it for a couple of months while the owner is in Europe. The owner is the mother of her best friend, as far as I know.' He added the last part because he was sounding as though he knew this girl way too intimately. Which was a possibility, or at least he hoped so. For the first time he'd been pondering how it might feel to have someone like Darcy by his side. Maybe he was getting old. At almost thirty-four years old, perhaps it wasn't only the odd grey strand of hair he noticed, but a softening of his ways and his heart.

'Well she seems a fine young lady,' said Ian.

'She is.' Myles felt his jaw tighten. 'Come on, Dad. Enough about the Inn. Why are you really here?'

Ian sat at the table again and gestured for Myles to sit in the seat opposite. It was as though the man couldn't do a conversation without the horizontal security of a piece of wood between them.

'Your mother thinks I'm here for a reunion with my old firm. They operate out of New York now.'

'But she booked you in here.'

'She did, and I think she was hoping we'd spend time together. But she has no idea that you're the only reason I came.'

Myles was stunned. Although his father hadn't mentioned the fake firm reunion before, he hadn't believed that he was only here to see him. He'd suspected there'd be another part of the schedule somewhere – perhaps a lunch with his former colleagues, tourist highlights, a stopover before he went to see relatives in Boston.

'You're not heading to Boston to see Auntie Pat?'

'Not this time, son. I have more important things to do.'

'How long are you here for?'

'Only a few nights. I'll be home for Christmas, like I always am.'

'Well that's not strictly true.' Myles couldn't help it.

'I guess I deserved that.' Ian pushed his empty cup away. His palms spread out on the wooden table in front of him, his fingers evenly spaced, his gaze on the age spots peppering the skin now. 'I wasn't always there, son. Nobody knows that more than I do, believe me.'

Myles stayed quiet.

'I see a lot of myself in you, too much sometimes, it's quite confronting. And I can't go back and fix what I did wrong, but what I can do is stop you doing the things I did. I had the career, I always pushed you boys to do the same. We're Cunningham men. Cunningham men are providers, they're responsible, they're strong. Somehow Winston got it exactly right. Goodness knows how he's managed it. I think he got half my genes, half your mother's.' He let out a long sigh. 'I suppose I'm here to try and bring you back into the family and to stop you making the biggest mistake of your life before it's too late.'

'What mistake am I making, Dad? Come on, you seem so sure, but I have no idea. I'm excelling at work, which is something you admit drumming into each of us boys, so is it marriage you're alluding to?'

'Not just marriage.'

'Then what?'

'A happy, functioning, two-way marriage, son. Your mother and I, we were a team, but I never gave her enough credit. She supported me, I excelled, but nobody was there to support her. She raised two healthy boys, but she largely did it alone. And when she was in trouble, when she needed me, I wasn't there.' His voice caught.

'We drove her to drink.' Myles looked at his feet, remembering the first time he'd smelt alcohol on her breath, the first time he'd realised what the strange overpowering smell was. 'I heard other boys at school talking about drinking and how it made you forget things, and I assumed that's what Mum did. She wanted to forget her life, her role as our mum. It would've been too hard for her raising us boys alone.' Tears appeared in the corners of his eyes and he refused to let them fall.

'She never once regretted having you boys.'

Myles harrumphed. 'Then why?' Myles had never questioned why one moment his mum wasn't drinking and the next she was. He'd never asked himself if there'd been one particular event that started it.

'Do you remember Grandma Cheryl?'

Myles warmed at the thought of her. His grandfather had died when he was too little to remember him and most of his and Winston's memories came from Grandma Cheryl. 'Of course I do, she was a big part of our childhood for a while.'

'Your mother was a lot like her. She had this energy, this sense of fun.'

The day Grandma Cheryl died, it was like a light had gone out in Myles's world. It was the first funeral Myles had ever been to and he'd hated every minute of it. He'd watched the coffin being lowered into a big hole in the ground, he'd listened to men of the cloth spouting words that were of no comfort to him or his brother because they made no sense.

Myles felt like a little boy all over again as his voice wavered. 'I never forgot her, you know.'

'That's because she stepped in when your mum started having problems. Sometimes she spent more time with you than either of us did.' Ian looked at his hands clasped in front of him. 'Your mum's problems all started when I was away on a work trip and the house was broken into.'

Myles froze. 'I don't remember.'

'You boys were in bed at the time, but Martha woke up. She made it downstairs but before she reached the alarm the intruder found her. He punched and kicked her as she tried to block the way to the upstairs. She hadn't cared about what he stole – if he'd asked she would've given him her entire jewellery box, the keys to the Porsche sitting on the drive. She just didn't want that man anywhere near her boys. You and Winston were both going through a stage of getting up at random times during the night. You'd go wandering. We called you our little sleepwalkers even though you were both awake every time. We even had to install a toddler gate at the top of the stairs because we were scared one of you would be so sleepy you'd fall down them in the middle of the night.' He lost himself in another memory. 'Martha was terrified you'd get up that night and the intruder would start on you.'

'What happened after that?' He swallowed hard. He wasn't sure he wanted to hear it.

'She got away from him and pressed the panic button on the alarm. The intruder came at her again and got a few more punches in. She made it to the kitchen with the alarm wailing. She grabbed a knife and he ran off. She was still clutching the knife when you came downstairs to see what the noise was.'

'I really don't remember any of it.' Myles shook his head through tears. Brave wasn't a word he'd ever associated with his mum. He had a few other adjectives to describe her but as his father recalled what had happened all those years ago his perception began to alter.

'Martha told me you were awake, but rubbing your eyes.'

It was a small detail but it somehow made Myles feel close to this mum he didn't really know anymore.

Ian had more emotion on his face than Myles had ever seen before. 'It was so dark you couldn't see the blood on her face, the way she was walking funny from where she'd been kicked in the hip, and she somehow got you up to bed, where you fell straight back to sleep. The police came, she gave a statement, and by the morning she'd cleared up the house so you had no idea.'

Myles could remember the toddler gate, he could remember getting up in the night on so many different occasions. But he berated himself for not having noticed anything else, because it felt like he'd failed his mum.

'I came straight home and stayed almost a month,' Ian went on. 'We updated all the locks, had a panic button put in upstairs in the bedroom, but I don't think she ever slept well without me at her side.'

'But you were barely there.' Myles got up and fixed himself a glass of water. He made one for his dad too, but Ian didn't touch it.

'When I met your mum she was a slip of a thing: delicate, fine features, pale skin, but with a warmth that was addictive. She'd never been a drinker. She'd have a small glass of wine with dinner, never much more. We used to joke that I had a full-time dedicated driver when I went to client dinners and took her along. But she never minded. I'd laugh at home if we ever had a few drinks because she'd fall asleep moments after, her head on my shoulder as we watched the television or sat talking when you kids were in bed.'

'I don't remember you two ever being like that.' Myles had only known them as being at the helm of a dysfunctional family. He'd never understood that they were a couple too. Once upon a time they would've done what every couple did, looking to the future, making plans. When had all that changed for them?

'After the burglary she started having nightmares.' The pain on Ian's face showed. 'They were terrible. She'd be up in the night, paranoid at every little sound. It was at the time when I was barely there. My career was going well, better than ever, and she insisted it was the way it should be and that she'd be just fine.'

'But she wasn't.'

Ian shook his head. 'Of course not. She'd lost her mum, she'd been beaten in her own home, all in the space of six weeks. She started to have a large brandy before bed, just so she'd sleep, and for a while I think it worked. It knocked her out until the small hours. But then one brandy turned to two, then three, then I caught her once having got up at four in the morning and she was having another glass to send her back to sleep.'

Myles shook his head. 'Didn't you think at that point that she might need help?' He didn't mean to sound angry, but somehow he did.

'I suggested she see a counsellor. I wasn't blind, I could see what she was doing wasn't normal, that she wasn't coping. But she brushed the suggestion off. She said to give her a couple of weeks and she'd see how she went. I took time off work and I whisked you all away to the Cotswolds for a week.'

'I remember.' Myles smiled fondly. Even though his grandma had died and they were all still so very sad, he recollected his parents being together, his brother and himself making up the family of four. It was one of the last genuinely happy family holidays he ever remembered. They'd eaten at a pub in the village, he and Winston feeling grown up as they were allowed to order from the big menu not the children's. They'd come back to the holiday house and played table tennis, his mum with an uncanny knack for whacking the ball as hard as she would do in tennis. They'd lost four ping-pong balls in the garden next door and no amount of crawling through bushes had found them. But they'd all laughed hysterically and it had been one of the best days Myles could remember.

'Your mum didn't drink a drop on that holiday,' his father told him. 'She refused wine at dinner, she was sleeping the entire night, she was happier than I'd seen her in a while. We'd even cuddled together on the sofa and talked about Cheryl, about the good times and the loss. She cried, something she hadn't done since the funeral, and she'd talked about the burglary and how she felt good with the panic button upstairs in the house. She said it gave her peace of mind and she wouldn't hesitate to use it.

'We returned home and had a lovely couple of weeks before I went back to work. My next stint was in Singapore and I was so worried about leaving her again, but she had you boys and you were her world.'

'When did you realise she'd turned to the bottle again?'

His dad hesitated. 'It was near Christmas, the year you turned nine. I came home a few days before and there was nobody around. Your mum had left a note in the kitchen to say you'd all gone out for ice-cream but you wouldn't be long. I was on a high at how happy my whole family was. I couldn't wait to see you all. I stood by the Christmas tree in the lounge. It was bare, stretching from floor to ceiling. The tip was even bent over at the top it was so tall, and I laughed remembering how you'd told me that very thing when we'd talked on the phone. You'd promised me that nobody would decorate it until I came home because it was a family tradition and I shouldn't miss it.'

'I remember.' But Myles's smile faded because he also remembered what happened afterwards. It was the Christmas that had changed everything.

'The boxes were all lined up ready to go. I could imagine your face, and your brother's. You'd both be desperate to decorate it, rooting through boxes, unearthing decorations from previous years. When the door went you both came running through, ice-cream smeared on your faces.'

'You'd been shocked we were allowed to eat it in the car,' said Myles.

'As soon as your mum walked into the lounge, her arms outstretched to me...' His voice wobbled. 'I knew.'

'Knew what?'

'That she was still drinking.'

'How?'

'I just knew. It was the way she sauntered, the smell of mouthwash rather than ice-cream on her breath when she leaned in for a kiss.'

His father's mood that night was beginning to make sense. 'You sent us to do our teeth. You said you were too tired to do the tree.'

His father looked down at the table, at the knots running through the otherwise smooth wood that had been varnished over to cover them up. 'I was angry, and I didn't want you to see it. She'd driven her boys, my boys, all over town to find an ice-cream shop that was open in the winter at that time of night. And she'd done it when she was drunk.'

Myles sat back in his chair, raked a hand through his hair. His mum had hidden her drinking well in those days. It was as they'd got older that she hadn't tended to bother. And now, he knew how the bad Christmas memories had started. They'd decorated the tree the next morning, with tension lacing every conversation. He remembered his dad looking tired, he'd assumed it was because he worked so much, but perhaps it was trying to support his family financially and pick up the pieces of the life that seemed to be crumbling around his wife.

'Christmas was never the same after that,' said Myles. 'She always drank, more and more every time, and if she ever helped with the tree it would end up a mess or she'd break something. A few years later, the tension reached an almost unbearable level, and I think I began to realise just how bad things had become.' A muscle in his jaw twitched. He felt sorry for his dad, but, still, he'd been the kid not the parent and he and his brother hadn't deserved their lives falling apart either. 'You'd come home really late Christmas Eve, flying in from Geneva. I remember because my friend Matty had come over for the afternoon and he was obsessed with the jet-set lifestyle you led.'

'Didn't he become a pilot?'

Myles shook his head and laughed. 'He did. No surprise there, eh?' Back to the topic of conversation, he said, 'You and Mum got up to see us open our presents and I remember hoping that this year it would be different. We'd all be a happy family and Mum would only drink grape juice not alcohol.'

Ian shook his head. He knew what was coming.

'I smelled it on her breath when she hugged me. I suppose I should be grateful she even did that.'

'She loves you, always has.'

'I'm not disputing that. But love also has to be earned in return, and my love was tested to the limit that year.' He took a deep breath as memories assaulted him from every angle. 'Every year Mum bought a huge turkey, and I'd seen it waiting in the fridge. I also knew that she usually took it out an hour or so before it needed to go in the oven. Something about bringing it to room temperature – I'd heard her talking about it with Grandma Cheryl once. But Mum was slouched in the armchair by the tree by then so I asked Winston to help me get the turkey out and put it on the table. It was so heavy I didn't trust my arms to be strong enough to lift it out without dropping it.'

'I thought you boys wanted to cook the Christmas lunch.' Ian's eyes glistened with the horrid realisation that that hadn't been their intention.

'We pretended that's what we wanted to do when you finally came downstairs after your sleep. We knew you'd worked hard and were tired. We didn't want another family argument, not on Christmas day.'

'You and Winston always did work well together.'

'We still do, Dad.'

Ian nodded as though glad something had turned out right.

'I tried to wake Mum,' Myles went on, 'but she was comatose. It wasn't even ten o'clock in the morning and she was out for the count. You'd gone back to bed so Winston and I got to work. We'd helped out with roast dinners before, we knew Mum always had her cookbooks out on the bench when she made Christmas dinner and she'd written out a menu plan the day before when she clearly had more intention of cooking it for us, or at least with us. The turkey was easy enough. We filled part of it with stuffing and collapsed into laughter not knowing whether we had our hands down a turkey's neck or up another part.' He almost started to laugh. Winston had been by his side for years and he loved his brother without question. It helped that someone else had been through the same crap as he had and at least one of them had come out the other side normal, and strong.

'However did you know how to make it all?' his father asked him now.

'Winston and I were both top of the class in maths so calculating cooking time was easy. Winston drew diagrams for each stage and we worked out the timings for when everything should be prepared. We looked at what was in the fridge to work out what vegetables we needed to prepare and we found cooking times for each of them. We tried to be quiet so as not to wake you upstairs and by then we didn't want Mum to wake either. Our best bet, we knew, would be if the dinner was almost done and she woke up, sobered up as much as was possible, and you woke up to be none the wiser about her behaviour.'

'I knew, son.' Ian rubbed the back of his neck with a hand that showed his age. The grey hair had come in his early fifties and Myles was used to it, but when Myles saw the backs of his dad's hands, not quite as steady as they once were, and wrinkled more than any other visible part of him, it reminded him of the reality. His dad wasn't getting any younger, and he'd had hard years just like Myles had. And here he was asking for a chance to put things right.

'When did you know?'

Ian grinned. 'Sorry, it's not funny, but I knew when I saw the gravy.'

Myles burst out laughing as he remembered. 'We made it too thick.'

Ian's laughter filled the apartment, his eyes gleaming as much as the shiniest bauble on the Christmas tree as he shared a less tense moment with his younger son. 'I tipped the jug up to pour it over my turkey and nothing came out for a while. It was like sludge.'

'I could almost cut it with my knife and fork.'

Ian's laughter increased. 'I remember boiling the kettle, adding water to the gravy to make it palatable.'

'Or at least thinner so we could pour it.'

'It had a good flavour, I'll give you that.'

'We may have added a considerable amount of gravy powder,' Myles admitted.

They let the memory settle between them and the laughter died down.

Myles's smile had faded. 'It was hard work for two little boys. I don't mean the cooking of the meal: it was more the stress of whether their mum was going to drink the rest of the day; whether their dad was going to have fun with them or focus his attentions on a huge row with his wife.'

'I tried to get her help.'

'You got us a nanny!' Myles was incredulous, the merriment gone from the room.

Ian shook his head. 'You don't understand. I paid for private counselling for your mother – she went once and then refused to go again. I tried to talk to her, but she didn't want me near her. She alienated friends along the way.' He spoke fast as though desperate to make Myles understand. 'Her own mother wasn't there to talk to, and I think that was the hardest thing for her. Somehow she'd got on this nightmare carousel with alcohol and couldn't see a way to get off. I despaired. I had to work, I had to keep the house we were in up and running, I had two boys to feed, clothe and send to school. I had to pay a nanny because I couldn't trust my own wife with our sons. I didn't want her to drive you all over the county to sports tournaments, pick you up from school, or, heaven forbid, have to react in an emergency. She loved you, but she was a drunk.'

The D word stung the most, but it was completely true.

'I did my best, Myles.' His father looked right at him, his bottom lip wobbling.

Myles had never seen him look so fragile and in that moment he knew his dad was telling the truth. For years Myles had laid the blame largely at his mum's feet, but he'd blamed his dad too and never once seen what the situation had been doing to him.

That Christmas he and Winston cooked, his dad really had been the life and soul of the party. There hadn't been a massive row as he and his brother had anticipated. His dad had been there for them, played board games, they'd been outside for a long walk wishing it would snow instead of rain. His dad had been with them all day long until the moment their heads hit their pillows, exhausted. His dad hadn't once focused on the fact that his wife had drifted off, away from the festivities, by mid-afternoon and found her solace in another bottle.

His sons had been Ian Cunningham's focus, and Myles felt shamefaced he hadn't realised.

# Chapter Fifteen

*Darcy*

*Five days until Christmas*

Darcy couldn't stop looking at her dress. Secure in the side of the closet that Sofia had emptied for her, it hung there as a reminder that she had a date. The last time she'd been on a date had been…well, she couldn't actually remember, which, she supposed, was why she really had to go on this one. Part of her still thought it unprofessional to date a guest – didn't it fall into the student/teacher or doctor/patient realm? But deep down she knew she was simply looking for excuses because she was afraid.

She took out the earrings from the drawer in the nightstand, unfastened one from the velvet insert and in front of the ornate white free-standing mirror she pushed it into her ear lobe. It shone as though telling her to put the other one in quickly before she changed her mind about the unexpected gift from Myles. When they were both in place she touched her fingers lightly to the jewellery, still scarcely able to believe he'd already given her diamonds before they'd even been out on a date. But when her gaze focused on her pale pink fluffy pyjamas instead, she plummeted back to earth. She was an ordinary girl, about to go out with a man who had plenty of issues and who felt way out of her league. She expected he usually dated women who dressed top to toe in Chanel or Gucci, not women who skipped the designer stores and found something for a fraction of the price. Myles's women probably wore silk nighties to bed, not pyjamas like hers, and a pair of diamond earrings most likely slotted in with an already sizeable collection of equally impressive pieces.

Darcy took the earrings off, put them back in their box and tucked them away in the drawer of the nightstand. She went through to the kitchenette, put the kettle on and as it boiled and rumbled and steam shot out of the spout, she knew she needed to get her head sorted and go back to business-Darcy, not going-on-a-date-and-fretting-Darcy, because today her all-important guest would be checking in and she wanted the apartment she was staying in to be utterly perfect.

When Darcy had managed to arrange this magazine editor staying at the Inn, it'd been a total fluke. It was a case of being in the right place at the right time. Darcy had been dropping off her résumé at a hotel on Broadway. She didn't want to send it in the mail because she knew that it made a good impression to hand-deliver it and whoever she spoke to would have a face to put to the name. And so, at the hotel, she'd confidently asked to see the manager and handed her documentation over. There was a possibility of a job opening in the New Year and Darcy was excited to have something, anything, in the pipeline after her stint at the Inn came to a close. It meant she'd be able to sort an apartment, have no unexplained gaps in her résumé, and carry on doing the job she loved.

With her résumé delivered, Darcy headed to the flower market. The sun was still struggling to get to the best position in the sky as she arrived at the entrance, giving the city a wonderful glow. She hadn't been to this market before but it was lovely and quiet right now so she had a chance to really look around. There was soft, delicate chocolate Queen Anne's lace teamed with marigolds and orange roses, another display filled with purple alliums, their colour a contrast to the green ball dianthus. Roses in as many colours as you could think of stood tall and proud, and the smell inside the flower market was a fragrant escape from the fumes of traffic and steam coming from grates outside on the streets.

She wondered how they could have so many different varieties of plants and flowers in here – did they all bloom in America, or had some of them been shipped in from other countries so customers had an enormous selection? She was taken by one particular display in a rectangular vase near the counter. 'Could you please tell me where I could get these?' she asked the assistant who had just pushed the cash register closed after serving another customer.

'They're popular this morning,' the girl confirmed. 'I think I've got more out the back – give me a sec and I'll check.'

Darcy leaned in to smell the white amaryllis, the red roses and the green hydrangeas. The arrangement had pine cones weaved between the stems of flowers and a type of red berry completing the look. It would be perfect on the side table in the hallway of the Inn, lift the dark wood and complement the garlands adorning the bannisters.

'You're in luck.' The girl was back, brandishing a practically identical bouquet except the flowers were nicely closed.

Darcy confirmed the price and took out her purse, when another woman said, 'They're gorgeous.'

'They are.' Darcy smiled.

'We'll have more in tomorrow,' the girl told the lady. 'That's our last one.'

'But I'm here so early,' the woman complained, though in good spirits.

When Darcy had paid and the assistant moved to help someone else, Darcy noticed the woman's finger was bleeding. 'What did you do?'

'Every rose has its thorn,' she laughed. Jackie-Onassis-style glasses were perched in amongst the auburn curls of her hair, ready to pull down to shield her eyes from the winter sun, and she wore a beautiful berry-coloured scarf around her neck. Dangly earrings jiggled as she laughed and her make-up was perfect, as though she'd just sat at a counter in a department store and had one of those makeovers they sometimes offered for free before persuading you to buy all kinds of skincare products and things you never had any intention of adding to your make-up kit.

Darcy fished in her handbag and took out a Band-Aid. 'Here, use this. You'll ruin your scarf if you get blood on it.'

'Thank you, that's really kind.' She took the Band-Aid and wrapped it around her finger. 'Enjoy those flowers.' She nodded to the arrangement nestled in Darcy's arms. 'I'll definitely be back tomorrow to get my own. I'm staying in an apartment that has quite possibly the drabbest four walls I've ever had to be in. I even started crying this morning. How over-the-top emotional is that? But it's all I could get at short notice.'

'Crying doesn't sound good, it must be really awful.'

The woman dismissed her concern. 'I came to see a friend who was in hospital and she died four days ago. We were going to spend Christmas and New Year's together.' Her voice caught before she waved her hands about to rid herself of the over-sentimentality. 'I'm sorry. It's just that we thought she would be home for

183

the holidays. We had it all planned out. I'd cook the dinner, she'd be waited on hand and foot. Oh god, I'm sorry.' She swiped at her eyes when tears came. 'I'm usually strong, I never cry. But she was only young, her whole life before her.'

Darcy ushered her out of the flower market. 'Don't apologise. Come on.' She took her into the café next door, bought her a coffee and they sat down.

'You don't have time for this, I'm sure,' said the woman, embarrassed at her outburst of emotion.

'I'm Darcy, and yes, I do have time.'

'I'm Holly. And I'm normally an astute businesswoman, not an emotional mess. It's nice to meet you.'

Darcy smiled. 'It's lovely to meet you too.' Holly looked to be in her early thirties and as she began to relax, seemed more of a peer or a friend to socialise with than the businesswoman she described herself as. Darcy wondered if other people thought the same about her sometimes. 'Tell me about your friend.' Darcy was used to this, being the ear to strangers with their woes. A lot of the time they came in to a hotel inebriated, laughing and joking about something or other; other times she saw emotional people, who were most often embarrassed the next morning – but it was all part of being in the service industry.

'How long are you here for?' Darcy asked as they finished their coffees and conversation paused.

'I'm staying for Christmas and New Year's, I have a party to attend a few days before that. My friend wouldn't want me to miss it.' She smiled. 'I can imagine her shoving me out the door, telling me to get on with it and stop moaning. She never did wallow in self-pity and hated anyone else doing it either.'

'Your friend sounds like she made the most of life.'

'She really did, although I'm not sure I want to hang around for the big day itself anymore. I'll have to cook my own Christmas dinner in that revolting apartment with nobody for company apart from the rats.'

'It sounds bad.'

'It is. I'd wanted to live like a true New Yorker, but I guess my plan backfired.'

'Can't you stay at your friend's place?'

She shook her head. 'Her family is there now and I don't want to encroach on their time together, their own grief. I might go to my parents perhaps, but I was all geared up for Christmas in New York.'

'Can't you have a word with the manager or the landlord?'

'The manager doesn't seem to be bothered about portraying the apartment as ten times better than it is. The adverts certainly used a lot of artistic licence. The pipes are noisy at night, one window is cracked, the water is lukewarm at best, there's mould on the ceiling and the light fittings are either broken or missing.'

Sometimes, the accommodation you got in a big city like this was pot luck. And it looked like the woman hadn't had much luck at all.

'You know,' Holly continued, 'Sarah also had a mischievous streak and she'll love my next move.'

'And what's that?'

'Revenge.' Her eyes twinkled.

'How?'

She leaned in and tapped the side of her nose. 'I'm a magazine editor and occasionally I write opinion pieces, the odd feature article, reviews when I travel around. I'm from Washington. I might put together an exposé. Other travellers really shouldn't have their vacation ruined in this way. I wouldn't mind if the landlord was helpful and at least a bit apologetic, but he isn't. He has the money, that's all he cares about.'

Darcy asked which magazine Holly was from and when she told her she tried not to let her shock show on her face. 'That's a major publication.'

'I know, and the review will be seen by thousands. Our circulation is huge.' Her voice went up an octave to illustrate the point. 'Sorry, do forgive me, I've gone into business mode. And I'm boring you.' She touched a hand gently to Darcy's arm. 'I'll leave you to it. Thank you for the inspiration for the flowers; I'll be sure to come back for some tomorrow.'

The smell of the blooms in Darcy's arms was intoxicating in a good way as she followed Holly out onto the sidewalk. 'Hang on a sec,' she said. 'I know this is a bit out of left field, but I know of a charming inn not too far from here that is streets ahead of the apartment you're staying in, by the sounds of it.'

'Give me the address and I'm there.'

'I've just started managing the place and we have capacity over Christmas and New Year's.'

'What's wrong with it?' Holly looked suspicious. 'Nowhere in Manhattan is available at that short notice unless it has something wrong with it. Rats? Blocked toilet? Neighbours from hell?'

Darcy laughed. 'None of the above. I'm managing this inn for a good friend of mine while she's overseas, but she isn't overly good on marketing and advertising so the place is rarely at full capacity.'

She still looked sceptical. 'Where is it?'

Darcy reeled off the address as they stood outside the café. 'We're in a side street but there are plenty of cafés, bars and restaurants nearby. And this year we're offering the full Christmas lunch if you're interested.'

'It does sound infinitely better than a takeaway for one in that grotty place I'm staying at right now. What's the room rate?'

Darcy told her that too. 'And I'll offer you a fifty per cent discount.'

'What's the catch?'

Darcy pulled her sunglasses down at the same time as Holly pulled down her own. She was squinting too much and the last thing she needed was a headache. 'There is a small one.' They stepped out of the way of a woman braving the Manhattan streets with a stroller. 'Is there any way we'd be able to have you review the Inn?'

Holly thought for a moment and then her eyes danced, her auburn hair bounced in enthusiasm. 'I'll do one better than that. I like you, Darcy. I'll review your inn, and I'll do a proper big feature on it too. I can jiggle things so come Easter you'll get a huge boost in advertising.'

Darcy was shocked. 'I wouldn't ask you to do that much. We don't have the budget.'

'This one's on me, it's sorted.'

And that was how she'd scored magazine coverage for the Inn.

Now, showered and ready to face the morning, Darcy had the cleaner do a thorough sweep of apartment number one. It had already been done last week but Darcy wanted to be thorough for their new guest.

'Do you want me to make up the bed?' Jill had done a wonderful job with the bathroom that sparkled already. She'd swept the floorboards and vacuumed the rug, she'd taken all the cushions off the two-seater sofa and cleaned beneath before replacing them strategically in the pattern they were usually in.

'If you could, that would be great.' Darcy smiled. Holly was going to love the Inglenook Inn, she just knew it.

'I'll give the stairs a once-over before I leave,' said Jill, 'and I picked up the flowers you requested. They're in the sink in the basement, in a bit of water but not too much.'

'Thank you.' Darcy beamed. Teamwork was what worked in this industry. She'd ordered the flowers from the same flower market she'd met Holly at that day. She'd remembered the same arrangement, reeled it off on the phone to ensure she got what she wanted. They'd add a touch of elegance the second Holly arrived. If she was coming from a posh hotel room then Darcy would have some competition, but as she was moving straight from that grotty apartment to here, Darcy knew she'd be in luck because anything would be better than that place sounded.

Darcy checked her watch. It was only mid-morning and her guest was checking in around dinner time. Darcy had already asked Rupert to cover for her – he was so much more than a chef – and sent Holly her enormous apologies. She hadn't said why she wouldn't be around later, she'd just said she had an important engagement tonight that she couldn't miss, but that she could be contacted if there were any problems, or else she'd see her tomorrow morning. Holly had replied back that it was of course fine, and she couldn't wait to be at the Inglenook Inn. She'd mentioned running a long, hot bath and Darcy thanked the heavens that her bathroom was the one with a free-standing tub. It was a bit of a squeeze in there but Sofia had put one in because a lot of guests asked for one, particularly in the winter months. Darcy had already put out a small bottle of fancy bath salts from Crabtree & Evelyn for their guest and some scented candles dotted around. She wanted the editor's write-up of the Inglenook Inn to give this place the biggest boost possible, for Sofia, for her, and for both of their reputations as independent businesswomen who could make it to the top without a man by their side.

'You're ridiculous,' Isabella had told her once. 'If a man wants to shower you with gifts and affection, let him!'

But that was the problem. Darcy was scared to let someone do that for her in case she forgot how to function on her own.

Darcy kept herself so busy that she blocked out thoughts of tonight's party until she saw Ian Cunningham coming through to the lounge. She was in the middle of sweeping up pine needles from the wooden floor after watering the tree – not an easy task to do elegantly when it involved getting under there to the root with a long-spouted watering can.

'Good morning,' he said, but then checked his watch. 'It's almost afternoon. Where does time go, eh?'

She had a feeling he wasn't just talking about today. 'Can I get you anything? Lunch? Drinks?' She plucked a pine needle from her sleeve and dropped it into the dustpan.

'No thank you, Darcy. I'm actually looking for my son. Have you seen him?'

'I haven't, not today.'

He smiled. 'I'll be in my room. If you see him, would you tell him I was looking for him?'

'I expect he's at work,' she said before he had a chance to leave.

'He works hard,' Ian confirmed and turned to leave again. Dressed in suit trousers, a shirt but no tie, with proper shoes befitting of an office worker, he seemed lost in unfamiliar territory.

'If it helps, he'll be back around six thirty.' She felt her skin colour. Most guests didn't tell their hotel host where they were going or what time they'd be back. 'I'm accompanying him to a work function this evening. He was stuck and so I volunteered.' With every extra word that came out of her mouth she cringed. They all sounded so pathetic and he could probably see through them completely.

'Are you dating my son?' The soft voice came from a man who was nothing like Darcy had expected. She'd imagined him to be serious, brash and unapproachable from the way Myles had talked about how he'd pushed his son's work ethic, but he seemed down to earth and, somehow, sad. 'I'm sorry, it's none of my business.' And then he smiled. 'But I'm glad. Myles – and I know he'd hate it if he heard me say this – doesn't let himself have much of a social life, and he needs one.'

Darcy held his gaze a moment longer and then realising she was still holding the pan full of needles and specks of dirt she disappeared off and deposited it in the trash. When she returned, Ian was sitting in the armchair scrolling through something on his cell phone. He stopped when she came in but she got on with her job in hand and laid a new fire.

'Would you like me to light it?' she asked Ian.

'Don't go to any trouble for me,' he insisted. He looked like Myles when he smiled. Their mouths turned up at the edges the same way, the right side ever so slightly more than the left.

'It's no trouble.' She arranged logs, took kindling from the shelves inset in the wall beside the fireplace. She positioned firelighters strategically and after putting a match to each piece it wasn't long before the fire took hold.

'You've got the knack.'

'I've prepared a few fires in my time,' she confessed. 'The damper switch helps too.' She pointed to the switch at the bottom that she'd adjusted. 'Once the flames get higher I can close the switch, and likewise, if they peter out I can adjust it to get them going again.'

'The benefits of modern inventions.' Ian spoke but he wasn't really in the conversation. His mind was elsewhere.

Darcy busied herself sweeping around the fireplace for any debris she'd created, which wasn't much. The white lights on the tree illuminated the window and as she replied to emails, paid another invoice and messaged Sofia with a brief update to keep her in the loop, she stole the odd glance at her guest, quiet and processing whatever it was on his mind.

She disappeared to apartment one and made up the bed for Holly. She used the white linen with intricate flowers stitched into its surface. She pulled on pillowcases and plumped pillows so they stood tall and proud against the headboard. She arranged a deep red runner across the bed three quarters of the way down, smiling when she realised it matched the colour of the berries in the flower arrangement she'd purchased.

Downstairs in the basement she found three vases and prepared the blooms, cutting the stems short for the smallest vase to go in the bedroom, medium length for the vase that could go on the side table, and left them long for the biggest vase that would stand in the centre of the coffee table opposite the sofa. She took each of them up to the apartment and once she was satisfied everything was ready for their guest, she returned to the lounge, where Ian was still sitting quietly.

'Can I get you anything else? A snack, or a drink from the bar? Coffee? Tea?' she asked.

He didn't answer but, instead, smiled. 'Would you look at that?'

She followed his gaze to outside the window and her insides filled with joy. 'It's snowing.'

'It's snowing.' Ian turned to her and beamed the biggest smile she'd seen from him yet.

'Welcome to New York,' she said.

'I think I will take that offer of a drink.'

'Coming right up.'

He ordered a bourbon and she brought it to him on a small tray. She'd taken the liberty of adding a couple of biscotti on a side plate, and she left him to enjoy the fire. She watched the snowfall from her position behind her desk, and with every flake that delicately fluttered from the sky, she began to get more nervous.

She had a date. In less than three hours.

And she wasn't sure she'd ever be ready for that.

# Chapter Sixteen

*Myles*

Myles left the office in plenty of time. He may be male, but he still had things he wanted to do before he went out tonight. His shirt and tux had been pressed and he'd picked them up days ago. They were hanging in his apartment on the top floor of the Inglenook Inn, all ready for his date with Darcy. That was what this was tonight. It had become so much more than a Christmas party, a chance to network for his boss and many of his colleagues. He was going out with the woman he'd been partly responsible for getting fired, but the woman who now made him struggle to think of things to say, who held him captivated whenever she spoke. And even though he had so much more on his mind now his father had shown up in New York, Darcy was a great distraction and a welcome one.

He got a cab from the office to the Inn. The snow had started to come down an hour ago but he was getting better at yelling in the street at the yellow vehicles and actually getting them to stop. At first, his stiff upper English lip had left him too polite to call out at random – shouldn't there be an orderly queue somewhere? – but it really was the only way to do it.

He paid the cab driver, tipped him, negotiated the parked cars near the Inn and went up the familiar brownstone steps. He slotted his key in the lock and stepped into a hallway that felt as far removed from a boutique hotel as it possibly could. It felt like he was coming home. It smelled familiar – the pine tree in the lounge, the scent of a rich, hearty meat dish coming from the kitchen, the smell of the fire he knew was going already.

What he didn't expect to see was his father sitting in the chair by the window as he pushed open the door. Myles had come from the opposite direction so Ian hadn't seen him approach.

What really stood out to Myles was how content his father looked. He was far removed from the desperate man he'd talked to a couple of nights ago, since they'd let words and explanations settle between them. Now, his face was illuminated by the glow of the fire and he was holding a glass of whiskey as he looked out at the snow falling from the skies.

Ian turned round as soon as Myles appeared in the lounge. 'Join me?' he asked, raising his glass. It was strange how alcohol still bonded the men, despite his mum's problems with the bottle. In some ways Myles had expected to hate it, but he didn't. He just wished his mother saw it in the same way they did, as something to enjoy in moderation, not as a way to dull the senses and avoid whatever else was going on.

He said hello to Darcy, who was at the desk, working away. It was hard to believe that very soon she'd go from being his landlady to his date. All day he'd been thinking about what she'd look like dressed up, wearing the earrings he'd chosen for her, those ice-blue eyes showing her excitement at being in a completely new environment to what she was used to.

He nodded at Darcy's offer of a drink and settled down on the sofa beside the armchair as he and his dad talked about the snow and watched it fall, hitting the sidewalk and the cars but not settling much yet. Cars passed by swishing it out the way, pedestrians avoided it touching their skin by wrapping scarves tighter and pulling hoods up over their heads. A young child with his mother walked past and tilted his head to the sky, opened his mouth and let a flake or two fall onto his tongue. Myles had done exactly the same as a kid and had this strange urge to do it again.

After Darcy brought their drinks over Myles wondered whether his mum had been in touch, but she hadn't.

Ian settled back against the armchair, swilling the drink in the bottom of his glass. 'I called this morning but no answer.'

He didn't need to say it. Myles knew what they were both thinking. Was she out and about and had simply missed the call? Or was she too drunk to answer it?

'Why did she start up again?' Myles still couldn't believe it. His childhood hadn't been a blast, but he'd thought she was well out of that stage of her life now.

'She feels like she's lost you, and she doesn't know how to get you back.'

'I came here for work, she knows that.'

Ian shook his head. 'It's not about your physical proximity to us, it's more that even when you're nearby, you're unreachable. You've never been able to move on from how she once was. You've never been able to forgive her. I don't know…perhaps it was because you were the youngest. You were always more sensitive and you threw everything into your career.' His face softened, as though he was completely deflated. 'You never stop to take a breath and look around you.'

'Of course I do. I've seen a lot of Manhattan since I've been here.' That wasn't what his dad meant and Myles knew it.

'Your mum and I were together, but we didn't have a good marriage. We had enormous obstacles in our path, but, somehow, we made it through. However, it took my retirement and me finally seeing her as a person, putting her needs as a priority, to do it.'

'You've always drummed the importance of career into us, the importance of taking responsibility and making a mark.'

'And I still stand by that. But you can have more than just a career. You can also have a loving, supporting relationship. You can work really hard, but your family can still come out on top. It's my one regret in life, Myles, that I couldn't quite manage it.'

Myles watched the snow get heavier beyond the window. He heard the family upstairs greet Darcy as they came back. 'It wasn't your fault, Dad. You can't blame yourself for everything that happened with Mum.'

He looked at Myles. 'I'd hate for you to go through life too afraid to commit, too scared your own relationships will fail or that you can't have it all.'

The muscle in his jaw tensed, because his dad was right. He'd trusted himself when it came to school work, then university, and then in the workplace. He had confidence, ability and end goals. But when it came to relationships he'd always feared the worst. Falling in love could happen in an instant, but love was more unpredictable than the world of finance. He'd rather have the fluctuations of the stock exchange on his mind than the ups and downs between each and every member of his family.

Ian leaned forwards and spoke more quietly. 'Darcy tells me she's escorting you to a function tonight. She's a lovely young lady.'

Myles turned to look at her – not that he needed to – to remember how beautiful she was, how well-spoken, what an approachable and genuine woman he'd found.

She was deep in conversation with the chef, reviewing menu items, discussing the plan for Christmas dinner.

'She's wonderful, Dad. But I'm nervous as hell.' It was the first time they'd talked about dating, let alone seen an admission of the feelings involved.

'I was nervous when I first met your mother.'

'You were?' Myles couldn't imagine it.

'I tried to pretend I wasn't at all. I was this confident man, or at least that's what I had her believe, but I still remember how dry my mouth felt the first time I spoke to her. I recall shoving my hands in my pockets so they wouldn't shake, I remember driving past her house the day before I was due to take her out to a dance at the local village hall just so I could make sure I knew where I was going and wouldn't be late. But that's how I knew, see.'

'How you knew what?'

'How I knew she was the one. I'd taken girls out before, but I'd never been that on edge. I knew then that she was special.'

It was funny, because Myles was already thinking the very same thing about Darcy.

*

Up on the top floor it was time for Myles to get ready. He was glad he'd seen his dad when he returned to the Inn. Things were far from sorted in their family, his mum could be sprawled out drunk back in England for all they knew, but this was a start. When Myles was growing up he'd wanted someone to sit him down along with his brother and tell them what was happening, explain that none of it was their fault. But, instead, his dad had tried to shield his boys and in doing so they'd felt as though they weren't considered in the equation. Myles felt sure his dad could see that that had been a mistake, and once upon a time Myles would've berated him for it. But not now. They'd started to make some progress and he didn't want to ruin that.

When Myles had said he really needed to get ready for his work party, his dad had ordered a hot cocoa to drink by the fire and taken out the latest Stephen King book to keep him company. Myles had almost wanted to stay there with him, get to know this man some more, but he knew they had plenty of time.

Myles showered, shaved until his jaw was smooth, pulled on his dress shirt and trousers and finally turned up his collar and draped his bow tie around the material. He fiddled with it and after two or three attempts got it right and shrugged on the jacket to his tux. Now he was standing in front of the mirror, ready to go, his heart skipped away inside his chest at the thought of meeting Darcy downstairs as agreed. He'd said he'd knock on the door to her apartment. She didn't want to wait around in the hallway in case other guests asked where she was off to. He suspected it had more to do with them asking *who* she was going with than anything else.

Nervously he went down the stairs, onto the landing, and checked his reflection one more time in the mirror on the wall with white lights draped around its frame. With his winter coat over one arm, he started towards her apartment but didn't get a chance to knock because she opened the door.

'Hey.' She smiled.

'Hey yourself.' He couldn't take his eyes off her. How could someone who dressed so smartly every day look so very different? She'd curled her hair and it hung in waves that fell across her shoulders, one stroking her collar bone. Bare, smooth skin on her upper arms that usually hid beneath a smart shirt or jacket was toned and the earrings he'd given her sparkled perfectly.

'I think it's going to snow again.' Why did he say that? He could've gone with 'You look beautiful', or 'Wow, you look gorgeous'. 'You'll be cold,' he added by way of explanation. He was dynamite in a boardroom, never hesitated to voice an opinion and get things moving in the way he wanted to, but opposite Darcy it was as though he'd forgotten basic social skills.

He watched as she dropped her key into a small, sparkly silver bag and then he saw she had something else draped over her arm. 'I have this,' she said. 'It'll keep me warm. Could you?' She held out her bag for him to hold while she shrugged on a furry-looking top that enhanced the line of her dress, nipped in at the waist to flatter her figure.

'You look beautiful, Darcy.' He relaxed now he'd finally said it and the way she smiled back at him made him even happier that he'd asked her to be his date tonight.

'You look pretty good yourself.' She led the way and they went downstairs, through the hallway and towards the front door. He did his best not to stare at long, toned legs, accentuated by her glittery high heels. 'I'm impressed with the bow tie,' she called over her shoulder, half turning in amusement. 'Unless you cheated and bought one on elastic.'

'Never, it's the real thing.' He moved past her and held the front door open for her to go first. 'I'll hail a cab.' The icy wind came straight for them.

'Listen to you, sounding like a native New Yorker already.'

'Careful.' He held out his arm so she could hook her hand through. 'The steps may be slippy.'

'They should be fine, I put de-icer on them earlier,' she said, but linked her arm with his.

'I'm trying to forget you're my landlady.'

She took the stairs gingerly. 'Now you make me sound old.' She looked up and down the street. 'We should've booked a cab in advance.'

'No need, I've got this.' He left Darcy waiting at the bottom of the stoop and stepped off the sidewalk and onto the street. He knew cabs came down here all the time and they were only waiting a minute before he saw a familiar yellow vehicle behind three other cars. Here was where he got to impress his date. He liked to be in control and tonight was no different.

'Taxi!' he yelled, his hand up in the air. But the damn thing went cruising on by and when he turned Darcy was laughing.

'Let me,' she said, ushering him back onto the pavement, and she stepped onto the street keeping behind the safety of a parked car. As soon as she saw a yellow vehicle approach, she leaned out and hollered 'Taxi!' in the New York accent that had fully returned now she'd got back into the swing of being on home turf.

'How...' He followed her and they climbed in the back while she took charge and told the driver they needed to go to The Plaza.

With a raise of her eyebrows, she swept a hand from the top of her body to the bottom.

'I'm a bit too male, I assume.' He whispered so the cab driver couldn't hear, and when he caught a waft of her floral perfume he was glad he'd had to lower his voice.

As the cab made its way from the Inn and through Greenwich Village before turning onto Fifth Avenue, they talked about some of Myles's work colleagues. He wanted her to have an idea of who people were. He told her about his boss and his wife, who were both good people and harmless. He warned her about Bobby's wife Krystal, who usually got drunk within half an hour of being at the function and would be looking for someone to either lean on or bore with talk of her apartment's very expensive renovations.

'Doesn't Bobby get embarrassed?' Darcy asked.

'I think she's done it so often that it's just part of the night now. And Bobby has been with the firm for years; it doesn't seem to have affected him or his work.'

'So I can feel free to get rolling drunk and dance on tables?'

As soon as she said it he noticed her cheeks flush, even in the limited light in the taxi. She turned to look out of the window and pointed out stores to him, the Flatiron Building, as they passed by. Tonight she was just a girl, he was just a guy, and the simplicity of it made him feel young, full of hope. His emotions had been all over the place lately but he felt as though they were finally getting back on track.

The cab took them past Madison Square Park, the Empire State Building, and when they crossed 34th Street he talked about the infamous *Miracle on 34th Street* movie he'd once watched with his niece and nephew.

Just before they hit 49th Street as it crossed Fifth Avenue, the traffic slowed and then came to a halt.

'What's happening?' Darcy asked the cab driver, but he shrugged. He had no idea.

'It's only another ten minutes' walk from here,' said Myles. 'We could just get out. Will you be OK?' He eyed her sparkly heels and tried not to let his gaze follow her legs for too long.

'I'll be fine, let's do it. We don't want to be late and it hasn't started snowing yet.'

Myles paid the cab fare and they crossed to the safety of the sidewalk. The air was freezing, but at least it wasn't windy. Making a lady walk in heels was bad enough.

As they walked they chatted about Christmas parties of old. She'd been to a few where staff had been so drunk they hadn't turned up to work the next day, she didn't do hangovers much these days because of her early starts and crazy shifts, and he admitted the last time he'd had too much to drink at a work Christmas party he and a colleague had Sellotaped their legs together and insisted on doing a three-legged race.

'It all ended in tears of course,' he explained as they came to another intersection. 'Mine mostly when we fell over and I cut my head open.'

'You didn't!'

As they waited for cars to slow and the sign to change so they could walk across, he pulled back the very front of his hair, leaning in close to her. 'I had a few stitches but the scar is almost gone.'

When she touched her fingers to it, to get a better look, he drew in his breath. He hadn't expected her touch and it threatened to send him giddy.

They crossed the street, avoiding the puddle where the tarmac dipped unevenly. He sneaked a sideways glance at his date for the night. She looked impossibly elegant in the classic black dress, which had a few ruffles on the skirt he'd noticed in the taxi. It was subtle detailing that you only saw if you were really looking and close enough. She held her silver bag against her body, crossing her other arm over either for security or because she was cold, and he made sure he didn't march as fast as usual so she wouldn't have to suffer sore feet for the rest of the evening.

'I'm really excited about going to The Plaza,' she admitted, almost coyly as though she shouldn't be broadcasting the information.

'Then in that case I hope tonight is everything you're wishing for.'

Darcy's hand rested against his arm as they approached the building that stretched across the corner with an impressive entrance, gold detailing and carpeted steps. 'I've seen it a thousand times before, but it's no less impressive.'

'It surprises me that you haven't been inside to check out the hotel part,' Myles remarked. 'You're in the industry after all.'

'When I was a little girl, my mum brought me here. We stood outside and I was amazed by the grandeur of the whole place. I can't even remember much apart from the food court and the lobby, but I haven't ever had a really good look around. Crazy isn't it? It's always the things on your doorstep that you see last. I met so many Londoners in my time over in your country and I think I'd seen more of England than they had. When you go somewhere as a tourist it's totally different.'

'Yes, I suppose it is. I guess I'm like that here. From the moment I arrived I've wanted to get the lay of the land, work out where everything is, get a feel for what it's like to be a New Yorker. When I moved around England with work, I pretty much arrived, went to the office and didn't think twice about the fact I was in a new city. England was my home so I didn't think outside the square enough.' He turned to her now as they stood aside to let others past as the impressive Plaza loomed in front of them. 'It's sad in a way, don't you think?'

'I suppose it is. We dream big and big usually means getting out there into the world, when sometimes what we need is right on our doorstep.'

The moment hovered between them and Myles wondered if Darcy was including him in the words she'd just shared.

'Would you want to work anywhere like this?' Myles wanted to know more about this girl. He wanted her to himself before they went inside. He wished they were going to an intimate restaurant to talk over a candlelit dinner, way into the small hours.

'You know, I never really thought about it. Travel was on my mind for a long, long time and I always assumed it would eventually end with me taking a job with a big hotel chain. I think part of the reason I wasn't overly interested in this place was because I knew it was the pinnacle of what I wanted to achieve. I needed to make something of myself before I so much as thought of approaching somewhere like this with a view to getting a job. Does that make sense?'

'It does. I guess I never dreamed big at the start either, but pushed myself daily, did the grind and eventually landed better and better jobs. It makes total sense to me.'

'Over the years I've begun to think about it more,' Darcy went on. And if she was cold, she wasn't showing it. She looked all lit up inside. 'I've seen both sides, worked in small establishments and large and I'm beginning to see the difference. I think I have an affinity for the boutique hotels, the quieter side.' Her eyes sparkled at the revelation. 'The Inglenook Inn has really opened my mind to the possibility of having my own place one day.'

'Here in New York?'

'I'm not sure. I'm not quite ready to leave Manhattan yet, so who knows.'

She may not be shivering but he noticed she was tense. He hoped it was the cold rather than nerves at being with him. 'Shall we go in?' he suggested. 'Are you ready for this?'

'I'm ready.'

He took her hand. It was a decisive move and she held his gaze until they reached the steps just as white flakes began to tumble down once again from the sky.

Neither of them rushed to escape it. 'Have you ever tasted snow?' he asked.

'What?' She giggled. 'Are you serious?'

'Yeah.' Holding her hand they both looked up at the sky, at the white flakes hurtling towards them in a rush but landing softly when they arrived.

'I was always told not to as a kid,' she said, 'especially if it was yellow.'

His laughter echoed into the night as other people hurried past to get into the warmth of The Plaza. 'That's revolting. No, I mean like this.' He tilted his head back and opened his mouth just enough to let a few flakes land and melt on his tongue. 'Go on, try it.'

'You're mad. These people' – she gestured around them – 'will think we're mad.'

'Who cares what they think?' He'd have to turn into a businessman in a few seconds and he just wanted a moment longer to be this man, outside, with a girl whose company was everything he could ever wish for.

Darcy tilted her head back and closed her eyes. Myles watched one flake land on her eyelashes, elegantly long with mascara, then another flake land on her tongue.

'It's weird,' she laughed, reacting to the sensation.

He felt almost incapable of moving. Watching her in the simplicity of the moment, he realised just how taken he was with Darcy Spencer.

But now, squeezing her hand and leading her inside, he knew he had to turn serious and try to put out of his mind the thoughts of what tonight could be in the long-term.

All he knew was that this was a start.

# Chapter Seventeen

*Darcy*


The carpeted steps bordered with gold handrails leading up to the doors of The Plaza swarmed with people, some coming out of the iconic hotel, others going in. Doormen wore black uniforms, hats trimmed with the same gold that appeared above the entrance and on handles. Gold lamps stood tall to the side with a cluster of glowing round bulbs illuminating the front on a winter's night.

Darcy was first in to a compartment in the revolving door and, her eyes wide with wonder, she couldn't wait to see what was on the other side. In the foyer was a big round wooden table with the most exquisite floral arrangements sitting on top. Two enormous glass vases contained deep red lilies, other smaller displays held red daisies and the scent filled the area as crowds gathered for another evening in the city. An opulent chandelier hung from the ceiling and ornate panelling on the walls left you in no doubt as to the luxurious hotel you were in.

Myles took Darcy's arm as they passed by the bar on their left and then a restaurant on their right, weaving their way through to get to their venue. Guests and visitors bustled inside the building, some on their way to the food court, others dressed up and heading in the opposite direction to go out in Manhattan, wafts of expensive perfume accompanying glitzy jewellery and colourful scarves. They followed signs with Myles's company name on them and stepped into the lift that would whisk them up to the floor with the Grand

Ballroom, and all the while Darcy thought she was going to have to pinch herself. It all felt too good to be true.

Once upstairs, Myles took her jacket and handed it to the hostess, who hung it in a cloakroom facility while Darcy headed in the direction of the ladies' restroom. They hadn't stood in the snow for long but she'd felt it land on her eyelashes and the last thing she wanted was to have panda eyes all evening. Truthfully she could've stood out there much longer. She hadn't even been that cold. She'd been so warm in the taxi with the heating cranked up to an almost uncomfortable level, that out in the fresh air she'd been happy standing next to Myles, the temperature of the evening not at the forefront of her mind compared to the businessman she was getting to know on a deeper level.

Darcy checked her reflection. Her mascara was intact and her deep pink lip gloss shimmered beneath the lights. Her foundation gave a natural coverage and the earrings Myles had given her shone proudly from behind the waves of her hair. She fished in her silver clutch and applied a touch more gloss to make sure and spritzed a little of her favourite Chanel perfume, which she'd bought in a purse-size bottle especially for tonight. It was an extravagance, but she'd count it as an early Christmas treat because it wasn't every day you came to a party like this.

Deep breath in and another out, she was ready to see Myles again. Outside the Grand Ballroom he was already in conflab with men in suits. Darcy was used to meeting new people so had no qualms joining them. She met Robert and Davina, colleagues of Myles's, as well as their respective partners, she met Neil and his wife, and another man was introduced with his fiancée, neither of whom Myles had met before, and Darcy was ashamed to admit she forgot their names straight away.

'You OK?' Myles leaned closer to her and she could smell the familiar aftershave that had wafted in and out of the brownstone every day he'd been staying there.

She turned her attention back to him. 'I have met people before you know.'

He smiled, his gaze flitting from her eyes to her lips, the promise of something else in his expression. 'I'll do my best to keep you company for as long as I can.' He discreetly steered her away from the main crowd and into the ballroom, where he plucked two glasses of champagne from the tray of a passing waiter and handed one to her.

'I know you'll have to do the work talk, you told me that's how your boss operates.'

'You make it sound so covert.'

They stood at the entrance to the ballroom and Darcy looked around her at the glitz, the glamour, the very different world she was a part of tonight. A warm glow enveloped the room filled with round tables. Similar floral arrangements to those downstairs stood tall and proud in the centre of each table, with a candle to complete the look. The room was framed with archways, expensive-looking material acting as drapes in each section, a stage was set up for a band to play and low music welcomed guests inside. The men were impeccably dressed in their tuxedos, the women were glamorous, sophisticated, in flowing gowns or cocktail dresses and they all looked a natural part of the set-up. If Darcy thought about it too much she'd realise she wasn't that at all, but, then again, maybe these women had just as many self-doubts tonight as she did. It wasn't easy being somebody else's plus one. You had to talk to their colleagues, make small talk with their wives or girlfriends, behave how you believed they wanted or expected you to.

'I've been to a few parties in my time,' said Myles, 'but none has ever been quite so grand.' He placed a hand in the small of her back as they moved past a couple of tables and into a space. 'Or maybe they have, and being in a new city makes it all the more exciting.'

'No, I agree. It's this place.' Her eyes took in the room again. 'It's something else.'

'It most certainly is.' He fiddled with his collar against his neck.

'You seem uncomfortable.'

'Something's scratching me.'

She raised an eyebrow. 'Now I'm getting flashbacks of how red your neck was that day.' She couldn't help the smile. 'I swear I haven't been putting itching powder in your bed.'

'Don't mention itching powder,' he grimaced. 'Oh no, now I'm scratching.'

'Hold this.' She handed him her glass of champagne with the faint trace of lip gloss on the rim if you looked closely enough. Darcy didn't think she'd ever perfect the art of keeping lip gloss on all evening, especially not tonight when there was food and drink involved. 'Let me see what's going on.' She stood on tiptoes and could just about make out a small piece of a plastic tag still on the neck of his shirt. 'We need scissors.'

He scratched at it again. 'I don't carry those. I'm not sure it'd be acceptable.'

Darcy took her glass and then grabbed his free hand in hers. 'Come with me.' She had a quick word with a hostess who was passing by tables ensuring everything was just so, and left Myles talking to his boss while she waited for the hostess to bring her a pair of scissors. Implement in her hand, she surreptitiously nodded to Myles and he made his excuses before meeting her outside the ballroom.

Darcy led him away from the crowd into a small corridor. 'We can't have you facing your colleagues with a neck like the one you ended up with in London.' When she laughed, he did too. She was glad they both could by now.

He stood facing the wall, holding both glasses again, and when her heels didn't give her quite enough height to be able to pull down the back of the collar and snip as close to the material as she'd like, she stood on tiptoes. Her fingers made contact with his skin and she wasn't sure but she thought he may have shivered a little. She snipped the plastic tag, announced it was all done, and he turned to face her, a glass in each hand.

'Thank you.' His eyes held hers.

'You're welcome.' She couldn't look away. She moved closer. She could feel the heat from his body, smell the crisply ironed shirt and its newness, she could see the smoothly shaven jaw with just a hint at where stubble would come through if he gave it permission. His eyes only left hers once to look lower, to her lips.

'There you are, Myles.' A jolly-looking fellow came along the corridor stifling any chemistry that was more than ready to erupt. 'Let me introduce you to Harry.' Another man followed behind.

The men shook hands, Myles introduced Darcy, and they all did a quick cover of the weather, the city, this amazing building and Darcy soon gathered this must be the new client Myles's boss was so desperate to impress. As they walked back to the Grand Ballroom she wondered whether this was what it was like to be a corporate wife, always on the edge, never quite a part of it until you were invited in to the inner sanctum.

The evening's preliminaries passed quickly and Darcy did her best to live up to what she believed Myles needed, talking to other wives and girlfriends, letting him use tonight for business as much as pleasure. She caught him looking over at her more than once and it made her insides flip over every time. She was filled with champagne, she'd absorbed the, at times, overwhelming, affluent atmosphere, and before she knew it they were seated, ready for a feast she had no doubt would be just as fancy as the rest of the affair.

Darcy was sitting opposite Myles and next to his colleague Geoff, who was a pleasant man. He seemed to be on the same wavelength and desperate to talk about anything other than work. 'I've had to do that for the last hour,' he told Darcy. 'Please talk about anything else and give me a break before I have to do it all over again with a stomach full of food.'

'It's not that bad, surely?' Darcy could see Myles relaxed in conversation with one of the wives.

'I do it all day, every day, and our boss expects it tonight. I don't know, call me old-fashioned, but a Christmas party should be about letting your hair down.' He reached up and touched a distinctly receding hairline. 'I don't have much, but I still want to enjoy the end of the year when I've worked so hard.'

'I think you're right,' Darcy admitted, and they started by talking about travel, a subject Darcy was more than comfortable with.

Their talk took them through the starters and on to the main course, with other people at the table joining in intermittently, and by the time they got to dessert and it was just the two of them talking again, Geoff said, 'Now tell me, what do you do, Darcy?'

'I work in hotels.'

His eyes widened. 'This one?'

'Not quite. The place I work is a little smaller.'

'And where is it?'

She told him all about the Inglenook Inn, her responsibilities in the short-term, her dreams for the future.

'You know, Darcy, my wife and I always try to stay at the boutique-type hotels whenever we go out of town. Last month we were in Vermont and stayed at a four-bedroom hotel in Burlington.' He put a hand over his wife's; she was on his opposite side and talking to a man whose name Darcy couldn't remember. 'What was the name of the hotel in Vermont?'

She told Darcy, smiled, and after Geoff patted her hand she went back to her conversation.

'I'd be lost without her,' Geoff grinned, earning himself a nudge from his wife. Darcy wondered what it would be like to be so close to someone that they finished your sentences, filled in the blanks when they got in the way of your memories.

'Vermont is beautiful.'

'It sure is,' he said. 'And the boutique hotel was much better for us. We could have our privacy but in the shared areas we got talking with other guests. It was so much more personal.' He leaned closer. 'I wouldn't want to stay anywhere this grand. I'd feel like I was being scrutinised all the time, afraid to make a sound.'

'That makes sense to me.'

'So, where else have you worked?' He was genuinely interested and Darcy knew it also took him away from the business a lot of people were still talking about at

213

their tables. She could hear Myles talking about a new venture for the company, someone on their other side talking about high risk strategies, and she could tell by the furrow of a man's brow on the table to the side of them that he would probably spend the entire night talking work.

Darcy told Geoff about some of her other work escapades and they talked about the hotel industry, the pluses and the minuses, about tourism in general, and by the end of the dinner Darcy felt thoroughly relaxed.

'Thank you, Darcy.' Geoff shook her hand as they stood to leave the table, and he handed her a business card. 'Give my brother a call. As I explained, he works for a global company and they're always on the lookout for good accommodation when employees relocate to New York.'

'Wow, that's great.' She took the card and slipped it into her purse. 'Thank you so much.' This is what the Inn needed, good corporate business that could become a steady, reliable source of income.

'Your young lady is like a breath of fresh air,' Geoff told Myles when Myles joined them from the other side of the table.

'She's definitely that,' he said. And when Geoff and his wife went on their way, added, 'You seem to be enjoying yourself.'

'I really am.' As she looked round, her glittering earrings caught the light and reflected in the mirror, and she realised she actually was a part of this tonight. 'You'll have to excuse me though. I need to go to the restroom. The champagne has been going down very nicely.'

'Of course.' Myles smiled warmly. 'Don't be long, though. And I'll meet you back here.'

Her heart leapt at his touch and the way he was looking at her tonight, and as she stood in line waiting for the restroom she found herself wondering what they could possibly do for their second date, because tonight was going better than she'd ever dared to imagine.

At the end of the line Darcy eventually made it into the toilet stall. She rested her purse on the hook on the other side of the door, careful to ensure it balanced, but a familiar voice caught her attention. It was Holly, the editor. She'd recognise that voice anywhere.

Darcy used the toilet, hoping she'd catch Holly before she left. She'd had no idea she would be here tonight and she wanted to ask whether she'd checked in at the Inglenook Inn and, more importantly, whether she was already impressed.

Holly and her companion had voices that travelled. Darcy smiled to herself. They were surely fuelled with champagne as they talked loudly about a man here tonight with a comb-over and rancid breath. Darcy only prayed the man's wife wasn't in here – if he was lucky enough to be married, that was.

But their next topic stopped Darcy in her tracks just as she was about to unlock the door.

'I've found a gorgeous little place, The Inglenook Inn.' Holly was answering the other woman's question about where she was staying in Manhattan.

'I've heard of it!' her companion announced with glee.

Darcy grinned. This was a good sign. Word of mouth was exactly what they needed. But she wasn't prepared for what came next.

'It's run by somewhat of a Cinderella, apparently,' the woman continued, starting to laugh now.

Myles's name for her made Darcy's hand freeze on the lock and she was shaking, deep down knowing that this wasn't going to be something she wanted to hear.

'Cinderella?' Holly's unmistakable tone was inquisitive. Darcy guessed she had to be that way in her job, finding out the good and bad about the world.

'The girl who runs it,' the woman answered as though it should be obvious. She elaborated. 'A colleague of Justin's is staying there now. He's over from England.'

Darcy had no doubt they were talking about Myles now.

The woman went on. 'Apparently this girl, who Justin's colleague has dubbed Cinderella, put up a Christmas tree in his apartment, which he hadn't asked for and hated – he has some issue about Christmas. She just let herself in and tidied around like she had a magic wand and could make everything perfect again.'

'This person obviously doesn't know his fairy tales very well,' said Holly. 'It's the Fairy Godmother who waves her wand, not Cinderella.'

The other woman harrumphed. 'Well anyway, he sent a long email rant going on and on about it, how she'd wound him up, how she interfered, how she lights the fires and sweeps the grate and is always there in the background, lurking. She sounds like a bit of a bunny boiler if you ask me.'

Darcy slumped against the door. She couldn't possibly go out now because Holly would know she'd overheard everything. Tears prickled her eyes and she felt her lower lip wobble. Usually she could take criticism, but not second-hand, or third-hand, and not when it had originated from the man she had begun to have feelings for. And Darcy valued honesty above all else. Lachie had never respected that and it looked like Myles was no different.

'I didn't find the manager like that at all.' Holly's voice drifted through the closed cubicle door. 'If we're talking about the same girl I think we are, I found her to be welcoming and friendly. I can't imagine she'd interfere.'

'Well, I suppose some people just clash.'

Darcy's heart sank even further. She wanted to run far away from The Plaza and forget she'd even bothered coming here tonight.

'I'm writing a feature on the place in the New Year,' Holly confessed, their extended conversation keeping Darcy exactly where she was.

'Well this will give you another angle. The Cinderella story.' The woman's cackling bounced off the walls of the restroom. Drunk or not, the words still had the power to hurt. 'How about I forward the email to you? I'll track it down – I'm sure Justin still has it.' Darcy didn't hear what else they said. All she heard was raucous laughter from the woman as the door to the restroom opened and then closed, leaving her hovering in the stall like a mouse too scared to come out and take a bite of the cheese in case the trap shut tight and finished her off.

Heart thudding against her chest, Darcy stayed in the stall until she was sure the restrooms were completely empty. Only then did she venture out. She was shaking, her eyes filled with tears. Angrily she swiped one away as it dared to topple out and across her cheekbone. How dare he? How dare he write about her in such a horrid way? Did he realise what he'd done? Holly could ask for the actual email and use it! Readers would love a juicy angle, especially when it came from a guest's perspective, and Holly wouldn't have made her mark in the editorial world without delivering a few of those types of stories. This had the potential to tarnish Sofia's reputation and her own.

And Myles was responsible for it all.

# Chapter Eighteen

*Myles*

Myles was about to go and find Darcy. She'd taken forever in the restrooms and he hoped she hadn't eaten anything out of the ordinary or drunk so much champagne that she was sick. When he finally saw her come back into the ballroom he could tell something was wrong.

He was at her side in seconds. 'There you are. I was about to come and look for you.' The sparkle had disappeared from her eyes. She looked right through him and he had no idea why. 'What's wrong? Have you had too much to drink?'

'Oh, you'd like that wouldn't you.'

He guided her by her elbow away from anyone who could overhear their conversation but as soon as he did, Neil appeared beside them, his wife on his arm. 'Myles, it's time to show us what you English men have in the way of talent on the dance floor.'

Myles tried to laugh it off and get back to Darcy but his boss was having none of it so he took Darcy's hand. 'It looks like we don't have a choice.' He led them over to the small dance floor that had opened up, tables having been shifted to the sides of the room.

The orchestra struck up a slow rendition of 'O Holy Night', following on from a faster number, and Myles took Darcy in his arms. But rather than looking into her eyes, feeling her close to him, bodies pressing up together, she was rigid as though he was making her do something unpleasant.

'What's going on, Darcy?' He moved her around the dance floor.

She pushed her hands against his chest in an effort to get away but he grabbed one hand, his other arm around her waist, and turned her again as they changed direction. 'Darcy, talk to me.'

'Darcy?' She pulled back enough with her upper body that she was looking right at him rather than her head resting against his chest to one side. 'I would've thought by now you'd know my name.'

He exhaled. It was already turning into a long night, with endless business talk that he really couldn't face much more of. He kept her dancing to the sounds of the piano and violin, smiled as they glided past the potential new client dancing with his wife.

When they'd passed them by, he whispered into Darcy's ear. 'Please enlighten me, because I've got no idea what you're talking about.' Even with a face full of anger, she was still beautiful. She had small frown lines at the top of her nose when she pulled the face she was making now, but it made her real, it made her honest. She was easily the best girl here, both inside and out, and he'd watched her from a distance as she warmed to his colleagues, chatted with people as though she'd known them years rather than minutes. He was in awe of her calm demeanour, the social graces she could carry off with skill and finesse.

'Cinderella. That's my name, isn't it?' She stopped now and as they were in the way of everyone else, he steered her off the dance floor over to a table, but she refused to sit down. 'I'm Cinderella. I want everything to sparkle. I fuss around, sweeping and adding unnecessary touches when guests would rather be left alone.'

'Darcy—'

'Don't Darcy me. In fact, don't bother talking to me.'

He remembered his long email rant he'd sent in a fit of rage right after he'd shut the door in her face that day. His colleague had picked the wrong time to tag onto the end of a business email a casual 'hope it's all good over at the Inn' and he'd unleashed his anger. He'd never once thought it would be shared or used against him. Especially not tonight, and certainly not by Darcy.

'How did you know?' he asked, his voice low.

'Does it matter?' Her voice didn't follow suit.

He took her hand and led her out of the ballroom. She resisted but a tight grip ensured the conversation didn't continue until they were alone, back in the corridor where she'd helped him remove the tag from his shirt, where her fingers had touched the skin on his neck and sent shivers cascading through his body.

When a member of staff passed them by Darcy described her jacket and the girl shuffled off to find it for her.

'You're leaving?' he asked.

She didn't answer.

'I sent the email when I was angry,' he tried to explain, ducking his head, moving it side to side in an attempt to grab her gaze, but she wouldn't look at him.

'You still sent it.' She looked hard at the wall.

He put his hand on the side of her face and tried to turn her to look at him and when she finally relented he saw the tears building in her eyes, more vulnerable than he'd ever seen her before.

'You have no idea what you've done, do you?' She tried to move past him but he stopped her. He had her against the wall and she almost relented, her body softening as the heat of his chest kept her there. But she soon remembered how she'd intended this to go and

221

pushed him away. 'I heard a woman telling Holly, the magazine editor staying at the Inn right now, the woman who will put together a feature on the Inn, on me.'

His hand grazed his jaw. 'I had no idea that would ever happen. I reacted in the heat of the moment.'

'The things you said!'

'Now wait a minute, I said the same things to you if I remember, when you put that tree in my apartment.'

'I was trying to help!'

When the girl returned with Darcy's jacket she shrugged it on and they didn't say another word until she'd left them alone again.

'I didn't want that help, I didn't ask for it, Darcy. All I can do now is apologise for sending the email. I'll talk to Holly, I'll let her know it was me, it was in my head, it wasn't you or the way you are with guests. To be honest, I don't really want my comments included in a bloody magazine article either. It'd be embarrassing.' His attempt at injecting a little bit of self-pity fell flat.

'She wouldn't be naming you, don't worry. She wouldn't need to. The damage would be done. The magazine has a circulation of thousands!'

She tried to walk away and he put an arm either side of her, against the wall, his face inches from hers. 'The editor won't use it, especially if I tell her the whole story.' He felt her breath – a breath of relief? – as he moved closer, convinced he had calmed her down enough. 'Come back and dance with me. This is a date, and I don't know about you but I'd really like it to continue.'

'You're an arrogant—'

He put his fingers across her lips. 'Don't say anything you'll regret.'

When he took his hand away she was momentarily flummoxed, but it didn't last long. 'This was a mistake, Myles. Mixing business with pleasure is always a bad idea. I never should've agreed to come.'

She ducked under his arm, left the corridor and by the time he rounded the corner she'd already disappeared into the elevator and the doors shut. The last glimpse he got was Darcy looking at the floor beneath her.

He ran to the elevators and pressed the button to call the other one, hoping to catch her downstairs. But as he waited impatiently, Neil caught him and asked where his lovely lady had disappeared off to.

'She's not feeling well, and apologises, but says to thank you for a wonderful night.'

Neil and his wife sympathised but if they suspected he was lying they didn't let on, and he had no choice but to conform and go to talk with the potential client, who, it seemed, was completely sold on the company.

Tonight he'd hoped to have the same effect on Darcy, but clearly it wasn't meant to be.

# Chapter Nineteen

*Darcy*

Darcy fled from the elevator, through the corridors, past the stunning floral arrangements in the foyer, out through the revolving door of The Plaza and into the December chill, which she felt fully now Myles wasn't by her side. She didn't want to talk to anyone. She kept walking, past a street vendor, past other people laughing and jovial as they enjoyed their night out. She gave a dollar to a homeless man on a step in a store doorway, she kept her head down as she walked on, and only slowed when she'd gone five blocks and the cold had sobered her up and calmed her down.

She stepped off the sidewalk and flagged down a taxi. The snow had stopped, the magical atmosphere was gone, and she climbed into the warmth, gave her destination and sat back to watch the city lights pass by in a blur. She'd been right not to want to get involved, right to stay away from a relationship that only introduced complications, right to make her career her entire focus.

The taxi wound its way through Manhattan and over to Greenwich Village, where the streets quietened at least a little. She paid the driver, stepped out and trudged up the steps to the entrance of the brownstone, her workplace, her home for now, the place she'd thought could be the next step to building her reputation in the industry.

Was she overreacting to what had happened?

She unlocked the front door and stepped inside to familiarity. The fire in the grate was almost out and she checked the damper was closed before ensuring the computer was off too. She looked at the clock. It was almost eleven. She texted Rupert a thank-you message for taking over this evening. She wouldn't need him to do it again. From now on, she'd be here, focused, the solid, reliable Darcy who was happy to look after everyone else's needs. It was easier than looking after her own.

'Am I interrupting?' It was Ian. He'd come downstairs so quietly he took Darcy by surprise. 'I'm sorry, I didn't mean to scare you. I was wondering if I could grab a nightcap. I know it's late.'

Darcy was back in business mode. Despite the dress and heels, at least she still had the bolero jacket on so it made her feel more professional.

'You look beautiful,' he told her and it almost finished her off because it reminded her of what tonight had started out as. It just hadn't finished that way.

'Thank you, it's very kind of you to say so.'

He looked around him. 'Where's Myles? You didn't leave him there did you?' He laughed but soon realised he'd pretty much hit the nail right on the head.

Darcy confirmed it was a bourbon he wanted, went around to the other side of the bar area and made up the drink. When she caught sight of her reflection in the splashback behind the bottles, she longed to take the earrings out, the reminder of the man she'd hoped would be the start of something different. She should've known he was too good to be true. All polished and shiny like a piece of jewellery, he wasn't quite the same underneath.

'Myles is talking business,' she replied simply. 'I've left him to it.'

Her cell phone buzzed and after she'd handed Ian his drink she checked her messages. Sure enough, as she suspected, it was Isabella, desperate to know how the date had gone tonight.

Darcy texted back: 'There won't be a second date, put it that way.'

Isabella wanted to know everything but Darcy replied that she was busy working with guests right now so she'd talk to her tomorrow. Isabella knew the deal. She knew her friend's job wasn't one she clocked on to at nine and off again at five. Darcy had a suspicion that even if Ian wasn't here right now, she would've said she was busy anyway.

'What did he do?' Ian asked when Darcy took out a broom to sweep the floor, an endless task at the Inn.

'He didn't do anything.' She refused to be drawn in to the conversation. In a few short days it would be Christmas Eve, her favourite day of the season. Or at least it usually was, but her enthusiasm this time round waned. She blamed Myles for that too.

'What did he do?' His voice softer, Ian repeated the question.

Shaking her head, she relented and told him all about the email, the Cinderella reference, Myles's anger at the Christmas tree. And it felt better than expected to offload it all on someone else.

'I must admit I was surprised to see it in his apartment,' said Ian. And he hesitated before he added, 'Christmas is a hard time for Myles.'

'It's no excuse.'

'It's not.' He shook his head, smiling. 'I told my niece only the other day, for goodness' sake, don't write personal things down. Don't text someone saying so-and-so is annoying you, don't email it or post it on social media. It'll only come back to bite you in the ass!'

His summation made Darcy laugh. 'Well yes, quite right. This one has bitten Myles very hard on the ass!'

'You know, Myles doesn't take dating women lightly.'

Darcy looked at him, trying to judge whether the comment was made flippantly or whether he was attempting to give her an insight into his son's character.

'He wouldn't date simply because he didn't have anyone else to take to this party. He would've asked you because he wanted to get to know you better. Myles rarely gets involved with anyone, so it would surprise me if he was anything less than one hundred per cent genuine where you're concerned.'

His words were just what a girl wanted to hear. But she'd seen too much collateral damage from relationships and she'd been hurt before by someone's dishonesty and disrespect. She had no intention of letting it happen again.

'I think we're just too different,' she concluded, leaving Ian and moving over to wipe down the bar counter, refill the pot of straws, clean down the board that had been used to slice a lemon earlier.

Her cell phone pinged again and when she saw Myles's name at the top she tapped on the message. It said he was on his way back to the Inn.

'That him?' Ian didn't miss much.

'Can I get you another?' She noted his empty glass.

'I'll make myself scarce. I think you two need to talk.'

Darcy took his glass, ready to deposit in the kitchen. 'I think we're done talking. I shouldn't have got involved with a guest in the first place. It wasn't professional, it was a mistake. Goodnight, Mr Cunningham.'

And with that she took the glass out to the kitchen and went up to her own apartment. She'd wait until all was quiet once again and she'd check the front door as she always did, ensure the Inn was ready to leave at peace for the night. But other than that, she just wanted to go to bed and forget that tonight had ever happened.

# Chapter Twenty

*Myles*

It was a long time since he'd confided in his dad. He'd gone to him in the past when he had a business problem to be resolved – they were good at tackling those – but they were strangers to any issue that could be classed as personal.

'I messed up,' Myles admitted as he made them both a cup of coffee upstairs in his apartment. He doubted he'd be able to sleep tonight anyway, with everything swirling around in his mind. From a work point of view tonight had been a total success. The client Neil had in his sights had been suitably wowed, which was more than could be said for Darcy. Myles knew it would be a battle to get back on her good side again and he wasn't sure he ever could. He got the impression she rated trust and honesty over everything else, and he wasn't sure how he could come back from this.

They sat in the lounge area on the Chesterfield sofas, from where they couldn't ignore the Christmas tree.

'It's a great tree,' said Ian.

Myles nodded. 'I'm afraid I wasn't too grateful when Darcy surprised me with it.'

'So I hear.'

'She told you?'

'I think she needed someone to talk to, although she shut down pretty quickly. She looked upset.'

'I think I've upset her one too many times.'

'The way I see it, is that she wouldn't be upset at all if she didn't care.'

Myles looked into the depths of his coffee, black, strong, just how he liked it. 'I met her once before you know. When I was still living in England. Remember that time I came over and told you about the itching powder in my bed?'

'That was her?'

'No, she didn't do it, but she lost her job as a result of my complaint.' He elaborated on exactly what had happened. 'So you see, I don't think she'll trust me now I've wronged her twice.' He leaned back against the sofa, trying to summon the same enthusiasm as the twinkly lights on the tree. 'This is why I don't usually do relationships.'

'She doesn't seem your type, I have to say.' Ian chose his words carefully, uneasy too at this kind of conversation.

'And what is my type?'

'Corporate, hard, expensive taste.' When his dad met his gaze, they both burst out laughing.

'High maintenance I think is the phrase I'd use, given my track record.'

'What was the name of that young lady you brought home a few years ago, the vegetarian?'

'Veronica?'

'That was it. Now she was definitely high maintenance.'

Myles sighed in good humour. 'She was. I still can't believe I asked her to meet the family – I'm not sure why. I think it was to prove to the rest of you that I was normal, that I could go on dates. It was round about the time Winston kept trying to set me up with friends of Victoria's and I wanted it to stop.'

Ian cleared his throat. 'Your mum and I didn't set a very good example, did we?' The question was rhetorical. 'I pushed and pushed for you boys to do well in school, to go on to get top jobs, be independent, but with your mum having her own problems, there was nobody there to balance it out.'

'I loved my work, Dad. I still do. I can't imagine ever being without it and I think I get that from you. It's not something I resent.'

Ian put down his coffee cup and sat forwards, arms resting on his knees. 'I met your mum and at the start everything was great, but I know I took her for granted. I was too busy concentrating on my work, and although I was doing it for my family, it was only in the last few years that I've looked back and can see that there's little point doing it for your family if it's only money you generate. Relationships need more. They need commitment, dedication, hard work, and your mum was by my side without question but she deserved more. It's why I'm here in New York, now.'

'What do you mean?'

'I can never give her back those years when I was absent so much, both physically and emotionally because my mind couldn't let anything else in other than the job. But what I can do now is help to bring her sons back to her. Winston is just about there, but with you taking off to another country, she feels like she's losing another part of you and won't ever get it back.'

Over the years Myles had become more and more distant with his family. Occasionally he tried to be a bigger part of it, like when he introduced Veronica to everyone, but his heart had never been in it. Closing that gap between them had always seemed insurmountable. And when Darcy had put the Christmas tree in his apartment it was like an oversized reminder that

231

something between him and his mum broke a long time ago, and perhaps it would never be completely fixed.

'Those Christmases will be etched on my mind forever too,' said Ian, and Myles knew which memories he was referring to. 'But I've put them behind me. It's the only way I stop myself going crazy with the unfairness of it all. I really think it's time you tried to do the same.'

In his head Myles could hear the carols that had played in the background all those years ago; he could hear Winston's excited voice as they took charge of their first turkey dinner; he could see his dad's face when he sent them to bed without touching the Christmas tree they'd waited so long to decorate; he could taste the chocolate ice-cream he'd savoured moments before the happiness had been replaced by this great big weight that settled over their lives for years to come. How could he simply move on? Was he to blame for their family problems too? Had his grudge driven a wedge between them that steamrolled his mum's emotions and drove her to the depths of despair all over again?

He couldn't think. He filled a glass of water and drank it down in one. He made another coffee and when it had been stirred, he set the spoon down on a napkin beside the mug.

'Darcy is special to you, isn't she?' Ian didn't let his son wallow in silence for too long.

Although things were a mess between them, hearing her name settled Myles in some way. 'She's different, like you say.'

'What's different about her?'

'She's kind. I mean really kind, from the bottom of her heart. She does things because she's thinking of other people. I've seen her with guests and this is more than a job to her, it's the way she is. She doesn't expect anything in return and she has this positive energy that can be frustrating.' He exhaled, his shoulders relaxing a couple of inches for the first time since he'd seen her walk into that elevator. 'But she's addictive to be around. She's beautiful too. When she smiles it's like a sign that everything will work out. It blocks out all else, stops me thinking about the negative and, instead, focus on the positive.'

Ian was smiling and Myles realised he'd completely laid his heart out in the open.

'I need to call it a night.' He patted the top of Myles's hand. 'Don't give up on her just yet,' he added. 'I have a feeling you'll both sort this out.'

Myles hoped he was right, but doubted it.

'There's another woman you need to talk to, son.'

Myles put both coffee mugs in the sink and said nothing.

'Call your mum.'

'I always do.' He faced his dad now. 'I've never lost touch with her.'

'You know what I mean. Have a proper conversation, really talk to her. It'll mean the world to her. Christmas is surely the best time to start over.'

'I thought that was what New Year's was about,' Myles grinned.

'I suppose it is, but why waste time?'

'I'll call her, Dad. But I can't make any promises.' If he detected she was drinking, he'd have to put the phone down straight away. No way did he want to have anything else to remind him of the way she'd once been. It might be happening, but over the years he'd got quite good at blocking it out. It was the way he carried on, the only way he knew how.

Ian put a hand on Myles's shoulder. 'Darcy will come round too. Remember, a relationship in your life will be one of the most important things you do. It's what makes everything else make sense.'

When his dad left him to it, Myles stood beside the Christmas tree looking into the dense foliage interrupted by ornaments. There was an owl clutching a book, a squirrel covered in white glitter as though a frost had settled on his fur, silver bells tied on branches with matching string, a jolly Santa Claus carrying a sack of presents. As kids, Myles and Winston had been allowed to choose a new decoration every year. Late November they'd trawl the shops and find that special something to hang on the tree. Myles could still remember the snowman on skis he'd bought that first terrible Christmas. He didn't remember seeing it after that. Perhaps it had been rehung every year, precariously dangling. Or maybe it had long since been thrown away, discarded along with his good memories.

Winston had once joked that Myles's inability to let go of the past could only be remedied by the love of a good woman. He'd been hopelessly in love at the time, had just proposed to Victoria, and his mind was filled with mushy thoughts that Myles simply laughed at. But perhaps he'd been right. Apart from his initial anger at seeing the tree Darcy had put up in his apartment, Myles had managed to tolerate its presence every day since. Perhaps it was all because of her. Perhaps she was the reason he could put up with the smell, the twinkling lights, the welcoming and homely feeling it generated every time he returned from the office.

This girl was special and if he had one wish this Christmas it would be that he could convince her to give him another chance.

# Chapter Twenty-One

*Darcy*

*Two days until Christmas*

Darcy refused to let what happened with Myles make her enjoy the season any less. The Inglenook Inn was at full capacity, the fire was crackling in the grate giving the lounge an ethereal glow, Christmas music played low on the speaker in the corner, and she'd just finished a FaceTime session with Sofia, Gabriella and Kyle. They were all geared up for Christmas in Switzerland and, although they missed New York at this time of the year, the backdrop they had shown Darcy was spectacular.

During her FaceTime call Myles had poked his head around the doorway on his way out to work. He'd hovered and she could tell he wanted to talk to her, but thankful for a reason not to, she kept chatting away. If it had been any other guest she would've paused the call, but not for him, not now. She'd seen him yesterday too, on his way out the door, but she'd been talking with the boys from upstairs at the time, listening to their stories about Central Park and how they wanted it to snow some more so they could build the biggest snowman anyone had ever seen.

The O'Sullivan family were next downstairs and settled in the dining room to a sumptuous breakfast of pancakes with maple syrup, hot buttered toast cut into doorstep-size pieces just like the kids wanted, and freshly squeezed orange juice. When the boys' attention was on Rupert, who had allowed them to watch through the old-fashioned hatch as he flipped more pancakes

235

high in the air with a practised ease, Darcy asked Adele when she wanted to start wrapping the presents.

'We're off out today,' Adele explained, 'going over to Brooklyn to meet up with friends, so how about tomorrow?'

'Sounds good to me,' Darcy whispered conspiratorially. 'I have wrapping paper, Sellotape, tags and ribbons.' She'd offered the additional service to guests and Adele had been delighted to take her up on the offer.

'This is such a lovely added extra,' Adele enthused, 'and between you and me, I hate wrapping!'

Darcy giggled. 'Good job I don't mind it then. We'll get it done in no time.'

Darcy cleared some of the breakfast dishes and cutlery, stacked the dishwasher, ordered some new towels for the Inn before she totally forgot – she'd noticed some were getting threadbare and while they had enough, they couldn't use a lot of them for guests and the last thing she wanted to do was run out. She paid another bill, scheduled a January inspection by the fire department, and then called Geoff's brother on the number from the business card she'd kept in the top desk drawer since the night at The Plaza. She crossed her legs, fingers and anything else she could think of but she needn't have worried because he'd been expecting her call. He scheduled a visit to the Inn for mid-January with a view to lining up corporate bookings soon after.

The snow had stopped for now, which was better for her guests even though Darcy knew the boys upstairs wouldn't be too happy about it. But at least it meant they would be able to get downtown and head to Brooklyn more easily. It made it easier for anyone who had last-minute gifts to buy, those who were still working until they stopped to enjoy their own Christmas.

Tomorrow, the snow could come. It could tumble down and blanket the Inn, because it was Christmas Eve, and it was going to be a wonderful Christmas. She could feel it.

Darcy checked through the refrigerator in the kitchen and the huge pantry, anxious to make sure everything was in place for the big day.

'You've done that a million times, Darce,' Rupert scolded, using the name he sometimes gave her, particularly when he was in a jovial mood.

'I know I have. I just want everything to be perfect.'

'It will be, don't worry.' He'd finished with the lunches so shrugged on his puffy jacket and picked up his bag, prepared to head out into the cold. 'I'll be back by four o'clock in time for dinner.'

'The O'Sullivans are out, I haven't heard from a couple of the guests, but Holly has requested dining in. I emailed you her selections.'

'That you did.' He smiled. 'Now stop fretting, we've got this. The Inglenook Inn is going to be the accommodation of choice. It'll be shouted from the rooftops with a review and a feature next year.'

'You didn't mention it to Sofia yet, did you?'

'No, but I think *you* should. She'll only see it as a positive step.'

'I'm not sure.' Sofia wouldn't be very understanding if Holly's article was published with comments about the manager interfering in guests' personal business. Darcy had a sudden panic that the woman in the restrooms at The Plaza would've told other people, and then each of those probably passed it on to more acquaintances. The

237

rumours could've multiplied and become totally out of control.

'Darcy, Sofia needs to step out of her comfort zone,' Rupert assured her.

Maybe he was right. And when he left her to it she wondered whether that was exactly what she needed to do in her personal life. Then again, she'd already tried. And look how well that had gone.

*

Darcy was busy sorting through wrapping and Sellotape and all the additional bits and pieces she'd need to help Adele, when Isabella popped in on her way to meet Jake to do some last-minute shopping. Thankfully she only had ten minutes to spare in which to quiz her friend about the night at The Plaza.

'So come on, out with it.' Isabella didn't hesitate in getting to the point. Her hat was still on, her scarf in place and coat done up. She'd only removed her gloves to allow herself some inside warming-up time before she ventured out into the depths of Manhattan again.

'Out with what?' Darcy stacked the rolls of paper below her desk, where she knew the kids never went. They'd been told by both parents they were never to venture round the other side and right now they were on their guard against Santa's elves catching them doing anything untoward. 'I told you, Isabella. It was a first date and it'll be our last. Men are complicated, and I've got too much going on right now to think of anything else.'

'You always put work first.'

'Well that's just about all we had in common, to be honest.' Darcy stacked scissors and Sellotape behind the rolls of wrapping paper. Ian Cunningham had already taken her up on her offer and asked her to wrap one gift, safely stowed inside a white, square cardboard box. She'd returned it to his room this morning, wrapped in red paper and tied off with a green satin bow. She assumed it must be for his wife and he needed it ready for when he left the Inn this afternoon to catch his flight back to England.

'Oh I do wish you'd give him a chance,' Isabella urged.

'It was his fault I ended up losing my job once upon a time, remember.' In simple terms, if Myles hadn't made a complaint, Darcy would never have been dismissed from her position.

'I thought you'd moved past that.'

'He also bad-mouthed me via email for putting up the tree and interfering in his life.' She watched her friend's face drop. 'And that email is more than likely winding its way to the editor staying in the room right above our heads, and therefore my feature write-up she promised could possibly end up being the worst decision I've ever made.'

'Oh.'

'Exactly.'

Darcy had been remiss in lighting the fire today because with one thing after another she hadn't even cleared out the grate. She got the brush and a pan and knelt down in front of the fireplace to do the job.

'Why would he ask you out if he'd been bad-mouthing you? I mean, if he just wanted to get you into bed, he wouldn't be likely to make you go along to a work function, surely.'

'Who knows, Isabella. I'm tired of trying to work some people out.'

'Did he apologise?'

'Of course.'

239

'And was the email sent a while back?'

'Yes, but it doesn't matter. He still said those things about me.'

When Isabella's phone pinged impatiently and she pulled a face, Darcy knew the interrogation had come to its conclusion.

'I've got to go, Darcy.' Isabella gave her friend a hug.

'Thanks, I needed that.'

'I thought so. You act like you're not bothered by the date that didn't turn into anything more, but I've known you a long time. I know you are hurting.'

'OK, agony aunt.'

Isabella stopped her from bending down to pick up the brush and pan again. 'I've seen the way he looks at you, Darcy. It's more than lust on his part.'

At least she made Darcy laugh. 'You can't tell that much from a look.'

'I can,' she shrugged, and then embraced her friend again. 'I'll see you a couple of days after Christmas, for lunch. I'll book somewhere – Italian?'

'Sounds perfect to me. I should be hungry by then.'

'I'll bet the feast you're planning for here is huge.'

'It certainly is.' She'd never made a Christmas lunch before, let alone been the hostess for multiple guests, and although she was nervous, she knew with Rupert at the helm she had no need to be. She'd be able to write it up on the website, advertise the event for future Christmases to come, add photos of happy guests, a sumptuous dinner with all the trimmings.

Isabella pulled on her gloves. 'Have a wonderful Christmas, my beautiful friend. I'm sorry we won't make the Christmas Eve Party.'

'You'll be far too busy with Jake to miss me,' Darcy smiled. 'Merry Christmas, Isabella.'

She drew in her breath and puffed it out again. 'Now wish me luck, I'm heading to Macy's. Jake, as usual, has left his shopping until the last minute.'

Laughing, Darcy said, 'I will wish you lots of luck, you'll need it.'

After she'd waved Isabella off, Darcy turned to carry on clearing out the grate. She swept out the ashes, she took them to the trash, she arranged logs and kindling in the familiar way she knew would allow the fire to evenly disperse. She pushed small pieces of firelighter in between logs at equal intervals to help it along and then got it going. Crouched down, she watched the flames take hold. Sometimes, late at night, when she'd closed the damper and all the guests had gone to bed, she'd sit here and daydream about running her own inn one day, as the last flickers of orange made everything glow.

She heard the door to the brownstone shut and Ian Cunningham walked in. With thinning hair, his scalp was as red as his face. 'You didn't wear a hat?' she queried.

'I'd already packed it.' He shook his head. 'I thought, not a problem, it's not even snowing.'

'Ah, New York can catch you out that way. It's a bit different from England.'

'Of course, I keep forgetting you were over there for a while and that you met Myles before.'

Darcy turned back to tend to the fire that was already capable of looking after itself.

'Darcy, give him a chance.'

'Mr Cunningham, I—'

'His issues with Christmas are something that have gone on for far too long, but he's making headway. We all seem to be.'

Darcy was surprised by this man's determination to help his son, but maybe he felt he owed it to Myles. His voice explained, yet his eyes pleaded and her insides knotted at the thought she was adding to his angst. But she had to stay focused. She didn't want to mess around. She wanted to keep building her career and with Myles causing trouble twice, she didn't have the time or the energy for anything else.

'I've made a lot of mistakes,' Ian continued, 'and he did well considering. He's not a bad person.'

Darcy had often been the sounding board for guests, but she'd never been embroiled in the complications before. She couldn't even tell him to stay out of it, because he was a paying guest and to do so would be impolite.

She said it the best way she knew how. 'I shouldn't have become involved with a guest. It wasn't professional of me.'

When the brownstone door creaked open again Darcy hoped it wasn't Myles, home early from work. She didn't think she could face both Cunningham men at once.

But it wasn't. It was a woman Darcy didn't recognise. Timid, with hair highlighted grey and blonde and drawn back in a bun, she immediately unbuttoned her coat as she met the heat of the room.

'Good afternoon.' Darcy stepped forward but the woman only met her gaze momentarily before she locked her focus onto Ian.

'My god! Martha.' Ian, flummoxed, didn't take long to step forwards and take this woman in his arms.

Darcy deduced it wasn't a potential guest stepping in off the street, but Myles's mum. She moved away and occupied herself with tidying the desk, shuffling papers, checking email. But when Ian and Martha didn't move from in front of the fire she had no hope of avoiding overhearing them.

'I'm flying home this afternoon,' said Ian, eyes still wide with surprise.

'Cancel the flight. Winston is having Christmas with Victoria and the kids. You, Myles and I are having Christmas together. I don't care where: at a hotel, at a local deli if we can find one open, a takeaway in Central Park if we have to. But I couldn't stand being there and Myles not coming home. I can't go back to how it was, not ever. Something needs to change.'

The desperation in her voice stunned Darcy. She watched Ian reach out and touch his wife's face. Darcy wanted to leave, give them privacy, but doing so would draw attention to herself as she passed them.

'Where are you staying?' Ian asked.

'I hadn't thought past getting here and seeing you both.'

'Don't worry, we'll sort something out.'

'What time will Myles be back?'

'I've no idea. We said our farewells this morning. Probably late, knowing Myles.'

Darcy could feel him looking at her and willed him not to refer to her date, perhaps suggesting she might have heard from Myles and know when he would return. She wanted to stay professional from now on. There was no room for tangled emotions to get in the way.

'Darcy…' Ian came over to the desk. 'Is there any way I could extend my stay here?'

Darcy hated giving guests bad news. 'I'm so sorry, Ian. I can give you an extra night tonight, but tomorrow I have new guests checking in for the Christmas period.'

'Not to worry. We'll figure something out.'

'I'll help you. How long do you need to stay?' It was going to be next to impossible to find something in the city at such short notice, but she could ring round for them. She'd already run her hand along a set of notebooks, pulling out the maroon one she knew contained details of other well-respected establishments they could recommend when they had no room. In turn, those same establishments often recommended the Inn when they were in the same position, so it worked both ways.

Martha spoke up so Darcy would know how long they needed. 'I have a return flight booked for December 29th.' She looked at her husband. 'We'll need to book you another seeing as you're missing your flight today.'

'We'll think about that later. But thank you, Darcy, for the extra night tonight, and it would be very helpful if you could make some calls to see if there's somewhere that'll have room at such short notice for the extra five nights.'

Ian suggested to Martha that they go up to his apartment. She looked shattered, they both did. There were so many emotions stirring beneath the surface that all Darcy wanted to do was find them a place to stay and take a weight off their mind.

She started with some of the smaller boutique hotels but no luck. She called hotels midtown, downtown, uptown, but still nothing. She called cheap hotels, mid-range accommodations, even the more expensive – but she might have known Manhattan itself was at full capacity, not just the Inn.

'How's it going?' Ian asked when he reappeared an hour later. 'I've left Martha upstairs taking a long shower. She's worn out.'

'I'll bet she is.'

'Any luck?'

Darcy shook her head. 'We might have to look outside of the city.'

'That could work, as long as it isn't too far. Martha is insistent we have Christmas together with Myles. I'm not sure how he's going to feel about it, but it's what she wants and, I think, what we all need.'

Darcy tried not to get lost in the emotions of it all. She couldn't empathise with Myles because it would make her weak, make her susceptible to being persuaded to give him another chance.

'I do have one idea, but I'm not sure how you'll feel about it,' she said. The fire crackled and spat out onto the rug so she went over to make sure the spark hadn't done any damage, and pulled the glass front down. Sometimes she liked to leave it completely open but it was roaring away from the extra log she'd put on as she waited to connect through to one of the major hotels in Manhattan.

'And what's that?'

'Myles has a sofa bed in the apartment on the top floor. It's an enormous space up there and I have all the extra bedding. And you have the Christmas tree,' she added with a flourish before remembering how that had instigated so much trouble when it was meant to bring joy. 'I'll charge you a minimal sum for the remaining nights, it'll be cheaper than any hotel, and it'll give you and your family some time together.'

When Ian roared with laughter Darcy asked, 'What's so funny?'

'I'm just picturing Myles's face in the mornings, when he comes out to see his parents on his sofa bed. Don't get me wrong. We do need family time, but I think we're under a lot of strain already, so I don't want to make it worse.'

'But if you stay somewhere else, especially out of the city, you won't have anywhere near enough time together.' She hesitated. 'I hope I'm not speaking out of turn…'

'Go on, dear.' He touched a hand to her arm. 'I'm happy to hear your opinion. Lord knows I've spent enough years too internally focused rather than thinking about life from everyone else's point of view.'

'Well, from what you've said, and what Myles has told me, the problems you've been having aren't going to be solved in one conversation.'

'Ain't that the truth?'

She grinned at the colloquial English 'ain't'. It was a long time since she'd heard one of those. 'Why don't you talk with Myles – give him a call and ask him?'

Ian shook his head. 'I don't want to tell him Martha is here yet.'

'Why not?'

'Because I'm afraid he'll stay out even later, avoid the whole situation. At least if he comes back to the Inn, which I know he will because he'll want to see you,' he winked, 'Martha will see him tonight and we can begin the process of talking properly with one another, putting the past to rest and moving on. At least that's what I'm hoping.'

'I think you're underestimating your son,' she said, buoyed by the comment about him wanting to see her, even though she knew she shouldn't be. 'Maybe he'll surprise you and want to sort things out as much as you do.' Here she went again, interfering. But Ian didn't seem to mind one bit. In fact, he seemed to appreciate having a neutral party to confide in.

Ian sat down on the sofa opposite the fire and stared into the flames. 'Let's hope you're right.'

With the rest of the Inn quiet for now, Darcy sat next to him. 'You look worried.'

'I just don't want this to blow up in our faces.'

'You'll be in trouble if it does.' She smiled and met his gaze. 'I don't want any fighting around the dinner table at Christmas.'

'God, I hadn't even thought about that. Myles is here for lunch isn't he?' He clasped his fingers together in front of him on his lap.

'Not a problem at all. Christmas lunch I can do.'

Martha appeared and came over to join them. 'Christmas lunch sounds good.'

Darcy stood up to leave them alone.

'Please, sit.' Martha gestured to the armchair beside them in such a maternal way that Darcy felt she had no choice. She reminded her of her own mum, wanting to make sure every visitor was looked after and didn't want for anything. 'How's the search going?'

She'd clearly been unable to relax upstairs, this playing on her mind. Darcy reiterated everything she'd told Ian, the suggestion she'd made.

Martha was thinking the same way as her husband. 'I think the relationship between Myles and me is far too delicate to survive an intrusion. I should've thought of this,' she berated herself.

'You were thinking with your heart not your head,' said Ian. 'It's a good thing.'

Darcy had to do something. 'Let me book you in somewhere. The subway and trains will run, even if it's a reduced service. The main thing is that you'll have somewhere to stay and there'll be no pressure on Myles.'

'We appreciate it. Anywhere will do.' But Martha wasn't looking at her, she was solely focused on Ian.

Darcy left them beside the fire, fixed them both a cup of coffee and then settled at her desk to start making the calls.

Less than an hour later the door to the brownstone swung open and in came Myles. By the look of his coat and the white dusting on each shoulder, the snow was starting to fall outside again.

'Hey,' he said, gingerly stepping into the lounge as Darcy finished on another call.

'Hey.' Darcy willed him to take another step so his view was no longer obscured. Right now it was all he needed to do to see his parents tucked next to each other on the sofa opposite the fire. Both of them had heard his voice and looked too frightened to move.

'I've been wanting to talk to you ever since the other night,' Myles began, striding towards the desk in the lounge, not even turning his head left to see who was waiting for him. 'I can only apologise again for something I had no intention of going any further than the person I emailed.'

'Myles,' she tried, but he went on.

'I was having a moan, went into a rant, I wasn't thinking clearly.'

'Myles, I think—'

'I don't know how else to say I'm sorry. I'll talk to the editor, I'll tell her the truth, how this inn is the best place I've ever stayed, the hostess one of the loveliest women I've ever had the pleasure to meet.'

Before Darcy could say anything else, Ian stood and when Myles heard a noise behind him he turned. 'Dad, didn't see you there.' It took him a moment to look past

248

Ian and to the sofa, where an anxious mother was waiting to see the reaction of her son. 'Mum?'

'I came to surprise you.'

Myles's face fell. 'You've certainly done that. Was this planned all along?'

Darcy could see exactly where this was going and she was powerless to stop it. Ian looked completely gutted, Martha looked devastated and Myles went on.

'You thought you'd send Dad out here to sweet-talk me, then join him later when he'd paved the way. Why can't you let me do things in my own time?'

Martha rose and came over to join both men. None of them seemed concerned that they were doing this in the lounge in front of Darcy.

'It wasn't planned, Myles. I can see why you would think that. But it wasn't. I let Ian come out here; I didn't want to, I thought it would be a bad idea. I did want to let you do things in your own time, but then I thought: you know what, if I do that we'll never sort this out. This mess will keep snowballing until there's no way back.'

She kind of had a point, Darcy thought. She went to move past them.

'I need a hot shower,' said Myles. 'Then we'll talk.'

His parents watched him go and Darcy was about to leave them to it when Holly came through the front door. She nodded to Ian and Martha as they went off to their apartment.

'Good afternoon, Holly.' Darcy tried to put aside the drama that had just taken place and, instead, pretend everything was normal. 'Or should that be good evening?' she smiled. Night had drawn a curtain over Manhattan already.

'It's really coming down out there.' Holly brushed the excess white flakes from her hair although as they met

249

the heat of the room they dissolved into droplets that soon made all traces of the weather outside disappear.

Darcy moved to the window and cupped her hands around her eyes to look out. 'It really is!' Perhaps they were going to get snow for Christmas after all. 'Are you a fan of the snow?'

Holly held out a hand, tipped it left and then right. 'Yes and no. At Christmas for sure. New Year's too. But after that, you can shove it where the sun don't shine.'

Darcy giggled. 'Pretty much the way I feel too.' Snow made Manhattan picture-postcard perfect for a while, until reality set in. Then it became hazardous on the streets, with pedestrians slipping on sidewalks, and the cold did a lot more than nip at your nose – it threatened your extremities and sometimes you wondered if you'd ever warm up.

'Great for the Inn though.' Holly had peeled off her coat, her gloves, an extra sweater and hung it all in the entrance lobby on the available hooks there for guests to use. 'I'll make sure I get some photos from across the street, this place covered in snow.'

'Don't you have professional photographers to do that for the magazine?'

'We do but I'm also a keen photographer. It's what I'd do if I ever changed career.'

'Is that likely?'

'Probably not. I enjoy my job for the most part. I can't be bothered to change.'

Darcy checked her watch. 'Rupert will have your dinner ready by six.'

'That's fantastic. Could you fix me a drink before then? I need something. And why don't you join me? I could use the company. I've been trawling the streets, had two meetings and I need to unwind.'

Smiling, Darcy handed her the drinks menu. 'Maybe after your dinner.' It would give them a chance to talk and Darcy knew she had to just jump on in and tell Holly what she'd overheard. From the conversation they were having, she didn't think Holly had any intention of bad-mouthing the Inn. But then you never knew, did you?

'Deal. I'll hold you to that.'

Holly ordered a Manhattan – when in Rome, she said – and Darcy added another log to the fire. She suspected this room would be used by guests all evening, especially those who didn't have much of a view from their apartment and wanted to watch the snow coming down outside. While Holly was having her dinner Darcy found availability in a hotel in Brooklyn for Ian and Martha. It was smaller than the Inn but priced similarly and at short notice an absolute steal at Christmas. She said she'd confirm the booking in the morning when she'd checked with Ian and Martha. She didn't want to disturb any of them tonight, because it appeared that family had enough going on already.

Holly raved about the food when she came through from the dining room after her dinner. 'Your chef is brilliant. The chicken tonight was to die for.'

'I'm glad you approve,' smiled Darcy. 'Same again?' She went behind the bar counter.

'Yes please, and tell me you're joining me.'

'I will, but mine will be a virgin cocktail. I have so much to do, and I'm still on duty remember.'

'Oh come on, you're a professional whether you've had a drink or not, and you'll be keeping one of your guests very happy if you join me. Come on, what do you say?'

Darcy shook her head. 'Just imagine my cocktail is the real thing.'

251

'Not even for me, a customer who could tell a hundred other people how she stayed at a beautiful Inn in New York, where the fire crackles and the hostess makes you feel so very welcome?'

Darcy grinned. 'You're very persuasive when you want to be, but it'll have to be another time.' She fixed two Manhattans – one virgin – and took both drinks over to the sofa in front of the fire.

She handed Holly her cocktail and put the other down on the side table. 'I've been meaning to talk to you.'

'Sounds serious. You're not throwing me out are you? Only I don't think I'll be able to find anywhere else at short notice and I don't ever want to go back to that apartment.'

Darcy grinned. 'I'm not throwing you out. It's about the party, the other night.'

'The one I went to?'

'Yes. At The Plaza.'

'Wait, how did you know it was The Plaza? I don't remember mentioning it.'

'I was there.'

'You were? Then you should've said hello! I was a plus one for a friend.' She looked intrigued. 'Were you with someone from the company? Who was it? There are some gorgeous men there – loaded, most of them, and some of them boring as hell, but a few good ones too.' Holly's personality was as fiery as her auburn hair, and Darcy only hoped it wouldn't be unleashed in that article. At least not in a bad way.

'I was with someone. It doesn't matter who. It's the conversation I overheard that I need to talk to you about.'

Eyes wide, Holly took another sip of her cocktail. 'This sounds like gossip. And I love gossip.'

252

It was exactly what Darcy had been afraid of. 'I was in the restrooms when I heard you.'

'It's something *I* said?' She looked worried, and put her glass down on the other side table.

'More something someone said to you.'

'OK.' She drew the word out slowly, unsure whether she was going to be in trouble or not.

'I heard someone telling you about this place, about me, about an email from a guest who said I was some kind of Cinderella, fussing and interfering.'

'You heard that?' Discomfited, she said, 'I can't imagine that was particularly pleasant.'

'It wasn't.'

'Do you know, I once wrote short stories, before my time at the magazine?' Darcy wasn't sure where this was going. 'They were reviewed frequently and mostly those reviews were complimentary. But some of them stank. What was it one reviewer said?' She thought hard. 'That was it. She, or he – I have no idea of the gender from the username – said: "This woman doesn't have a creative bone in her body. Her stories are dull, she should get a real job." Nice, huh?'

'Jeez,' Darcy exhaled. 'They didn't hold back, did they?'

'I know, not nice to read. That was my first bad review and it always stuck with me. But do you know what I did?'

'What?'

'I went and looked at reviews for some of the best pieces of writing around and they all, without exception, had scathing reviews amongst the many good ones. That woman at The Plaza? Well, if I could review her and her behaviour that night I would say, 'This woman should learn to stop drinking champagne after the tenth glass and should probably go to a good lingerie store because she wasn't wearing a bra beneath that gold dress and there was way too much side cleavage on display.''

Darcy burst out laughing.

'See, it's one opinion, Darcy. She was ranting on and on about this email but, to be honest, it all went way over my head. I knew you already, I was staying here, I hadn't had the experience that this person had clearly had.'

Darcy sipped her cocktail, nervous about confiding in a guest, a woman who had the power to slate the Inglenook Inn should she see fit. And if she talked to her about her personal life, was that overstepping the mark? Surely it was backing up the claim that the manager at the Inn wasn't professional.

'Do you know who the guest was?' Holly asked.

Darcy hesitated. 'I do.'

'Why do I get the feeling there's something you're not telling me?'

Darcy only hesitated for a moment. She was so comfortable talking to Holly that it all came flooding out: how she'd known the guest on the top floor in London, how she'd put up the Christmas tree, how he'd despised her for doing so and then seen the light, how they'd gone on a date and it was all going well until she'd found out he'd sent that email.

'Whoa.' Holly downed the rest of her cocktail. 'I'm gonna need another of these.'

Darcy did the honours and when she was sitting down, said, 'He's a man with a lot of issues. He's apologised over and over.'

'It sounds as though he regrets saying what he did.'

'Maybe he does, but it's too much drama. I don't need drama.'

'Hey, you're preaching to the converted. I don't do drama either, at least not when it comes to my own life. Now other people's lives…perhaps I do, but not my own. I can see why you're backing away.'

'But…' She knew there was more.

Holly grinned conspiratorially. 'But…he's hot! I've seen him a couple of times. Mmm…Mmm…'

Darcy shook her head and laughed. 'That simple, huh?'

'I didn't say it was simple, but he's hot. Fact?'

'Fact.'

'And he likes you, a lot, I'd say.'

'How do you know?'

'Because men like him could get any woman they wanted. That party at The Plaza was filled with trophy wives, wives who are way more attractive than their husbands. Sorry, I tell it like it is,' she said when Darcy refused to comment. 'Your Myles—'

'He's not my Myles.'

'Oh he is, you take my word for it. Your Myles could get a woman like that any day of the week, and there he is putting himself on the line and dating not only his landlady, but also a woman who pissed him off right from the start by putting a Christmas tree in his apartment. How dare you, by the way? What a terrible thing to do,' she admonished in good humour. 'Putting up a tree for someone, taking the time to try and make their Christmas as magical as you believe it can be.'

Her sarcasm made Darcy laugh hard. 'I still shouldn't have done it.'

Holly got more serious. 'Maybe not, but I think if he didn't really like you then he would've yelled at you, sent that email, and never bothered to pass the time of day with you again. But, he put himself out on a limb,

I'm guessing, and asked you out. And he's apologised more than once, you say, which means he's not giving up quietly. I've had a few relationships in my time and one thing I've learnt is that men, outside of the boardroom, don't tend to revel in conflict. It would've taken a lot of courage and dedication to keep on at you for forgiveness.'

Darcy watched the snow falling gently from the sky outside, creating a winter wonderland. She could just about make out a light coating on top of some of the car roofs, the railings on the brownstone on the opposite side of the street. 'I've seen women rely on men and it's one hell of a risk.' There, she'd said it.

'So have I, believe me. My sister for one.'

'Really?'

'She met a man who travels all over the world. She left her corporate job because she didn't want to live as a single woman even though she was married. It was a huge sacrifice. At the time I thought she was crazy, but when I'm not being so cynical, the romantic in me says that sometimes, for the right person, it's worth it.'

'I'm not arguing with that.' Darcy's cocktail glass was empty and she toyed with the stem between her fingers. 'But when it all goes pear-shaped, what is a woman left with? I decided early on that I wasn't going to ever let it happen to me.'

'Shit happens everywhere. Well it does.' She refused to accept Darcy's protestations. 'Whether you're in a relationship or not. My sister, she's beyond happy. It's sickening really. She's never looked back and wished she'd kept her job. Then you've got my best friend, Lynne. Now her husband gave up his job to look after the kids while she was the one with the career, and that suits them just fine. Both these women could fall flat on

256

their faces, or they could end up having the happiest of lives. There's nothing to say your life won't go to shit even if you're on your own, completely independent.'

'I suppose you're right.'

'You know I am.'

'I'm not sure you've made me feel any better.'

'I'm sorry, I tend to tell it how it is. Which is exactly what I shall do when it's time for the article write-up. The Inglenook Inn will be reviewed from my point of view. I'll talk about the wonderful, honest, down-to-earth manager called Cinderella,' she teased. 'Just kidding, I'll call you something else. I'll tell readers about the way the brownstone looks from the street, like any other façade, but once you step inside there's a glowing welcome with a cosy fireplace. I'll talk about how if you stay at Christmas you can have a real tree in your own apartment, I'll rave about the food from your brilliant chef, and your Christmas lunch.' She patted Darcy's hand. 'How does that sound?'

'It sounds good. I can try to get you a tree if you'd like.'

'For my apartment? No. I'd rather socialise in here with this beautiful tree. I think I need other people around me. It's what Christmas is about after all.'

'You're right.' Darcy understood. 'I'm glad you're settling in here.'

'And I'm glad I bumped into you.' She smiled. 'Give the man a chance, eh?'

Darcy let out a long breath. 'I don't know.'

'Haven't you ever done anything you regret? It's Christmas, and everyone deserves a second chance at this time of the year.' She took her glass and Darcy's over to the bar.

'That's *my* job,' said Darcy, getting up to follow her as the O'Sullivans came bustling through the front door, colourful coats jostling together as they chatted amongst themselves.

'I'll say goodnight,' Holly smiled. 'I'm going upstairs to spoil myself with a bubble bath.'

After she left Darcy chatted with the boys from upstairs as they speculated as to whether Santa Claus would realise they weren't at home this Christmas.

Rupert came through from the kitchen. 'All done for the night,' he said as the O'Sullivans warmed themselves in front of the fire. 'And I've left you a chicken dinner.'

'You're a star, I'm famished.' Darcy hadn't realised it'd been so long since she'd eaten, what with Ian, Martha and Myles and the complications that went with them, and then her conversation with Holly. 'Did you get my note about extras for Christmas lunch?'

'I did. Now stop worrying. We're all set.'

'That's a relief, thank you. Are you OK?' He looked exhausted.

'Just tired, that's all. Early night for me and I'll see you in the morning. We're almost there,' he smiled. 'Christmas at the Inglenook Inn for the first time, and it's going to be wonderful.'

Darcy crossed her third finger over her index finger on each hand. 'I really hope so, Rupert.'

# Chapter Twenty-Two

*Myles*

Myles finished up in the shower. He pulled on a pair of jeans, a white T-shirt and a navy cable-knit sweater. He was emotionally spent from everything with Darcy, and his dad, and seeing his mum had almost been too much. But he couldn't delay this any longer. It was time to face them both.

He went down a floor, along the corridor to the end, and knocked at the apartment his dad and now also his mum were staying in. His heart pounded as he waited for someone to answer and he berated himself for letting loose with the accusations earlier. It was no way to start mending the broken relationship between them all. He'd begun to make some headway with his dad and being here in a different country, in accommodation that was neutral territory, he just hoped the same would happen with his mum.

It was she who opened the door. She stepped forwards and hugged him – which wasn't out of the ordinary. She'd probably been too scared to do it earlier.

'Come in, Myles.' She stood back to let him in. The apartment was small in dimensions compared to his own but it was functional, with a bedroom off to the right, a living area with a television and a kitchenette.

'When did you get in?' he asked her, as his dad switched off the TV. By the sounds of it he had the news on. Myles could imagine them both sitting there, waiting and waiting for him to come down, not knowing what would happen when he did.

'My flight arrived early afternoon and I got in a cab and came straight here. We were going to order takeaway tonight; have you eaten?'

He shook his head.

'Would you like to join us?' she prompted.

It was as though he were a kid all over again, afraid to say a word, scared to fracture the fragile atmosphere. 'As long as it's Chinese, I'm in.'

His words broke the strain in the atmosphere and Ian took out a menu from a pile on the table. They sat like any normal family, selecting items from the menu folded into thirds, Myles ringing through the order on his phone ready for delivery in an hour. It would give them a chance to talk.

'Cup of tea?' his mum offered.

He'd rather have a beer, or a big glass of red, but, he supposed, from a woman who'd drunk herself into oblivion way too many times, it would be torturous and completely inappropriate to offer him alcohol right now. 'Tea would be great. Black, no sugar, thanks.'

He sat at the only sofa, tucked on one end while his mum made the tea, tapping the teaspoon on the edge of the cup exactly five times as she usually did after she'd stirred it. The ritual used to irritate him when he was younger and still living at home, but there was something strangely comforting about it now.

Martha handed Myles his cup of tea and gingerly sat down at the other side of the sofa with her own. His dad sat on one of the kitchen chairs opposite so it was easier to talk, so they weren't all sat like ducks in a row, making it more like an inquisition.

'It's wonderful to see you, Myles.' She looked nervous, her voice came out quieter than usual. 'And this inn is lovely.' She blew across her tea. 'I can stay tonight but we'll have to move as of tomorrow, which is a shame. But I'm not surprised it's fully booked.'

'You didn't book anywhere else?' Now wasn't the time to be critical and Myles knew if each of them didn't tread carefully, they'd get nowhere. So he didn't say anything more.

'The lovely girl downstairs has been calling around and said she'll do her best, so fingers crossed. I really want us all to be together at Christmas.'

The tension in Myles's hands made it almost impossible to lift his mug to sip his tea. What was he supposed to say? That yes, it would be nice?

'If it's OK with you, that is,' Martha added.

Throughout, Ian had stayed quiet, hovering on the sidelines in case his input was needed. Myles looked over to him and realised what he really needed was to have a conversation with his mum, on her own. He couldn't remember the last time they'd done that without anyone in the background and, although he hadn't realised before, now he knew that he desperately needed it to be that way.

'Dad, would you mind giving us some time?'

'Martha?' Ian looked torn between giving his son what he wanted and staying by his wife's side. He'd told Myles how guilty he'd felt for not being there for Martha, not seeing her, so asking him to stand aside now was a tough request.

Her voice shook. 'It's fine…I'm fine. Go and enjoy that beautiful lounge downstairs and you can intercept the Chinese food.'

Myles put his cup of tea on the table. He hoped he could work up an appetite because in the few minutes since placing their order, he'd suddenly lost all desire to eat.

The door clunked shut as Ian left them to it, but the silence now was louder than any other sound: the buzz of traffic outside, a yell from someone walking past in the street, the hum of the fridge in the corner of the kitchenette.

'Are you drinking again?' He may as well come straight out with it. She wasn't today, he could already tell. She'd hugged him and there wasn't the faintest whiff – and although she usually tried to disguise it, she could never do it so well that he couldn't guess. He'd caught her out many a time.

'I was.'

'I appreciate the honesty.'

'Myles…I know I hurt you a lot over the years and I'm not asking you to pretend none of it happened. I don't think any of us can do that.'

'I know I can't,' he admitted, unable to look at her. She stayed at her end of the sofa and he at his. He felt like a pre-teen, unable to process his emotions and see the bigger picture. 'So you're not drinking now?'

'I haven't had a drink in more than a week. I didn't reach the depths I'd reached before either, because your father has been there for me, he wasn't going to let it happen on his watch.' Myles's shoulders sagged in relief. 'I'm not making light of it. I know I need to be strong so I never go down that path again. I joined a support group.'

'You did?'

She was smiling now. 'I've made a couple of lovely friends and we're all there for each other. Your dad is right by my side but it helps to have outsiders to talk with as well.'

'You and Dad do seem much better than ever before.'

'We're getting there.' She coughed to clear her throat. 'We did a disservice to our children. To you and Winston. We should've been setting an example, paving the way for you two to grow into happy, rounded young men, but instead our own problems got in the way.'

He noticed her hand stray to her side, a few inches closer to him, but she put it safely back in her lap again. 'Some of those days are so foggy I can't remember them.'

'I can. I remember every last detail.' Silence hung between them. 'I remember finding you passed out in a chair on more than one occasion, having to cook an entire Christmas dinner with Winston when we had no idea where to start. The funny thing was, it wasn't that we were incapable or we didn't enjoy it. It just would've been nice to have you a part of it.'

'After the house was broken into I was terrified.'

Myles was catapulted to the other side, the side that showed all this from her perspective. 'Dad told me all about it. Why did you never say anything? Winston and I could've handled it.'

She shook her head vehemently. 'It wasn't what I wanted. In hindsight it may have been better to be honest, but at the time I just wanted to protect you from all harm. That man, he was terrifying. All I could think about that night was you two boys. I thought I'd get over the break-in after a couple of weeks. We had locks changed, a high-tech alarm installed, we even redid the windows on the ground floor to make it next to impossible to break one. But, still, I rarely slept. I had a prescription for sleeping pills for a while, and they worked at the start. I don't know, maybe I got too used to them. I started to have a glass of wine in the evening. It was the only way I could relax and not be paralysed with fear in my own home. But one glass soon turned into two, which soon turned into many. If you asked me to pinpoint exactly when I went from enjoying a few drinks to an alcoholic, I couldn't even tell you.'

'Why didn't you get help back then?'

'I was ashamed. I was failing as a mother. Plenty of people lived alone while their husbands worked away, but I was unable to hold it all together.' She fiddled with the bottom buttonhole of her cardigan. It looked new and he found himself wondering whether she'd bought it especially for this visit. Some days back when she was drinking she'd looked so bedraggled in tatty old leggings and threadbare jumpers that he had started buying her clothing for Christmas and birthdays because it broke his heart to see her looking so bereft.

'There's no shame in being scared,' he said.

'I felt like my mum was the only one who understood me. She didn't lecture me, she saw all the hurt and fear deep down, and she did her best to come in and support my children while I tried to sort myself out. The counselling your dad arranged should've been a turning point, but I was too blind to see it. I'd got myself into this state, this rut, and getting out of it was going to take a lot more than I ever realised.

'When your grandma died I reached new depths, Myles. It made me realise how I'd shut myself off from everyone else, including your father and my boys. You were both doing so well but I couldn't take any credit for that. I saw what my mum did with you two, I saw the encouragement from your father, but I thought I was just an embarrassment. Sometimes I'd think, right, today's the day I'm going to talk to them both. I'll sit Winston and Myles down and I'll tell them everything that happened. I'll let them know that none of it was their fault, that this was my doing, and that I loved you both very much. But I never quite managed it. You were both at that age where any frank conversation with your parents was beyond embarrassing.'

Her wry smile made him grin too. 'Winston has all that to look forward to with his kids. He says they're already monosyllabic at the dinner table and he has to coax information out of them.'

Martha nodded. 'I think kids grow up much more quickly these days.' She looked at her youngest son. 'I hope you have that to look forward to one day as well.'

Myles shrugged. 'Who knows.'

'That's my biggest regret, you know.'

'What is?'

'That I ruined the idea of family for you.'

'I'm not stupid, Mum. I know that not all families are happy, some have plenty of problems.'

'That's the common-sense approach, but I think you absorbed a lot of negativity over the years that you've never been able to step away from. You've battled on in your career and come out on top, and we couldn't be more proud of you. But with every promotion, every move up the career ladder, I had a pang of sadness that I couldn't instil in you the importance of having other things in your life.'

'You didn't completely fuck up my life, Mum.'

She raised her eyebrows. 'I'm still your mother and I can still tell you off for your language.'

'Sorry, it just seemed the easiest way to describe what you feel you've done. But it wasn't all you. Winston seems to have coped with it all, processed it and moved on. It's me who couldn't see past everything that happened.'

Her fingers stilled on her lap. 'You know, I sometimes wonder if it was because you were the youngest. I think Winston partly saw it as his responsibility to grow up and set an example for the both of you. You always were close, and I'm so glad it stayed that way.'

'Me too.' He relaxed back into the sofa.

'Do you ever talk? You know, about the years when I was…'

'An alcoholic?'

She looked down at her fingers rather than look at her son. 'It took me a long time to admit I was one. That I'll always be one.' Her eyes didn't leave her hands. 'I went through the denial for a long time. But then, one day, something snapped and I couldn't keep doing it. Your father was there for me and helped me through it all. I think I saw all those wasted years flash in front of my eyes, the mess I'd made for my two sons, and instead of sinking further into depression, finding solace in a bottle, I made the decision that no, this wasn't it. Not for me, not for us – me and your father – and certainly not for my boys.'

'So why did you start drinking again recently?'

'I didn't go back to being as bad as before, but I could've easily done so. We've shared Christmas many a time, but the tension has been…well, at times unbearable. I guess lately it's all I've been able to think about.'

'I thought you'd put everything behind you and were just carrying on as normal.'

'I tried to, but who was I kidding? You can't go through the stuff that we all dealt with and then assume it'll just fizzle away without addressing it. I needed to sit both you boys down and damn well apologise. That

266

should've been the first thing I did, back before Winston got married. But I was pathetic. I was scared you'd both turn around and throw it all back in my face. I saw Winston get his happy ending and assumed you'd follow suit, but the more time went on I saw the animosity you still held on to about those years you'd seen me in a state – when you'd taken over basic household tasks if I was too far gone to do them, the things you'd missed out on because of me – and, well, I knew you were going to be different from your older brother. Sometimes, when you came into the room I'd say your name with every intention of having the conversation that needed to start with 'I'm sorry', but it never happened. There was always my fear that you'd run even further away.'

'Is that what you thought I was doing by taking the job in New York?'

Her face had already given it away. 'I thought you needed to get far away from me.'

'You're not completely wrong.' He risked a glance at her. She looked so hurt, fearful, desperate for reassurance. 'It wasn't why I went for the position and took it up, but it was an added bonus.'

'Oh Myles…' She trailed off, pulled a tissue from the box on the countertop.

'All those Christmas days when you were drinking were hell for me. Decorating a tree without your mum was wrong. She was the person who should've been leading the proceedings. Dad tried to be that person but I started to resent him not being enough to make up for the missing piece.

'Do you remember the year the stockings were ruined? I was fifteen.' When he heard a sniff he knew she remembered it too well. 'It was Christmas Eve and you'd hung our stockings, stuffed full of presents, and

267

for the first time in a long while I thought, at last, she's pulled herself together and we're going to have a proper family Christmas. Dad was coming home early that evening and we were all excited about the next day. We'd said we'd cook together, Winston and I argued over who got to do the most and you were so proud of us. "My boys", you said, "My little chefs." We were so excited.'

'And then I ruined it.'

'It was a disaster. You'd had a couple of drinks, which I think Winston and I didn't notice because we were too happy and you weren't that far gone. You kept adding logs to the fire, piling them up, and, boys being boys, we thought it was fantastic. We kept saying it was an indoor fire that would make Guy Fawkes proud. You kept it going long after we went to bed, and then you fell asleep.'

His mum carried on for him as though reiterating the words helped her process what she'd done, one of the many things she must regret now. 'Your dad came home and the stockings had fallen down, the flames had caught the material alight, the presents were all ruined, and if he'd been much later it could've been so much worse.'

'Do you know what I remember the most?' Myles couldn't look at his mum. Instead, he stared at the wall opposite, with the single painting of the Empire State Building standing tall and proud in Manhattan, tiny dots of people scuttling around on its viewing deck. 'First of all it was the smell, the unmistakable stench of fire mixed with plastic, the reminder of another ruined Christmas. But then it was the shouting, the yelling, the crying.'

'Your father went mad.'

'Are you surprised?'

268

Taken aback by the way he snapped at her, she said, 'I'm not excusing it. He had every right to be angry.'

'You could've burnt down the house, Mum.'

'That wasn't why he shouted, Myles.' She was looking at him, he could feel it. 'He yelled because I'd put you two in harm's way, yet again.' She took a deep breath. 'Did you know he threatened to leave me?' Myles looked at her now. 'He was going to take you and Winston and walk out. And you know what? I'm glad he said it to me. I'm glad he didn't pussyfoot around and treat me kindly. He told me the way it was going to be. I think his fear drove him to say enough was enough, and I needed it.'

Myles got up, paced, and settled against the countertop.

'I know you can never forgive me for all of those years, Myles. That's not what this is about. I'm not asking you to wipe those memories away. But what I am asking for is another chance, with you. To start again with my son and make some new memories, if you can let me.'

Could he do it? He'd held on to his anger for so long, half the time without realising it, that he didn't even know how to exist without that grudge. It'd been ingrained in his psyche, become a part of him, and it was hard to shoehorn himself out of it.

'Your dad and I have something for you.' She stood up, went into the bedroom and picked up a small wrapped box, which she brought over to him. 'Merry Christmas, Myles. And thank you for the hamper you sent, it's beautiful and it'll be something to enjoy in the New Year for us.'

'I should put this beneath my tree upstairs,' he said, distracted, still clutching the gift. 'It's not Christmas yet.'

'Trust me, you want to open this before the big day.' She managed more of a smile than she'd been able to give since she'd arrived.

Myles tugged at the green satin material tied around the gift and the bow unravelled. He pulled the Sellotape until it peeled away from the red paper and allowed him to remove the box from inside. When he opened it, he reached in and when he realised what it was his eyes filled with tears.

'Where did you find it?' Looking back at him was the snowman on skis ornament that he'd chosen as a young boy. He'd thought it long gone.

'It was never lost, Myles. I kept it safe every year.'

'But I thought it'd been broken, thrown away.' He ran a finger along the black painted ski, the white leg of the snowman, careful as he handled it for fear it would break now it was so old.

Martha shook her head. 'I knocked it off when I was drunk, remember. It crashed to the floor, and I still remember your face when you saw it happen. It was as though it was another piece of your life I'd taken, thrown away without a concern, and smashed to pieces. You examined it, it was fine, but you took it and wrapped it in tissue paper and pushed it in a drawer in the study. I found it there once when I was looking for something else.'

'I forgot I put it there,' he said. He couldn't remember her knocking it off. Perhaps it was something he'd refused to let surface in his mind. 'Why didn't you get it out the year after and hang it on the tree?'

'Because…' Her voice faltered. '…because after that year, Christmas was never the same again. You had so much anger inside, so much fury, and I'd caused it all. I thought that if I put that ornament on the tree, you'd smash it up yourself in a fit of rage at everything that had happened.' Her tears came and instead of standing there waiting to see if he said anything in reply, she turned and fled into the bedroom and shut the door.

Myles waited. He looked at the time. He wondered whether the Chinese takeaway had arrived yet and his dad was too scared to come back up.

After another ten minutes passed he went over to the bedroom door and knocked tentatively.
'Mum…Mum…'

She didn't say come in but he opened the door anyway. She was over by the window looking out. 'It's snowing,' she said, her voice soft, exactly how he remembered it from the very early years. There was no pleading for forgiveness now, no apprehension at what his reaction might be.

He stood beside her. 'It means a lot to me that you kept the ornament all these years.'

'Perhaps you could put it on the tree in your apartment here.' She looked out across the street, the snow illuminated in the golden glow of the streetlamps.

Down below, a group of people huddled together against the elements, hurrying to wherever they needed to go, and finally Myles felt as though he was in a place where he'd needed to be for a very long time but hadn't known how to get there.

'Mum…' He put a hand on her arm. 'Would you like to come up to my apartment and hang the ornament with me?'

He heard her voice catch. 'Yes, I'd like that very much.'

'And, Mum…'

'Yes, Myles?' She waited for him to switch the light off in the room and shut the door behind them.

'Can we eat soon? I'm bloody starving.'

She pulled him into a hug, a hug that felt like the first real affection they'd had between them in far too many years.

# Chapter Twenty-Three

*Darcy*

*Christmas Eve*

Darcy sat up in bed. It was still dark, but she knew exactly what day it was. Christmas Eve. Her favourite day of the year.

Last night she'd made s'mores for the O'Sullivan boys, who were still trying to convince their parents they should try it when they got home to Ireland. She'd also told Ian Cunningham he had accommodation in Brooklyn, for which he'd been eternally grateful. Vanessa and Zach had enjoyed cocktails at the bar, Holly had headed out to a show at Radio City Hall with the sister of her friend who passed away, and she'd not heard anything from Myles or Martha Cunningham, but Ian's face had said it all. And when he'd taken delivery of a Chinese takeaway and finally made his way upstairs to where the sound of voices told Darcy the family must have made some headway, she hoped this Christmas was going to run smoothly for everyone.

She climbed into the shower. This Christmas needed to go without a hitch and she felt confident she could pull it off. Strong, independent, and without the tangles that came with a relationship, it was the way she had always worked best.

After her shower she pulled on her stockings, a French navy dress with a scooped neckline and knitted ribbed trim. She ran a brush through her hair and twisted it up into a chignon. She had plenty to do today and went over it all in her mind. She needed to run through the food list again with Rupert and ensure they left nothing out. She needed to go to the Chelsea Market and pick up her seafood order. Tomorrow's entrée would be a choice of either prawn cocktail or baked mushrooms with a ricotta stuffing.

She laughed to herself when her tummy gurgled at the thought of the feast they had planned, and it stopped her insides plummeting at the prospect of sharing a Christmas lunch with Myles. She wasn't angry about his email anymore – largely because Holly had been so lovely about it – but regardless of that, what had happened had only served to remind her that rather than playing games and trying to battle her way through a relationship, her career was her main focus, her independence meant everything to her. All she had to do was push out the niggling voice that said she could always have both.

The Inn was cloaked in the remaining fragments of night and it was quiet when Darcy went down to the lounge. She loved this time of the morning before anyone else woke up, the start of Christmas Eve, the feeling of magic that hung in the air. She pushed the socket into the wall to switch on the tree lights and gazed into them. The smell of last night's fire hovered in the air, reminding her she'd need to clean out the grate once again and lay another. When she'd seen Sofia doing it all the time she'd thought it a pain, but she knew now exactly why her friend's mum had made the effort. The Inglenook Inn was at its absolute best in winter, with a roaring fire, and decorations all around with the promise of Christmas.

The sound of the front door opening brought her out of her trance. She turned to see Rupert. 'You're early.' She kept her voice low even though once they were tucked away in their apartments guests probably enjoyed a relatively quiet night. Or at least as quiet as you could in Manhattan. There was always some level of noise, but living here you grew accustomed to it. The sound of traffic going back and forth as though it was still daytime, voices from people who wanted to become like the city and not sleep themselves, the blare of a car alarm, the distant hum from the bakery on the next street that started its day in the small hours with deliveries and noisy machinery to get the day's baking underway.

'Lots to do,' he said with a cheer that didn't quite reach his eyes. 'First up, the gingerbread cookies.'

'You'll have everyone awake in seconds when the smell of those wafts through the hallway.' She once again noticed how he didn't seem quite himself. 'You look shattered, Rupert.'

''Tis the season. Another early night for me again tonight I think. I'm getting old.'

'Rubbish. You're in your mid-forties, that's nowhere near old.'

'Thanks, I'll try to bear that in mind.' A broad smile spread across his face deepening the creases at his temples. 'It's Christmas Eve, Darcy.'

'It's Christmas Eve.' Like a small child she felt all lit up inside.

'And you'll be doubly pleased of course.' He hung his coat up, looped the scarf from his neck onto the hook, pushing it in so it wouldn't fall off. 'You'll want to get a lot of photos. It's almost light so you should do it while there's not too much traffic around.'

'What are you talking about?'

He grinned. 'The snow!'

'It's snowing?'

He let out a laugh but then covered his mouth when she waved her hands to remind him people were still sleeping. 'Sorry, forgot I'm on a different timeframe,' he whispered. 'But seriously, it's lucky I only live three blocks away.'

Darcy dashed to the front door of the brownstone, pulled it open, and peeped out. There it was. A winter wonderland.

The whole neighbourhood was blanketed in white. The sidewalk was inches deep, the cars parked on either side of the street were like part of a painting, their colours hidden and shapes only outlined in white as snow spread across bonnets, up over the roofs and along the sides, allowing the odd wing mirror to stick out. Snow balanced on the top of streetlamps, on railings opposite, on bare trees that had long since shed their leaves. Down the middle of the street were grey tracks where cars must have cut through the white, and the pine trees in pots on either side of the front door had a dusting of snow to make them all the more Christmassy.

Darcy shut the door when she finally felt the cold. Dressed minimally and for inside temperatures only, she briskly rubbed her hands together and then rubbed her palms against her arms. She was still smiling when the door opened again behind her, and this time she was surprised to see it was Myles.

Clearly he hadn't expected to see either of them standing there either.

'Good morning,' he said, looking quickly to Rupert and then focusing his attention on Darcy.

'Good morning, Myles.' Rupert scarpered off towards the kitchen.

Uneasy in his presence, Darcy offered her greeting and then said, 'You're up very early. Been for a run?' She indicated the gear he was wearing.

'I couldn't sleep.'

She took the dustpan and brush out from the cupboard. Sometimes she felt as though she may as well have the tools tied to a belt round her waist she used them so much. 'Isn't it hard to run in the snow?'

He shrugged, still panting slightly from the exertion. 'It's not so bad.'

'Well that's dedication.'

'I'm afraid if I stop I'll never get going again. I make sure I go a few times a week.'

She smiled, the light conversation a relief. 'Are you working today?'

'I'm taking the day off.'

For some reason it pleased her to hear. 'I'm assuming that doesn't happen very often.'

'You are exactly right. I was all set to work, especially with Dad leaving, but now both my parents are here we're going to have family time.' He pulled a face. 'It feels weird saying that.'

'How's it all going?' She could tell by his expression that something had changed. He no longer looked harried. He looked open, receptive, and it unnerved her.

'It's going better than I expected. When Mum showed up I just thought there would be tension, a big shouting match, and then we'd all go our separate ways. I think I was so shocked she and Dad are both here that it forced me to make the effort to really listen for a change.'

'I'm glad it's all working out.'

'Mum thought I'd come to New York to get away from her.' He seemed to want to talk more and she couldn't ignore him. He followed her into the lounge,

277

where she bent down to clean out the grate. 'The job came first, but she was right. I was trying to get away rather than face up to everything.'

Darcy carried on sweeping, making non-committal grunts along the way. She willed the smell of gingerbread to waft from the kitchen so she could rave about the Christmas cookies that would be served, the plans they had for tonight's Christmas Eve menu, what was on the list for tomorrow.

'Darcy, please look at me.'

She did, but only on her way to take the bag she'd filled with ashes down to the basement to throw in the trash.

He stopped her before she could pass him, his hand settling on her arm. He smelled of the outside, of the cold air and the icy blast, a subtle hint of laundry detergent on his clothes even though he'd been out running. 'Darcy, please.'

'Myles, I don't think we need to say anything else. I've cleared it with Holly and she isn't going to use the email information, so the Inn should get a good review and write-up – providing I can pull Christmas off.' She added the last bit to try to inject a bit of humour, light-heartedness, in the hope he'd just let this go.

'I don't think there's any doubt is there?' His voice had a nervous edge to it, a vulnerability usually disguised beneath a well-cut, expensive suit.

'We should be fine. But I need to get on, there's so much to do.'

He accepted it for now, and didn't try to push her on the issue of them. 'I wanted to thank you for finding somewhere for my parents to stay,' he said.

'It was my pleasure. I've found them a room in a delightful hotel over in Brooklyn so not too far. I did suggest you all stay in your apartment.' He pulled a face that made Darcy laugh. 'Your dad reacted in pretty much the same way.'

'Us three, all under one roof, in such close proximity?' Myles shook his head and she noticed a snowflake, which had hovered on the surface as long as it could, disperse as it gave up resistance to the ambient temperature. 'Now that's a recipe for disaster.'

Darcy excused herself and Myles headed on up to his apartment. She went down to the basement and threw the remnants of last night's fire into the trash, wondering how many more times he'd mention what had happened between them, how many times he'd try to make up for his mistake. On the one hand she longed for him to do so; on the other, the thought terrified her. When she stuck with work and her career, she knew what was what. When relationships came along, her mind got muddled and it was all too much.

By the time the scent of the gingerbread cookies made its way through the downstairs of the brownstone, the O'Sullivans were up and about, Vanessa and Zach were seated in the dining room, and Darcy had taken Ian and Martha a breakfast tray upstairs with freshly baked croissants, a fruit salad and squeezed orange juice.

The snow continued to fall and Darcy managed to get outside and take plenty of photos of the Inn, capturing the way the snow lined the outsides of the window panes, settled over the little arch on the front door, with the pine trees standing tall and proud and the railings bordering the stoop. She emailed them to Holly for inclusion in the article and sent a few photographs to Dylan to add to the website. He responded less than an hour later to say he'd added them, and suggested she write some short, snappy paragraphs about Christmas at the Inglenook Inn to explain the pictures, what customers could expect. Darcy got straight to it and, lo and behold, the changes had not even been live an hour when they generated a couple of very speedy emails from people enquiring about bookings for next Christmas. Giddy with excitement, Darcy took their details and said she'd talk with the owner and be sure to get in touch. She forwarded everything to Sofia and hoped she would see it as the opportunity Darcy believed it was.

With Christmas music in the background, a tray of gingerbread cookies on the side table for guests to help themselves, and the intense concentration she needed to place an order for some items on her inventory and ensure she didn't order a ridiculous number of light bulbs or ten times too many miniature soaps, Darcy didn't hear Myles come into the lounge until he was standing in front of the desk.

He smiled and it reminded her of the way he'd looked at her when he met her outside her apartment the night they'd been to The Plaza. She cleared her throat, thinking of something to say. 'Have you been out again?' He was freshly shaven, his hair neater than it had been this morning after his run. He had on jeans, a Canada Goose jacket different from the long, tailored coat he wore when he went out to work. It was almost like a different Myles standing here now.

'I have. I love walking around when it's snowing. It seems especially fitting at Christmas. Am I disturbing you?'

'Myles, it's not like you can't talk to me. I run the Inn, you stay at the Inn. Our paths will inevitably cross.'

'I'm glad you feel that way.' From the cardboard tray he was holding he took out one cup. 'My folks are having some time together and I needed a really good cup of coffee. This other one is for you.'

She stood up from behind the desk. She'd thought the two coffees were for his parents and he'd drunk his on the way. It was one of Darcy's favourite things to do – grab a coffee while out and about on the streets of Manhattan and let its warmth slide right through her as she battled the weather to find her way home.

'Thank you, Myles.' It was a gift from a guest. A festive gesture. Nothing more. She took a grateful sip and, surprised, said, 'It's a caramel macchiato. How did you know?'

'Lucky guess,' he shrugged.

How had he known? 'Well, thank you very much.' She shut her eyes and, although unnerved, sipped again. 'You've no idea how much I need this today. I might even treat myself to another when I go out later.'

'Venturing anywhere nice?'

She could do this. He was just another person out of the many staying at the Inn. And she wasn't thinking about kissing him, not at all. She gulped and did her best to keep the conversation platonic, at least out loud. 'Not likely. I've got to get to the Chelsea Market to collect a seafood order for tomorrow. Rupert did mention that he'd go after he'd finished with breakfasts but some guests have ordered lunch, he'll have this evening's food to prepare and then there's tomorrow. And he looks exhausted.'

'I guess full capacity means more work for him.'

'It does. He's juggling this and another job. Hopefully this will eventually become his sole focus, but it's something the boss herself needs to make plans for.'

The music shifted and soothing sounds of Michael Bublé's 'White Christmas' played out on the speaker in the corner.

'Kind of appropriate,' Myles commented. 'White Christmases were rare in England.'

'It's funny. I'd always expected one when I went there. I blame the movies. Name one Christmas movie that doesn't feature snow.'

He laughed. 'You know, I can't think of any. Wow, I haven't seen a Christmas movie in ages.'

'You're kidding me.'

'I never usually have the time.'

'Or you never usually make the time.' She hid behind another sip of coffee in case her comment cut too deep.

He took the remark well. 'You're right, and I can't guarantee my work ethic will change, but I will try from now on to remember that there are other things that are just as important.'

Maybe they weren't so different from one another after all.

The words hung between them until Adele appeared, ready to get going with the wrapping.

'They're on their way out now,' Adele whispered, 'over to Central Park to enjoy the snow. I'll join them later.'

Darcy tapped the side of her nose as footsteps pounded down the stairs announcing the arrival of both boys.

Myles leaned in and Darcy didn't miss his glance to her lips before he lifted his focus. 'What's going on?'

She drew her lips inwards in case she had coffee froth lingering anywhere. 'Operation Santa,' she said with a wink.

When the family bustled out of the door Darcy grabbed the wrapping paper, Sellotape, scissors and labelling accessories and went into the dining room with Adele. She'd cleared it with Rupert that they could use the big dining table. Lunch wasn't for a while so they could spread everything out here.

Adele retrieved gifts from wherever she'd hidden them and they got to work. It took far longer than Darcy had estimated and by the time they were wrapping the final few pieces for the stockings, she remembered she had an errand to run.

'The seafood.' She got up from the table, flustered. 'Damn, you'll have to excuse me, Adele, or else we won't have a key ingredient for tomorrow.'

'Don't apologise. I could never have wrapped these so quickly without your help. I'll do these last few, then bag them all up before I head out to meet my family. Is there anywhere I can hide them?'

'In the basement, it's perfect. But it's locked right now as I don't want guests going down there. The staircase is ridiculously steep.'

'Anything I can do to help?' Holly stepped into the room. 'Whoa, that's a lot of gifts.'

'Santa has been crazy generous this year,' Adele admitted. 'Lucky we were under the limit with our luggage weight or this would send us over the edge on the return trip.'

Holly gestured to a chair. 'May I?'

'Of course. You any good at wrapping?'

'As a matter of fact, I am. I'm one of those weird people that finds it soothing.'

Darcy grinned. Soothing wasn't exactly the description she'd use. 'I'll leave you two to it,' she said, but they were already deep in discussion about gift tags and what made the best ribbons, impossible shapes to wrap, what Adele had bought for her boys. Holly even offered to stash all of the presents in her apartment out of the way of prying eyes until very late tonight. The place was too big for just her anyway, she'd said.

Darcy bundled up warm and stepped out onto the snowy Manhattan streets. She couldn't stop smiling. It was almost Christmas, magic was in the air, and everything was going perfectly. She headed straight for the Chelsea Market complex, where she first collected their pre-ordered prawns. Then she went to the fruit and vegetable markets with her list from Rupert and picked up anything else they needed, and less than an hour and a half later bustled through the doors to the Inglenook Inn and the ringing telephone.

She dropped the bags to the floor, rushed to get it and found it was Mr and Mrs Pendleton, who were stranded in Toronto. Their flight had been cancelled and they wouldn't make it to New York for Christmas after all. Darcy was apologetic on behalf of the weather even though there was nothing she could've done about it, but as soon as she hung up, she called through to the hotel in Brooklyn and cancelled the emergency booking she'd made for the Cunninghams. Myles and his family could all have Christmas under the same roof and for some reason it lifted her spirits to an impossible high.

She unbuttoned her coat, hung it up, took the food through to the kitchen where Rupert was in full flow preparing for that evening.

'How did the gingerbread cookies go down?' he asked as he perused the food she'd bought to check he'd be working with the best ingredients.

'Well, there's an empty tray upstairs – that should tell you something,' she smiled.

She helped unload the food, emptied the dishwasher so Rupert could focus on preparations for tonight, when guests would be served canapés and champagne over the course of a few hours as and when they wanted to indulge. It was what Christmas Eve was all about for Darcy. A chance to sparkle, dress up and talk with guests, feel that small-town spirit even here in the big city.

She only hoped she could manage to think of Myles as she would any other guest. But she knew that wasn't going to be easy. Making a decision not to take her feelings any further and to be professional was one thing, but actually going through with it and keeping her distance was something else entirely.

# Chapter Twenty-Four

*Myles*

Myles couldn't remember the last time he'd seen his parents laugh so hard. It was cathartic, a tremendous relief from the tension over not only the last couple of days but all the years since he was a little boy.

At an ice rink on the east side of Central Park, with a city backdrop and the snow continuing to fall, they'd rented skates and gone from an unsteady, teetering Bambi-like trio to three reasonably competent skaters – unless you looked at some of the kids who were skating backwards, twisting this way and that, or even doing some kind of spin with one foot off the floor.

'Come on, Myles!' Martha wobbled on her ice-skates as she came round the rink again, holding on to Ian's hand. 'Show us oldies how it's done!'

Myles had skated enough loops that he'd snuck off, not only for a rest but to allow his parents this time together. What they didn't realise was that as well as enjoying their company, what he was revelling in was seeing their relationship so strong, so different from how he remembered. It was great to see, and he'd already texted Winston a photograph as evidence.

'I'll join you again soon,' he called after them as his mum laughed away and his dad, a fierce concentration on his face, was the one to wobble this time. They'd stayed upright thankfully. The last thing he wanted was to have to take either of them back to the Inn with broken bones or kaput hips.

Darcy had texted Ian a couple of hours ago as they walked over to the rink, to say that the move to Brooklyn tomorrow was off because a couple had cancelled their stay at the Inn. Myles' parents were welcome to stay for a few more nights. Ian and Martha had been ecstatic and Myles had felt an excitement he hadn't experienced in years. Pre-Christmas was usually a time filled with dread, but, now, it was like being a child all over again.

The air was freezing standing here by the rink. Myles hadn't quite known cold like it before, but it was part of the New York experience, and the only other thing he really wanted here, the only thing that could make it extra perfect, would be to have Darcy by his side. But she'd made a firm decision and he got the impression she wasn't the type of woman to be easily swayed. His mum had tried to talk to him about her as they'd made their way towards Central Park, but although they'd sorted out a lot of things, he wasn't quite ready for those kinds of discussions yet.

Myles joined his parents one last time and when their legs ached from the effort to balance, their faces were red and sore from the onslaught of the cold, it was time to recuperate with hot drinks at a café on their way back to the Inn.

'I was impressed with you both today.' Myles cradled a coffee as his mum unwrapped her scarf, took off her coat and his dad hung it on the back of the chair for her.

'I haven't done that in a very long time.' The cold, still evident on Ian's face by his red nose and cheeks, hadn't driven away the look of delight that Myles had waited years to see. He looked relaxed, ready to take on whatever life threw at him.

'I think the last time I went ice-skating was with Winston,' said Myles, 'when we took his kids to the rink in Richmond. Remember, they went through a craze of wanting to learn and take lessons?'

Martha smiled. 'Didn't last long, then it was onto indoor climbing, wasn't it?'

'And don't forget diving – wasn't that Lulu's dream after watching the Olympics on television?'

'I guess kids have their dreams, don't they?' Martha stirred a sachet of sugar through her coffee.

'I always wanted to be a pilot,' Myles confessed.

'I never knew that.' The happiness on Martha's face wavered for a second.

He hadn't meant her to feel guilty. They were chatting about inconsequential things, but he guessed it had been around the time she'd started drinking and his dad was away a lot. 'I was fascinated. Actually, I still am.' He'd make a joke, lighten the mood. 'I mean, how *do* planes stay up in the sky?'

It worked. His mum smiled. 'I sat looking out over the wing on the way here and found myself wondering the same thing.'

Conversation turned to flying, destinations, holidays, hopes and dreams they'd all had. Myles learned his dad had wanted to make cars once upon a time and that his mum had always dreamt of having her own wool shop.

'You know, it's called yarn here,' Myles told her, glad they could talk about something she was comfortable with. He realised over the years he'd probably punished her, subtly, mostly without thinking about it, but now he was conscious to turn things around and make just as much effort as she was. He'd gone to sleep last night thinking what if she'd died and they'd never made peace, and the thought had had him tossing and turning until the small hours, because it was unbearable.

'I haven't knitted anything in years,' Martha told them. 'I saw Darcy knitting yesterday and almost asked her about it but she looked like she was finally having a few minutes to herself so I left her to it. I'll have to ask her about it later.'

'I'm sure she wouldn't mind,' said Ian. 'I think she sees it as part of her job to make customers feel almost like they're at home rather than away in a strange place. She'll go far that one.'

Myles didn't miss the look from his dad but chose not to mention it. Instead, they talked about the gathering at the Inn tonight. He wondered whether Darcy would be there the whole time, or if guests would be left to their own devices. The other people staying under the same roof seemed pleasant enough, but it was Darcy who interested him the most. He had a while left staying at the Inn and hoped in that time she'd still be there too, although when the owner returned she was bound to move on to something different. And in a city the size of New York, he might never see her again.

'I think it'll be far nicer than finding a stuffy restaurant with hordes of other people and not being able to talk above the noise,' said Ian.

'You did well to find the Inglenook Inn, Myles.' Martha put her teaspoon into her empty mug.

'I've been happy with it. The apartment I'll be moving into should be ready soon.'

'Oh, you must take us to see it! Please, before I leave.'

'I promise I will. There's too much snow today to trudge over there but we'll do it after Christmas, how does that sound?'

'It sounds pretty good to me.'

And for the first time in forever, Myles felt like he was part of a fully functioning family.

*

When the skies outside grew dark, they congregated outside his parents' apartment ready to head downstairs and join everyone else. His dad looked dapper in black trousers – although he supposed he should get with the New York lingo and call them pants – and a burgundy shirt. His mum had on a cream silk top with an indigo scarf tied in a loose knot at the front and the necklace with a single pearl drop at the end that she'd always worn. Myles wore jeans teamed with a white shirt beneath a charcoal sweater. He'd splashed on his usual aftershave, checked his reflection more than once, and he hoped he'd get to talk to Darcy at least a little bit tonight.

'Merry Christmas!' Holly greeted Martha the second she stepped off the bottom step. Myles grinned. She was clearly in the Christmas spirit and goodness knows how much champagne or eggnog she'd had.

He stopped his dad while his mum was otherwise occupied. 'Is Mum going to be OK tonight?'

'What do you mean?'

'The alcohol, Dad.'

'The liquor?'

Myles's head tipped back when he laughed at his dad trying to get in with the way New Yorkers spoke. He'd started saying he was nipping to the restroom instead of the bathroom, he'd filled a glass of water from the faucet rather than the tap, and now he was talking about liquor. 'Very Manhattan.' He patted his dad on the shoulder.

'She'll be fine, son.' His face softened, despite the seriousness of the topic. 'She is being incredible, strong, and you have a lot to do with that.'

'Me?'

'Yes, you. If you hadn't wanted to hear her apologies, if you'd chosen not to go some way to forgive her, then

I'm not sure how she would've reacted. I like to think we could've handled it together, but I'm just glad we didn't have to.' He patted his son on the shoulder, just once, but firmly, before joining his wife as she sipped from a glass of orange juice, a strawberry pushed onto the side of the vessel.

Myles took a glass of champagne rather than eggnog, a drink he wasn't sure he ever wanted to experiment with. He nodded hellos to the O'Sullivans as the father and sons admired the Christmas tree. He watched the young couple, Vanessa and Zach, twirl one another in time to the music, slowly in the compact space now filled with guests but enjoying the moment nonetheless, and when he finally battled his way through he found Darcy standing with a silver platter of canapés resting on one forearm.

She held out the platter to him. 'Myles, Merry Christmas.'

'Merry Christmas, Darcy.' He didn't take anything but when she pushed the platter closer he asked, 'What do we have here? They look delicious.'

'These are sausages covered in a hoisin sauce with sesame seeds. They're good.'

He picked one up. 'I don't doubt they are.'

'Try it.'

'Are you trying to make me eat so I can't talk and ask you any questions?'

Her cheeks coloured. 'Of course not.'

'You're wearing the same dress,' he said, his eyes not looking away, his fingers twiddling the cocktail stick and the sausage still in one piece on the end of it. 'The dress you wore to The Plaza.'

'I like to make the most of my clothes.'

'I didn't mean it as a criticism. You look beautiful.'

She went to move past him but Holly came up behind her and said, 'Point me to the champagne, Darcy.'

Darcy tipped her head. 'Over there. I left some fresh glasses lined up on the bar.'

When Holly left, Myles lowered his voice. 'How many of those has she had?'

'No idea, but she was first here tonight.'

'She's having fun.'

'She is.'

'Good for your write-up next year.'

'Let's hope so.'

Damn, he shouldn't have made any reference to the editor's write-up. Darcy had already turned with the platter to offer the sausages to Adele and her elder son. They both took a couple and when the youngest son helped himself and almost put a half-eaten one back after realising it wasn't to his taste, Darcy leaned in and asked him very nicely to drop it in the trash near the bar. She had a way with everyone it seemed.

Myles chatted with Zach about ice-skating in Central Park. They'd been earlier too and Vanessa had come off the worst with a bruised hip and a graze up her arm that was irritated by the bangles she was wearing.

Myles talked with his dad some more, he spoke to Holly about anything other than the Inn and his email, and he exchanged pleasantries with Rupert when he came out to deliver another platter of food to Darcy and take away the one that had been emptied in a few short minutes.

Christmas music played softly in the background and the ambience tonight was so right that Myles was glad to be a part of it.

When he got another orange juice for his mum, he happened to be right next to Darcy, who was greeting two newcomers who weren't staying at the Inn. Darcy kissed each of them on the cheek and asked after someone called Grandpa Joe, as well as asking about the kids and sympathising at tales of sleepless nights while the couple's baby was teething. She thanked the man for updating the website and told him she'd already had further enquiries about booking in for Christmas next year.

'Myles, these are two very good friends of mine,' Darcy explained as she held a platter of pumpernickel bites with a beetroot and cream cheese topping. 'This is Dylan and this is Cleo, and they have a much-needed night off from the kids. Now, I'm really sorry, but I have to circulate and feed the masses. Cleo, don't leave until I've shown you my progress with the sweater. Promise?' When Cleo agreed Darcy was off again and Myles watched after her, unable to avoid admiring her figure in the dress that hugged every curve of her body.

Myles turned and shook Dylan's hand. 'It's nice to meet you both.' He did the same with Cleo, unsure of the etiquette. He never knew whether it was better to kiss a woman on the cheek or go with the handshake, but she didn't seem to mind the avenue he'd chosen. 'And you look like you're enjoying a night out.'

'Oh, we are,' Cleo replied, her cheeks still rosy from the cold outside. 'We don't get much free time, but when we do, it's all the more special.'

He could tell these two were completely in love and felt a pang of regret that he'd never found that. 'So where are you guys from? Here in Manhattan?'

'Actually,' said Dylan, 'we were both living in Manhattan but now we live out in Inglenook Falls, Connecticut. And Cleo is from England.'

'You are?'

They talked some more about the Cotswolds, a region he was familiar with and where Cleo had lived too.

'Are you liking New York?' Cleo wanted to know.

'I'm liking it more than I thought. I had a suspicion the city would be too manic for me, but it kind of works if you know what I mean. Do you miss being here?'

'I don't,' Dylan admitted, a bottle of low-alcohol beer in his hand. 'I moved out a while before Cleo because I got to the point where I needed to. I still love coming back here, like tonight. It's a real treat now, especially when we come here kid-free.'

'You sound like my brother. He has kids and on the rare occasion he gets his wife to himself he says it's as though he's living a different life.'

Dylan chuckled. 'Sounds about right.'

'I haven't had much of a chance to miss Manhattan either,' Cleo admitted. 'Family life is a bit crazy and then my knitting store keeps me busy whenever I dare to think I might have a free moment. But I'm the same as Dylan, I like coming to the city occasionally and I remember it for all the fabulous things it offers.'

When Darcy walked by, Dylan told her to send on any more photos and he'd update the website as soon as he could. 'Sorry – I promise, no more work talk,' he told Cleo.

Cleo turned to Myles with a frown. 'He loves web design a bit too much sometimes. Careful or he'll start talking about it with you.'

'I'm not that bad,' Dylan admonished. 'And I know you want to tell Darcy all the latest about your work.'

Cleo smiled. 'Actually he's right, I'd be a hypocrite if I told him off for talking about websites.' She linked her arm through Dylan's and told Myles, 'I run a store and a Christmas market stall and next year I have a much bigger plot at the Inglenook Markets, so I'm already a bit over-excited.'

'That's an understatement,' said Dylan.

'How do you manage both?' Myles asked.

'This year it hasn't been too bad as the stall is quite small. My former assistant, Kaisha, went travelling around Europe when she finished college – Paris, London, Milan – but she's back in New York in the spring and has promised me she'll help out next Christmas.' She crossed her fingers. 'She's a godsend.'

'Work is always better if you have a team you can rely on,' said Myles. 'And don't apologise for talking work, I get it. I usually eat, breathe and sleep work, but took the day off today.'

'I wish Darcy would do that.' Cleo watched after her friend, laughing with a couple of the guests. 'Sorry,' she said to Dylan and Myles, 'just thinking out loud. You know' – she leaned closer – 'the girl is all work and no play.'

'Cleo,' Dylan warned.

'What? I'm not being mean. Believe me. I've been there before, hid behind my work rather than putting myself out there, I know all the signs. She says she's happy, but she deserves more, you know?'

Myles nodded but she hadn't finished.

'Do you know, she had her first proper date in years the other night, and it was a disaster?'

'Really?' Should he admit it was him?

'It sounds as though she was really smitten but for reasons I won't go into, it was the only date they'll ever have. Shame really.'

His heart sank. He looked over at Darcy, her lips glossy and teeth white when she smiled, oozing a confidence he knew hid a softer side, one she built a wall

295

around so she could focus on her independence, what she knew she could rely on.

As his eyes roamed the room he noticed his mum hovering awkwardly by the Christmas tree as Ian talked with Mr O'Sullivan. She seemed to be having a good time, but she was also a little lost. 'Mum, over here.'

She gladly came over and he introduced her to Dylan and Cleo. 'Mum, Cleo owns a knitting store out in Inglenook Falls. It's not too far from here, is it?' He was sure Connecticut was reachable from Manhattan.

'That's right, not far on a train,' Cleo confirmed.

Martha moved closer to Cleo, and Myles made room for them. 'I was saying to Myles earlier today that it's been far too long since I picked up any knitting. I loved it.'

'You'll have to come by the store. It'll be open again after New Year's.'

'That's a shame, we'll be home in England by then.'

'Not to worry,' said Cleo, her eyes twinkling, 'come by next time you're in New York.'

When his mum glanced nervously his way, Myles nodded to her. Rather than wishing he could put more distance between them, he now welcomed ways of bringing his family back together again. 'I'll make sure she does,' he said.

The rest of the evening went well. The champagne flowed in the right direction – he couldn't help checking his mum wasn't drinking anything alcoholic and he sensed she knew, but didn't mind this time – and over in one corner near the tree a few of the guests played a game of charades. Even Ian and Martha joined in. Canapés came and went. Darcy flitted to and fro relishing the ambience that came from the party she'd hosted and the warmth she'd created, and by the time the last guests filtered off to their rooms Myles was left saying goodbye to Dylan and Cleo in the hallway. Cleo had passed him the details of her knitting store in Inglenook Falls and he'd promised to have his mum call her when she was next in New York so they could sort out a visit. Cleo told him she ran workshops for all levels if his mum wanted to attend one and he knew she'd leap at the chance, if only to get involved in something new.

Myles gathered glasses to take through to the kitchen. He was wired rather than exhausted and there was no way he'd be able to sleep yet.

'You don't need to help,' said Darcy, although not ungratefully.

'Have you seen this place?' Glasses and napkins everywhere, the trash can overflowing and spills on several surfaces, it had been a successful but messy party. 'It's the least I can do. And remember I'm not used to taking it easy. This is a day off for me.'

'Well I appreciate it.' Her hair fell in waves around her shoulders, across smooth skin he remembered what it felt like to touch in those fleeting moments at The Plaza, where they'd been closer than they'd been since.

'It sounds as though Cleo's store is a real success,' he said as he followed her through to the kitchen.

'The Little Knitting Box?'

'It even sounds a winner by its name.'

'It's a lovely store. And Cleo knows a thing or two about knitting. I'm still surprised she was impressed with the sweater I'm knitting. I showed her and I thought she'd think it was terrible. Did you know the Little Knitting Box was originally in the West Village?'

'Really?'

She set down the cluster of glasses she'd brought out, tapped Rupert on the shoulder and thanked him for all

297

his hard work tonight. 'You go home, Rupert, I've got this. And I've got a helper too.' She looked to Myles. 'You're not going to rescind your offer are you?'

He shook his head.

Rupert gratefully dried his hands, bid them both goodnight, said he was going home to collapse into bed and he'd see them in the morning.

The two of them alone again, Darcy got busy stacking the dishwasher. 'Cleo's shop was in the West Village for years.'

'What happened?' Myles began washing up some of the larger platters.

'Dylan put her out of business.' Smiling at the look on his face, she added, 'Long story but it ended happily. She now owns and runs the Little Knitting Box out in Inglenook Falls. You should go some time. Now you know Dylan and Cleo, go say hello. They have a wonderful Christmas market every year, which we're too late for this time, but next year. And it's not all about shopping. It's also about the mulled cider, gingerbread and roasted chestnuts.'

'You're inviting me?'

She hid her face by stacking cutlery in the dedicated section inside the dishwasher. 'We've talked about this, Myles.'

'I don't get it.'

She looked at him. 'Get what?'

'Why you won't give me another chance.'

'Because I've spent a long time building my career. I like my independence, I value it. I want to keep it. Surely you must know how that feels.'

Before she had a chance to end the conversation he said, 'Cleo thinks you're doing what she once did.'

'You spoke about me?'

He shrugged. 'Do you mind?'

'Depends what was said.'

'She thinks you work too hard.'

She bristled. 'Yeah, well if we'd had this conversation when she was first building up the Little Knitting Box a few years ago, I suspect she would've understood exactly where I was coming from.' She went through to the lounge again and wiped down the bar top, the ring mark on the desk where someone had placed a cold glass of champagne.

He followed her. 'Thank you for this evening. Mum, Dad and I all had a brilliant time.'

'It was my pleasure.'

He watched her as she plucked crumbs from one of the armchairs, a discarded napkin from the floor. 'It means a lot that we can have Christmas together.'

She still didn't fully engage.

'Darcy.' When she stood to take out the trash she'd picked up he put a hand on her arm to stop her. And then he smiled. He reached up and hooked her hair behind her ear. 'You're wearing the earrings I gave you.' The diamonds sparkled as much as her smile had tonight.

'Myles, I—'

'Can we talk? I mean properly.' He nodded to the sofa. 'Over there, sit down together.'

'Myles, I've too much to do. And I'm exhausted. It's going to be a big day tomorrow. A day that means a lot, personally and career-wise.'

He placed his hands against each of her cheeks, looking down into ice-blue eyes that shone as they focused on his, her lips still coated with gloss he wanted to kiss away. 'Cinderella, all this won't disappear or turn into a pumpkin if you stay up past midnight.'

299

Her eyes held his a split second longer before she pulled away and picked up the garbage bag in the corner and tied it at the top.

'Darcy?'

'Go to bed, Myles.'

'What the hell have I done now?'

'Cinderella?'

'It was a joke!' He'd done it again, but all he'd wanted to do was lighten the tension between them, get this girl to open up to him.

'That's the whole problem though, isn't it?' The garbage was heavy and she used a second hand to steady it. 'It's all a joke to you. You go out in your expensive suit, dine at fancy restaurants, flatter women with gifts like earrings, but I've known men like you. They want the dream, the woman who'll be by their side and support them. Don't get me wrong, that's fine for so many, but I can't ever be one of those women. I don't have a longing to be spoilt, a wish that I didn't have to work the hours I do. I like the way I've built my life and I won't ever give it up.' Her eyes darted to his as she tried to reiterate how serious she was with everything she said. And then her hands went to one ear lobe and then the other.

'What are you doing?'

She handed him the earrings she'd removed, the one thing he'd given her.

'They won't take them back, remember?'

'Myles, take them.'

'They were a gift.'

'And it wasn't appropriate.' Her hand hovered, earrings ready to drop into his.

He put his hands behind his back, a cheeky smile forming on his lips. 'I won't take them.'

He almost thought she'd relent and put them back in but he should've known by now that backing down wasn't something Darcy did. 'Fine,' she said. She put them down on the side table. 'But I can't keep them.'

'Darcy, please.'

She moved towards the door leading to the basement just as they were joined by footsteps on the stairs.

'Adele.' Darcy was shocked to see the other guest this late. 'Is everything OK?'

'It's a disaster. Holly hid all the boys' gifts from Santa in her apartment and I've knocked on her door over and over, but I think she had so much champagne she must be comatose in there. If I don't get those presents under the tree tonight, Christmas will be a catastrophe.'

Darcy left the garbage bag, went back to the desk and called Holly's mobile. Mrs O'Sullivan was fretting, telling Myles how the elder boy was beginning to doubt Santa Claus existed and that if the presents weren't there tomorrow morning, that would be it for good.

Darcy finally got an answer. 'Holly, it's Darcy. Yes, from downstairs. I'm sorry to wake you.' She went on to explain the predicament and Myles had no choice but to leave them to it.

He watched the snow fall outside the window in the lounge, standing inside in the room where he wished the fire was roaring and Darcy was by his side so they could sort through this. He'd tried to make jokes to ease the atmosphere between them but it had backfired, and now he really didn't know what he could possibly do.

He picked up the diamond earrings from the side table, pushed them into his pocket and went upstairs to bed.

301

# Chapter Twenty-Five

*Darcy*

*Christmas Day*

Darcy opened her eyes and it took her a moment to realise what day it was. She'd slept soundly, pushed out all thoughts of Myles and tried to focus on the job ahead.

When she threw back the covers she shivered. At five in the morning the brownstone was dark and very chilly. The heating usually kicked in around five thirty so she rubbed her hands against her pyjama top before braving the cold wooden floorboards to retrieve woolly socks she'd left on the chair at the side of the room. She slipped them on but not before peeking out from behind the blind to see what the weather was like. She pressed her face right against the glass it was so dark out, but with her hands on either side of her eyes, she could see enough.

A huge grin spread across her face. She could imagine she looked a state – dark hair sticking up on end, maybe a crease down her cheek where she'd buried herself into her pillow last night with a determination that probably caused a frown the whole night long. But if anyone saw her standing there at the window, she didn't care. Snow covered the street, flakes fluttered down from the sky seeking out their landing spot, and the city felt quieter than it had been in a long while. All that would change once Manhattan woke up to Christmas Day, but, for now, it was a sight to behold.

She made a cup of tea in the kitchen and back in the bedroom pulled the curved-back armchair closer to the window. She opened the blind fully to the top, turned off the lamp by the bed, and gazed into the darkness. She could see enough from the glow cast by streetlamps on her side of the street and opposite, and she sat that way watching flakes cascade down from up above until the familiar clicking sounds told her the heating was getting ready for the day and the radiator started its progression from cold, through to lukewarm, and finally to hot.

And now it was time. It was time for Christmas at the Inglenook Inn, and she couldn't wait. She jumped into the shower, singing away to the Michael Bublé album playing from her cell phone balanced on the shelf by the mirror, and when the bathroom was all steamed up, she stepped out and wrapped herself in a fluffy towel, using another to twist up her hair. She tried not to plough through all of today's tasks in her head as she got ready. She needed this down time before the hectic day began. She and Rupert had made a detailed plan of all the cooking that needed to be done and first up was breakfast, with guests able to choose between omelette, eggs Benedict, sausages and maple bacon, the usual cereals, a selection of fruits. All of the guests had opted for breakfast and lunch so Darcy knew the kitchen was going to be operating at full capacity today.

She dried her hair, turning her head upside down to get all the layers. Today she'd dress in a pair of dark jeans with a deep-navy sparkly top and then she'd change again this afternoon. She already had an apron in the kitchen too because she knew she'd be helping Rupert, especially when it came to service.

Hair done and clothes on, Darcy took her cell phone and went downstairs, excited to be doing this, finally!

The brownstone was warm now but no familiar sounds greeted her as she reached the lounge and headed towards the kitchen. She checked her watch. Six thirty. Guests would be getting up soon.

She poked her head around the kitchen door expecting to see Rupert in full chef mode, slicing, dicing, whipping, stirring, preparing whatever he could. But he wasn't there.

'Rupert, where are you?' she said out loud and tapped out a text to him. He'd said he would be here by six at the latest. He was also joining them for lunch. He'd bring a change of clothes and the second all that food was served, he'd sneak into Darcy's apartment, spruce himself up and join them all. Then he'd make do with an apron as he served desserts and provided any after snacks. Darcy had fully supported the idea. He worked hard all year round, they'd never had any complaints about him, and she knew the Inn wouldn't be the same without him.

When Rupert still hadn't replied to her text after fifteen minutes, Darcy called him. He picked up on the fourth ring. Relieved, she leaned against the closed kitchen door. 'Oh, Rupert, thank goodness.' He'd overslept. She could hear it in his voice. 'How long will it take you to get here?' When he grunted she said, 'Rupert, wake up.' Her voice softened. Clearly he wasn't a man who woke up easily. 'It's me, Darcy. It's Christmas Day.'

'Can't.' It was the only word she could make out.

'You can't? What do you mean?'

'Flu.'

'You have flu?' OK, now wasn't the time to panic. Except it was! 'Is it man flu?'

'Darce, it's the real thing.' She could hear it in his voice, the way he spoke as though every syllable made his head pound and was agony in his throat. 'I can't get

304

out of bed. My flatmate has been bringing me painkillers and water all night.' He stopped talking and Darcy wondered if he'd already fallen back to sleep. 'I'm sorry, Darce. I must've slept through my alarm. I meant to call earlier.'

Her coping mechanisms fired up even though she was terrified of how the hell she was going to do this. 'What am I going to do?'

'We planned it all, my recipes are all there.' His words struggled to come out coherently. He was in a bad way. 'You can do this. I'd be there if I could.'

Her heart sank. 'I know you would.'

'I'm sorry.'

She needed to pull herself together. She couldn't let herself fall apart. She wouldn't. 'Don't apologise, you can't help it. Now, go back to sleep, look after yourself. Drink lots of fluids.'

'Yes, Mum.'

When he tried to apologise again she wouldn't hear of it. 'I'll be fine. Don't you worry.'

But when she ended the call her spirits slumped. How could she possibly be fine? This was going to be the world's biggest disaster.

\*

Darcy coped with breakfast. She'd done it enough times and making an omelette wasn't overly difficult. Luckily for her, guests came down at different times, almost as though they'd planned it that way. She put out cereals and fruits, made boiled eggs for the O'Sullivans, whipped up an enormous omelette that could be cut into thirds for Myles, Ian and Martha, and squeezed oranges to make juice. Holly came downstairs looking fresher than everyone else. Darcy prepared a poppy-seed bagel for the guest she needed to impress the most and Holly took over the spreading of the honey as Darcy set a coffee down beside it.

'Where's that lovely young chef of yours?' Martha asked. The sun had only just come up outside and although she'd been going through the motions until now, wishing guests a very Merry Christmas and being joyful and triumphant as guests would expect their host to be, Darcy was already willing people to disperse so she could get on with the mammoth task of food preparation.

'He has the flu.' She leaned in because she didn't want anyone else to hear. There was no way she wanted to alert the whole room to the fact that this sumptuous Christmas lunch they'd all ordered and paid for could end up being one epic failure.

Martha picked up on the need to keep calm. 'Do you have a substitute chef?'

'You're looking at her.'

'Well, I bet you'll do a brilliant job, and I'm already looking forward to a home-cooked Christmas lunch.'

'You've cooked a turkey before, right?' Myles must have been listening in. Trust him to ask the obvious.

She frowned at him. 'Of course.'

'It must be a big one for today, given all your guests.'

Her eyes widened playfully in an attempt to disguise her trepidation. 'It's enormous.'

'So you'll have put it in the oven already then,' he said.

Her eyes fixed on his. She didn't answer.

'Yes, you must put it in, or it won't be ready,' Martha went on, her voice mildly hinting at panic-mode on Darcy's behalf.

'It's in,' she said. 'Now, can I get you anything else?'

'I'd love another coffee if I may.' Ian had finished every last morsel of his omelette.

'Coming right up. Cream on the side?'

'You have a good memory.' He smiled at her.

She smiled back right until she got out of the dining room and into the kitchen, where she shut the door and leaned against it. She immediately took out her cell phone in a fluster. 'Mum, thank god. It's me, Darcy.'

'Merry Christmas! It's Darcy,' she called into the background and Darcy could imagine her dad pushing himself up from the armchair and making his way over. But she didn't have time for this.

'It's a disaster, Mum.'

'What is?'

Darcy told her everything. 'I don't know what to do.' Tears pricked at the corners of her eyes and for the first time she felt as though everything was falling apart. If this was the huge failure she suspected it was about to be, Darcy wasn't sure Sofia would ever forgive her. She wasn't sure she'd ever forgive herself either.

'You need to get going with the turkey, Darcy.' Her mum's firm instruction came down the line. 'I've got your brother and our neighbour coming so I can't even hop on a train, not that I know whether they'll be running in all this snow.'

'Just some instructions would be good.' Darcy gulped back tears but when her cell phone cut out in the middle of her mum talking about trussing the turkey and she looked to see the battery had died, she almost lost it. She ran out and upstairs to her apartment, got her charger and then came back and plugged it in on the cabinet at one end of the room. She waited for it to get enough power to make the call and while she waited she leaned against the kitchen door again, looking around Rupert's domain, one she could use now and then like she had for breakfast, but not one she had a vast experience of.

Someone was pushing the door from the other side and then there was a knock. 'Darcy?' It was Myles.

'I'll be out in a minute,' she called, trying to make her voice sound as normal as possible. Guests rarely knocked on the kitchen door. It was an out-of-bounds area. She'd also made sure she'd locked the hatch so nobody would be able to peer in and see her fear building.

She swiped the tears and pulled open the door, feigning nonchalance. 'Can I get you anything?'

Myles looked past her and sniffed the air. 'I don't smell turkey.'

She couldn't hold it in any longer. The tears spilt over. 'I've never cooked a turkey in my life. I've never made a Christmas dinner. Nobody will get their Christmas lunch, we'll get a horrid review, Sofia will never talk to me again, I'll be out of a job, and the Inglenook Inn will be no more.'

Myles puffed out his cheeks when she finally looked at him. 'That's a lot of information to give me when all I said was I don't smell turkey.' She managed a smile. 'That's better.' But then her face crumpled again.

She waited for him to seize his moment and pull her into him, take control, but he didn't.

He stepped past her, into the kitchen, shut the door behind them and took Rupert's apron from the back of the door. He put it over his head and fastened it at the back. 'Take it from someone who made their first Christmas dinner at a very young age – and under extreme pressure, might I add? – that it's hard, but not impossible. You can do it. I'm not doing it for you.' He held up his hands. 'I'm here to help, not take over. Do you have a full menu for today?'

She wiped her cheeks, blew her nose and then washed her hands. He did his hands too and then, after he'd taken the turkey from the refrigerator and switched on the oven to preheat, they went through the plan she and Rupert had made, step by step. There were vegetables to prepare, the meats to make, gravy, side dishes.

'Dessert is almost covered,' said Darcy confidently as she wound her loose hair up into a high bun to get it out of the way. 'And by the time everyone has eaten the enormous lunch, we could play for time and gather them all in the lounge by the fire for Christmas songs, or games of charades.'

'Great idea. I'll get Mum and Dad to run that. They have a weird fascination for charades that I don't even want to think about.'

Darcy laughed, the first time she'd smiled genuinely since she'd spoken with Rupert that morning. 'It'll give us time to finish the desserts.'

'What do we have?'

'Rupert made salted-caramel pie, which should be in the refrigerator…' She pulled open the door to check she was right. '…Yes, it's there. He also planned to make a cinnamon-and-cardamom-spiced apple pie.' She looked at the recipes Rupert had left beneath their plan and thanked goodness her chef was so organised. 'It says here that it'll take forty-five minutes to cook, and, looking at this, I estimate twenty minutes to prepare.'

'Too easy,' he said without looking up from what he was doing with the turkey.

'What are you doing there?'

He pulled a face. 'Sorry, am I taking over?'

She waved her hands. 'I'm not going to fight you. Not today anyway.'

'I'm almost disappointed.' His gaze lingered on her until she ushered him into continuing with the turkey. 'This is going to be a maple-syrup-glazed turkey, which we'll serve with a white-wine gravy.'

'You're following Rupert's recipe?'

'To the letter,' he said. 'And I'm impressed he left recipes.'

'He doesn't always, but for the Christmas dinner I made him write them out.'

'Now why doesn't that surprise me?'

Rupert hadn't wanted to, he'd told her to trust him, but Christmas was a big thing, the first time the Inn had hosted it, and she needed to be able to visualise what would be served, how guests may react, the whole parcel of Christmas at the Inglenook Inn.

The atmosphere between them started off tense, but the more Darcy let Myles help and they worked together, the better it became. Rather than feeling she was losing control, she felt she was gaining it, because letting him in to help out was the way she was going to maintain the integrity of the Inn. And that was her end goal after all.

They made a stuffing and filled the cavity of the turkey with it, they seasoned the bird and then used a cheesecloth coated in melting butter to drape over the meat while it went in the oven, to keep it moist. The word cheesecloth had been scribbled on Rupert's recipe but without Myles's input Darcy would never have known what it meant. 'I didn't do it the first time I roasted a turkey,' he'd said, 'but over the years I learned it as a good trick to keep the bird moist at the start of cooking.'

Darcy peeled potatoes, Myles washed and prepared carrots and chopped beetroot. 'I smell of food,' she laughed. She'd given up trying to stay clean. Her sparkly top had been mostly protected by an apron, but cooking a meal of this size came with risks and she had a spill of melted butter on her jeans, starch from the potatoes up her arms. She'd even managed a smear of beetroot colouring across her jawbone that Myles had helped her wipe off with kitchen towel.

Christmas music blared out from the corner of the room and every now and then Darcy went out to ensure guests were happy enough and didn't need anything. Her cell phone was charged, she spoke to her parents – who were confused when they heard how chirpy she was now – and she sent Rupert a text to say that everything was in hand. He didn't reply. He didn't need to.

'Oh crap!' Darcy put a hand across her mouth when she went to the refrigerator and saw the racks of venison. 'We haven't done anything with this yet.'

Myles turned the flame on beneath the pan of potatoes and came over, leaning so close to Darcy as he peered into the refrigerator that her insides took a tumble.

'Relax,' he told her, going over to the collection of recipes. 'I read the plan and it won't take anywhere near as long as the turkey. You go and set up the dining room, make it look stunning, and I'll move on to the sauce.'

Darcy squeezed past the countertop, meeting with Myles's body momentarily, each of them reacting to the close contact for a second before they continued with the job they needed to do. Darcy surreptitiously watched Myles combining stock, port, bay leaves and thyme after checking and re-checking the recipe. He was in control and rather than resenting it, she found having someone else take charge alongside her rather than instead of her gave her a sense of encouragement.

'And Darcy?' His voice stopped her before she left the room.

'Yes?'

'Make sure the fire is crackling in the lounge. It wouldn't be Christmas without it.'

She gasped. 'I completely forgot.'

Without turning round he said, 'Like it or not, I know things about you, and I know that fireplace is part of the ambience of this Inn because you make sure it's going for as many hours of the day as possible, even if it means a late night.'

She shifted, uncomfortable, but he still didn't turn round. She was waiting for a Cinderella remark, but it didn't come. And when she made her way to the dining room she almost wished he had made a reference to the email again, because it would make it easier not to like him.

In the dining room the tree in the corner stood tall and proud. The colours from decorations and baubles shone as the lights twinkled and Darcy shifted the smaller tables together to make one long structure. She put chairs around it until they had the right amount of place settings. She went down to the basement where the tablecloth had hung so that it didn't crease, and back upstairs she laid it on the tables to create one piece of furniture. On top of the red tablecloth she laid a gold runner that stretched from one end to the other. She arranged a holly, pine-cone and red-berried centrepiece with a candle and then two smaller versions of the same arrangement at intervals along the Christmas table before rolling emerald-green napkins inside shimmering silver rings that she set down next to the polished heavyweight cutlery.

Leaving everything in Myles's capable hands back in the kitchen, Darcy went to welcome guests in the lounge, where they were congregating for pre-Christmas drinks. She relaxed in her role because she'd already seen the turkey was looking golden and succulent and ready to carve, the venison smelled delicious, potatoes were crisping up in the oven and the vegetables were ready to have garnish and finishing touches added. Guests would choose which meat they wanted, opting for both or none as they so desired, and then would get the standard fayre added to their plates. Nobody would go hungry today, Darcy thought. Not on her watch.

She smiled. This morning she'd thought it was a disaster, but Christmas Day was beginning to really take shape.

'Did Santa come?' she asked the boys, who came running down the stairs and excitedly exploded with details of everything he'd put beneath the tree. They turned to speculation at whether he'd used the front door or whether he'd braved the chimney like he should do.

Holly came over all smiles. 'Thank you, Darcy. For everything.'

'You're welcome.'

'It looked like I was going to have a terrible Christmas but you saved me from a rat-infested apartment and a lonely meal for one.'

'I'm sorry about your friend. Christmas is a hard time for anyone who has lost someone special.'

Holly smiled humbly. 'She wouldn't want me wallowing. She'd tell me to stop being miserable and live my life.' And then her eyes twinkled as her

Christmas-tree earrings swung from behind her auburn hair. 'Have a glass of champagne,' she encouraged.

'I will later, I promise.' She swept effortlessly away to the next guest. She kept glasses of water circulating, served champagne or eggnog, and for Ian, a beer. The guests chattered amongst themselves and her smile only wavered when she was on the other side of the kitchen door and back to work. It wasn't quite time to relax yet.

'Could you finish those potatoes?' Myles looked frantic, darting this way and that.

'These?' She indicated the bowl on the countertop.

'Yep. I wasn't sure how Rupert prepares potatoes but this is what I'd do.' He said it as though waiting for her approval but she didn't question him so he carried on. 'Take the whisk, give it thirty seconds on low speed, then crank it up to medium and slowly drizzle the hot milk from the jug into the potatoes, then add the softened butter from the plate, gradually. It should go nice and fluffy and I'll come and add some salt to taste. Or you could, it's your call.'

She got to work, smiling when Myles found a few seconds to turn up the music. 'White Christmas' came over the speakers and neither of them could help but bop to the music as they put the finishing touches to lunch.

'The gravy!' She looked around until her eyes fell on a jug.

'It's done,' said Myles, picking up the enormous platter with the turkey on it. He'd taken off the sweater he'd had on at breakfast that morning. The heat of the kitchen wouldn't allow for it, and even Darcy had pushed her sleeves up and opened the window further as the temperature became uncomfortable. She watched the strong, manly tendons of his arms strain under the weight of the bird.

'Cranberry sauce?' she asked, just so she could look around the kitchen rather than focusing on his physique.

'Done. Why don't you go and get changed?'

'We don't have time for that.'

'Darcy, this is your day as much as anyone else's. You've pulled this off. You have a few minutes to go and change and make sure you enjoy the rest of today.'

'I…I don't know how to thank you.'

'I can think of a few ways.' His cheeky smile was back and it almost had her.

'Myles, I…'

'Go on, get changed, or you'll run out of time. I'll take this into the dining room. I'm putting everything but the turkey and gravy onto plates. You can't deny guests the chance to watch the carving. Just tell me where the carving knives are.' Her face told him she had no idea and with a laugh he said, 'I'll find them.'

Darcy skittered off to her apartment. She had the quickest shower she'd ever managed, dried herself and spritzed perfume. She pulled on a bottle-green velvet crush skirt with side zip pockets that finished a few inches above the knee and a black roll-neck top. She took her hair out of the bun and let it fall around her shoulders and with a bit of teasing it looked as good as it had that morning.

With another spritz of perfume and her high-heeled black suede Mary Janes with snap fastenings on her feet, it was time. This was it. What she'd worked so hard to convince Sofia she was capable of doing. Christmas at the Inglenook Inn. And she'd done it.

She stopped just outside the dining room, took a deep breath. Yes, she had done it, but she'd only done it with Myles's help.

The kitchen door behind her opened. 'There you are.' Myles had changed his shirt too.

'How did you have time?' She could smell his subtle aftershave that was so familiar by now.

'I'm fit. I ran up the stairs and down again.'

'Shall we?' she asked, turning back to push open the door to the dining room.

Myles stopped her by laying a hand on her shoulder. When she turned he said, 'One more thing, before you go in.'

'What's that?' Their faces were inches apart. She saw him reach into his pocket and he took something out. When he opened his palm it was to show her the two diamond earrings she'd handed back to him last night.

She looked down into his hand. And without another word she took the earrings, put one in, and then the other.

'You look beautiful, Darcy,' he said, but didn't do anything else. He didn't try to kiss her, he didn't ask her to give him a chance.

But she almost wished he would.

*

Christmas lunch started with Myles standing at the head of the table after Darcy had insisted she was more than happy for him to carve the turkey. Just as he was about to plunge the fork into it and run the carving knife back and forth he said, 'I'd like to make a toast first, if I may?'

Darcy nodded her approval.

Myles picked up a glass of champagne and everyone followed suit with whatever they were drinking. The O'Sullivan boys were feeling very grown up with champagne glasses filled with grape juice.

'I'd like to make a toast to the Inglenook Inn,' said Myles. 'And also to our hostess today. To Darcy.'

Everyone charged their glasses and Darcy felt the intense appreciation in the room. 'Thank you,' she said modestly, but Myles hadn't finished.

'I think we can all agree that this young lady has given us all a Christmas to remember so far. She's pulled together this lunch – with a little bit of help,' he smiled, 'and I'll bet none of you would've known the disaster she was faced with this morning.'

Murmurs of agreement were heard around the room and Darcy had to say something. 'I couldn't have done it without help,' she smiled. 'You ask my mother, I called her in tears.' She raised a laugh and sounds of sympathy. 'I want to wish each and every one of you here a very merry Christmas.'

Glasses clinked mid-air, well wishes were exchanged, and between the merriment Darcy met Myles's gaze across the table. Whatever had gone on before, they'd somehow worked as a team today. A look of understanding passed between them, and Darcy wondered whether she was the only one who didn't think he deserved a second chance.

*

Christmas lunch went without a hitch. There was a charged atmosphere filled with chatter, laughter and most of all new friendships the guests at the Inn had secured. The O'Sullivan boys told jokes from the books Santa had given them, Holly had everyone gasping in shock when she told them about her brother who tried to be Santa one year and went as far as climbing onto the roof and was about to attempt the chimney when their dad put a stop to it. 'I thought he was going to dive head first,' she said. 'I was terrified!'

Darcy sat next to Martha for the dinner and managed to switch off from being the boss, the hostess, and enjoy the occasion for what it was: a gathering with new friends, full of good food and cheer. She wasn't sure she'd ever work in a big hotel again after this and wondered whether this job would be the trigger for a lot of changes in her life.

Nobody backed off when it came to clearing the table. In fact, guests were clamouring to be helpful taking plates away, glasses to the kitchen, picking up debris from the floor.

Myles and Darcy left the dessert preparation for now. Every guest was too full to eat more food and some went out to see the snow in Manhattan, others went for a walk in Central Park, and the Cunninghams settled in the lounge to enjoy the tree and fireplace.

Back in her apartment with the laptop, Darcy snatched her chance to FaceTime Sofia and Gabriella. Their Christmas looked as spectacular as the one Darcy was experiencing, with a white scene playing out beyond the warmth of the house. Kyle spent most of the conversation tugging at his grandma's arm to try to persuade her to take him out in the snow.

'Darcy, you've done really well. I'm proud of you,' Sofia's voice beamed all the way from Switzerland.

Darcy hadn't told her about Holly yet. She'd save that for when Sofia returned, once the piece was finalised. Holly, albeit under the influence of champagne, had agreed to read the article to Darcy over the telephone before it went to publication. She did it for a select few, she'd told her, but not many, and Darcy had thanked her profusely, although she doubted she needed to worry any more after today's celebrations. Holly seemed to be

318

embracing the day entirely and already seemed a more laid-back version of the woman Darcy had first met.

'I need to make some changes, don't I?' Sofia was still smiling, but clearly the time away from the Inn had made her see it in a new light.

'Not too many, but we'll talk about some ideas when you're home.'

'We will. And I've been thinking about making this a bit more permanent.'

'Living in Switzerland?'

'No, no.' She shook her head. 'I'm talking about you working at the Inn. I've enjoyed this time with Gabriella and it's made me realise how many hours I put into my job. Don't get me wrong, I'm glad I've done it, but I need to make sure I prioritise other areas of my life. Maybe we could talk about you having a part share in the Inn. I have no idea how we could work it out, perhaps we need to see a financial advisor.' Sofia threw her hands up in the air the way she did when she had no idea what was going on. 'But whatever happens, what do you think? Could you see your involvement in the Inglenook Inn becoming more long-term?'

Darcy grinned at how excited Sofia was. 'I would absolutely love that.'

'Then it's settled. We'll talk. But for now, I must go. I have snow angels to make. And Darcy…Merry Christmas.'

'Merry Christmas, Sofia.'

Darcy checked her hair, added some lip gloss, smoothed down her skirt and popped her heels back on. She'd kicked them off whilst she lay on the bed chatting with friends across the miles.

Downstairs the Cunninghams were laughing around a laptop resting on Martha's knees and Darcy gave them

319

space. But it didn't seem that Martha wanted any and she called Darcy over. 'Come and say hello.'

Darcy saw they were Skyping someone and she waved to a man, a woman and a couple of kids. She realised it could only be Myles's brother and his family. 'Merry Christmas,' she said to them.

'Merry Christmas!' they all chimed back. The woman moved closer to the camera. 'So you're the infamous Darcy.' She earned herself a nudge from the man, who must be Winston, and she lost her balance and ended up falling onto the kids' laps, which they found hilarious.

'Sorry about her,' said Winston, 'but it's lovely to meet you.'

'Thank you. It's nice to see you all.' She was aware of her proximity to Myles and wondered if it was making him as nervous as it was making her.

'I hope my family are behaving themselves,' Winston continued. 'They have a tendency to make Christmas an interesting affair.'

Martha giggled and Myles seemed pleased that the teasing was taken in good spirits.

'They've been on their best behaviour,' Darcy confirmed.

'They're loving the Inglenook Inn. Careful, or we may all come over next year. How about it, kids? Christmas in New York?'

Wide eyes and yelps of 'Yay! Oh please, can we?' rang out and Darcy laughed, leaving the Cunninghams to it.

The O'Sullivans came through the door brushing off snow, chattering about the snowman they'd made a few blocks away with some local kids; Vanessa and Zach came in from a walk and said they needed at least another hour before dessert because they were so full.

Darcy swept the hallway with the broom. She longed to step outside and walk a few blocks, take a deep breathful of the season and enjoy the feeling of snow on her cheeks, look up at the sky while flakes cascaded down at her and twirled round. She settled for hovering at the top of the stoop, with the front door open to the world. She wished a merry Christmas to Mrs Armstrong from number twenty as she came home from wherever she'd been to, she waved at a stranger on the other side of the street, because it was Christmas after all.

When she felt someone behind her, she knew it would be Myles.

'We did it.' He was standing so close she could feel the heat from his body against the cold of the outside, and she wasn't shivering at all.

'I'm sorry, Myles. I've not been very pleasant to be around.' She looked down at the top step, clear of snow where it was protected by the arched doorway above. The rest of the steps were white with a collection of footprints slowly being covered by fresh snowfall.

'No, I'm sorry. I'm sorry I got you into trouble in London. I'm sorry I sent a horrible email because I was so ungrateful when you were only trying to help.'

'I was interfering and it was wrong.' They both gazed out across the street. It was easier to talk this way.

'You were, but your intentions were right. I overreacted. I'm so used to being the one in charge, nobody putting a foot wrong around me.' He leaned closer. 'Except my family, but that's another story.'

Darcy smiled. 'You all seem really happy now.'

'Mum needed my forgiveness, but she couldn't ask for it.' He swallowed hard. 'And I couldn't give it until I understood what had really gone on. And that has taken more years than I care to admit.'

She turned to him. 'So you're converted? You love Christmas again?'

'I wouldn't go that far.' He grinned. 'But it's growing on me. Mum gave me a gift.'

She'd noticed him holding a small present wrapped in gold paper with an ice-white bow. 'What is it? Haven't you opened it?'

'I did open it. But I re-wrapped it myself.' At her confusion he said, handing her the gift, 'I'm giving it to you.'

'What is it? Another caramel macchiato?'

Smiling, he said, 'Like I said, I know things about you.'

'I still can't work out how you knew that little bit of information. Were you inspecting my takeaway cups after I'd thrown them in the trash?'

'Not quite. It was your friend Isabella.'

'Isabella told you it was my favourite coffee? When?'

'She slipped a note under my door suggesting it may be a way back into your heart.'

'The sneaky thing.' Darcy shouldn't be surprised. Her friend had suffered the frustration of Darcy's insecurities when it came to relationships for a long time now. She probably saw it as a last resort. 'So what is it then?' She looked at the gift once again.

'You don't understand the present ritual if you're asking me that. Open it, Darcy.'

She took a deep breath as the wind picked up and blew the waves of her hair across her face. Myles reached out a hand and moved the strands out of the way as she pulled back the paper.

'It's...cute,' she said, looking at a little snowman on skis.

His laughter filled the muffled sounds of the street. 'It was mine when I was a little boy. I thought it had been thrown out, but Mum kept it all these years. It means a lot to me and I'll tell you the whole story another time, but I wanted you to have it.'

'Why?'

'Because it isn't an expensive pair of earrings, Darcy. This is something you could probably pick up for a few dollars at a bargain store. But it means something to me. It has enormous sentimental value, and…well, I guess I'm trying to show you that I'm not trying to extinguish your independence. What we did in there…' He tilted his head back towards the inside of the Inn. '…that is what I want. It's been a long time since I let anyone into my life. I think we're more similar than you realise. I want someone who will be my partner, who I can support and who supports me. I guess what I'm trying to show you is that you can still be you, Darcy, but it doesn't mean to say you can't let anyone else be a part of the bigger picture.' He looked down at the ground beneath their feet. 'I'm making a mess of this, aren't I?'

Holly picked up the tail-end of the conversation as she arrived back at the Inn and trudged up the steps, her boots collecting snow. 'You could be doing a better job, Myles,' she said.

Darcy grinned. They were all very much on a first-name basis after last night's festivities and today's lunch.

'Here,' said Holly, reaching into a plastic bag. 'I think I can help you both. I bought this because I thought it might be fun,' she said with a mischievous smile. She took out something Darcy instantly recognised, stretched up above the doorway but couldn't find anything to push the mistletoe into.

Without taking his eyes from Darcy, Myles reached out a hand and Holly, understanding, placed the mistletoe onto his palm. Standing even closer to Darcy, he lifted it above both their heads as the breeze swirled snowflakes their way, landing on the shoulders of his sweater and fluttering onto her miniskirt.

Darcy was vaguely aware of the other guests crowded in the hall of the Inglenook Inn, as keen as they both were to see how this worked out.

'What do you say, Darcy Spencer? Do you want to be part of a team?'

She smiled. 'Well now, that really does depend.'

He closed the gap between them some more, the warmth of his body now against hers, his lips inches from her own. 'Oh yeah? On what?'

'On whether I'm the boss or you are.'

His hand reached up through her hair and clasped the back of her neck as he gently pulled her closer still. 'Oh I think we all know who's the boss.'

And with that he kissed her deeply. And Darcy knew she'd been right all along. This was going to be the most perfect Christmas ever.

## THE END

# Acknowledgments

I'd like to thank my friend, Pam, for an unforgettable trip to New York. Neither of us realised we were going on a walking holiday but we covered so much ground in Manhattan clocking up a total of almost eighty miles in six days! Thank you, Pam, for letting me take a ridiculous amount of photos along the way and for selling me as an author when it looked as though I wouldn't be able to see the Grand Ballroom at The Plaza. You'd make a great PR person!

Thank you  Katharine Walkden for the brilliant editing job. You are so thorough and I'm learning lots along the way, which can only be a good thing! I'd also like to thank my proofreader, Edward, for catching punctuation mistakes and helping me polish the manuscript to the final version I can share with everyone. Thank you, Berni Stevens, for a beautiful cover design that fits perfectly for book two in the series. It's exactly what I wanted, and I love it.

As always, thank you to my husband and children for their unwavering support even when I get stressed when deadline time is looming. I love you all to bits and hope I continue to make you proud.

And lastly, a huge thank you to all of my readers who support me along the way. I love hearing from you via Facebook, Twitter, my website or when you review on Amazon, and I can't wait to hear what you think of Snowflakes and Mistletoe at the Inglenook Inn.

Helen J Rolfe

## Christmas at the Little Knitting Box
## (New York Ever After, Book 1)

Christmas is coming and New York is in full swing for the snowy season. But at The Little Knitting Box in the West Village, things are about to change …

The Little Knitting Box has been in Cleo's family for nearly four decades, and since she arrived fresh off the plane from the Cotswolds four years ago, Cleo has been doing a stellar job of running the store. But instead of an early Christmas card in the mail this year, she gets a letter that tips her world on its axis.

Dylan has had a tumultuous few years. His marriage broke down, his mother passed away and he's been trying to pick up the pieces as a stay-at-home dad. All he wants this Christmas is to give his kids the home and stability they need. But when he meets Cleo at a party one night, he begins to see it's not always so easy to move on and pick up the pieces, especially when his ex seems determined to win him back.

When the snow starts to fall in New York City, both Cleo and Dylan realise life is rarely so black and white and both of them have choices to make. Will Dylan follow his heart or his head? And will Cleo ever allow herself to be a part of another family when her own fell apart at the seams?

# In a Manhattan Minute

It's the most wonderful time of the year… but when the temperature dips, can Manhattan work its magic?

Jack exists in a world that has seen its fair share of tragedy, but also success and the wealth that comes with it. One snowy night, he crosses paths with Evie, a homeless girl, and it changes everything.

Three years on, Evie's life is very different. She's the assistant to a prestigious wedding gown designer, she's settled in Manhattan, has her own apartment and friendships she holds dear. But the past is lurking in the background, threatening to spoil everything, and it's catching up with her.

Kent has kept a family secret for two decades, a secret he never wanted to share with his son, Jack. And even though she doesn't realise it yet, his life is inextricably tangled with Nicole's, the woman who was his housekeeper for thirteen years and the woman who helped Evie turn her life around.

It's Christmas and a time for forgiveness, love and Happy Ever Afters. And when the snow starts to fall, the truth could finally bring everyone the gift of happiness they're looking for.

## You, Me, and Everything In Between

Against all odds, a Happy Ever After could be just around the corner ...

Lydia and Theo face the unthinkable when a knock at the door changes everything.

As Lydia begins to pick up the pieces, not every part of the puzzle fits together as neatly as it did before, and as she discovers the truth about the man she loves, she finds herself stuck in limbo.

When Theo finally wakes up from a coma, Lydia is faced with an impossible choice. She has a history with him, the man she thought she'd spend the rest of her life with, but has too much happened to be able to forgive and forget?

## What Rosie Found Next
## (Magnolia Creek, Book 1)

One house, two strangers, one very big secret...

A shaky upbringing has left Rosie Stevens craving safety and security. She thinks she knows exactly what she needs to make her life complete – the stable job and perfect house-sit she's just found in Magnolia Creek. The only thing she wants now is for her long-term boyfriend, Adam, to leave his overseas job and come home for good.

Owen Harrison is notoriously nomadic, and he roars into town on his Ducati for one reason and one reason only – to search his parents' house while they're away to find out what they've been hiding from him his entire life. When he meets Rosie, who refuses to quit the house-sit in his parents' home, sparks fly.

Secrets are unearthed, promises are broken, friendships are put to the test and the real risk of bushfires under the hot Australian sun threatens to undo Rosie once and for all.

Will Rosie and Owen be able to find what they want or what they really need?

Made in the USA
Columbia, SC
22 October 2021

47673728R00202